Book # C

MYSTERIES
of SILVER PEAK

Dear Reader,

Writing this story took me back to my teenage years, when I rode for hours on trails and dirt roads. I loved horses. For several years, I was blessed to either own one or stable someone else's horse with riding privileges. I never had a scary adventure like Sara's in this book, and for that I am thankful.

Having the freedom and suitable places to ride for hours was priceless. As Winston Churchill said in his memoir, *My Early Years*, no hour of life is lost that is spent in the saddle.

The part of the story that was *not* fun to write was the part about Alice. I had to delve deep into a mother's agony. With six children of my own, I understood her anxiety for a child. I am so glad Alice has Sadie and other loving people around her when difficult times come her way. For Alice, as for most of us parents, the "not knowing" was the worst part of the ordeal. Realizing God is there with us and also with our child, watching over him or her, is the comforting part.

I hope you enjoy Sara and Alice's story.

Susan Page Davis
writing as Carole Jefferson

Mysteries of Silver Peak

A Mountain of Mystery
Nobody's Safe
Silver Surprise
Wildfire
A Lode of Secrets
Time Will Tell
A Code of Honor
Empty Saddle

MYSTERIES
of SILVER PEAK

Empty Saddle

CAROLE JEFFERSON

Guideposts

New York

Acknowledgments

Every attempt has been made to credit the sources of copyrighted material used in this book. If any such acknowledgment has been inadvertently omitted or miscredited, receipt of such information would be appreciated.

Scripture quotations are taken from *The Holy Bible, New International Version*. Copyright © 1973, 1978, 1984, 2011 by Biblica, Inc. Used by permission of Zondervan. All rights reserved worldwide. www.zondervan.com

Cover and interior design by Müllerhaus
Cover art by Greg Copeland represented by Deborah Wolfe, Ltd.
Typeset by Aptara, Inc.

Printed and bound in the United States of America
10 9 8 7 6 5 4 3 2 1

Prologue

DEAR LADY,

    I take pen in hand to thank you, and to humbly beg your forgiveness for the wicked thoughts I once harbored toward you, and for the words I spoke against you. I owe you my life, and I have come to see that what you did was best. You truly have a gift for ministering to those in need. May God bless you,

Tom Klein

1

SADIE RAISED HER BIDDING CARD TO CHIN HEIGHT AND CAUGHT the auctioneer's eye.

"One-twenty-five over here," he said. "Who'll give one-thirty?"

Sadie's friend Roz leaned toward her. "Isn't that an awful lot for a dusty old doctor's bag?"

"It's the stuff inside it that intrigues me," Sadie said as the auctioneer continued his patter for a few seconds.

"Going once, going twice." He paused with his gavel raised, then pointed it toward Sadie. "Sold, to number forty-three for one hundred and twenty-five dollars."

Sadie grinned at Roz. "Oh boy!"

Roz chuckled. "I never knew anyone so excited about a few old scalpels and clamps. Are antique medical instruments a hot commodity at your shop?"

"Not really," Sadie said. "I suppose I could get quite a bit if I sold the instruments separately, but I'd rather keep the whole kit together. Especially if I can find out who the owner was and get some provenance on it." In antiques, an item's provenance—its history of ownership—could make a huge difference in its value and appeal.

The black leather satchel had the initials *RMT* engraved on a small brass fitting near the top opening on one side. Sadie had examined the bag and instruments earlier, and she was quite certain they were relics of the nineteenth century.

"Who will want to buy it?" Roz asked.

"Lots of people." Sadie waved her card at the runner who carried her prize down the aisle to her chair. "Thank you." She took it on her lap and ran her hand over the dry old leather. "Some people collect antique doctor's tools, especially people in the medical field. And if I discover that RMT lived in Colorado, lots of people who live here will be interested."

"I suppose so." Roz glanced toward the platform at the front of the auction hall and arched her eyebrows. "Look! It's my quilt."

Sadie smiled. "Getting awfully proprietary about it, aren't you? You haven't even started bidding yet."

"I just love it," Roz said. "I hope I can get it and not go over my budget. Roscoe wouldn't like it if I drained the bank account for an old quilt."

"I hope you get it. I'm waiting for that old sword to come up." Sadie sat back, content to watch Roz vie for the double wedding ring quilt. Roscoe was easygoing, and he probably wouldn't object if Roz treated herself to something she liked.

"Here we have a beautiful, hand-stitched quilt that I'm told was made by the estate owner's mother around 1910. What am I bid?"

A few minutes later, the auctioneer declared Roz the new owner of the quilt for a hundred and twenty dollars. Roz pushed back her shoulder-length gray hair and settled down in her chair with a satisfied smile. "There! That wasn't too bad."

"Not at all," Sadie said. "In fact, I think you got a steal. It's in wonderful shape. I could probably sell that for more in the shop."

"Keep your hands off it," Roz teased. "It's all mine." She took it eagerly from the runner, set it on her lap, and lifted one of the folds. "Just look at that stitching."

"You got a real gem." Sadie settled into her bidding mode once more and waited eagerly through several sales until an antique sword came on the block. She'd had her eye on it since the viewing hour before the auction started that morning, and she knew it was of Civil War vintage. The silver hilt and chasing, as well as the engraved name of the officer who had owned it, made the sword a rare find. She hoped she could get it for less than a thousand dollars, but she was prepared to spend a little more if she had to. Several customers regularly bought Civil War artifacts from her, and one man in Denver was particularly apt to want that sword for his collection.

An hour later, as the sale wound down with box lots of leftovers, Sadie and Roz paid their tabs and loaded their treasures into the back of Sadie's red Chevy Tahoe.

"That was lots of fun," Roz said as they headed back toward Silver Peak, their tiny town perched on a Colorado mountainside at 9,600 feet. Though the old mining town was no longer booming, the residents wouldn't trade it for any other location on earth.

Sadie loved the drive up the winding mountain road from Breckenridge. The aspen leaves were turning yellow, and the late September nights dropped to nippy temperatures. This was a beautiful time of year in the mountains.

Sadie parked in front of her antique shop, which she had christened the Antique Mine. It sat squarely between Roscoe

Putnam's hardware store and Arbuckle's Coffee on the pictur-
esque main street.

"Hi," Sadie's daughter, Alice, called from behind the counter
as Sadie and Roz entered the store with their arms full of bundles.
"Did you have a good time?" Alice often helped out at the shop on
Saturdays, though her teaching job kept her busy on weekdays.
She had gladly offered to fill in today while Sadie and her friend
went to the auction.

"It was great," Sadie said. "I got three boxes of dishes, a hand-
carved whatnot shelf, an old sword, and look at this." Sadie held
up the leather satchel.

"What is it?" Alice eyed the bag as Sadie set it on the
counter.

"A medical kit. It has antique doctor's instruments in it."

"Interesting. Did you eat lunch?"

"Roz and I had sandwiches at the auction," Sadie said.

Alice glanced up. A customer was approaching the checkout
counter with several small items in her hands. "I'll get this while
you unload the rest."

"Thanks." Sadie put her purse in a drawer of the antique desk
that formed the base of her checkout counter. She and Roz went
outside, and Roz took her quilt from the backseat.

"Thanks for taking me," Roz said. "That was great fun."

"I was glad for the company," Sadie said, pulling out a box of
china.

By the time she had brought in the sword and other treasures,
Alice had rung up the customer's purchases.

"You'll love this sword," Sadie told her. "It has an officer's
name engraved on it, and silver chasing."

"Civil War?" Alice guessed, studying the scabbard with a practiced eye.

"Yup. And Julie will go nuts over the china, but I think this is my favorite." Sadie rested her hand on the leather medical bag. "It's the most mysterious thing."

"Mysterious how?" Alice asked.

"The people at the sale had no idea to whom it belonged. The bag has initials on it, but the last initial isn't the same as the estate owner's, and the auctioneer had no clue where it came from. He said it was in with all the other stuff, and the family didn't give him much to go on."

"What about this?" Alice seemed more interested in the sword, and she slid it halfway out of the scabbard.

"At least I have his name," Sadie said. "George Watson. With his military record, he shouldn't be too hard to track down. And I got it for a good price—less than I was afraid I'd have to pay." She looked around the crowded room, stuffed with treasures she loved. "Now I have to find a place for the whatnot."

"It will make a great display for some of those dishes," Alice said. "How about near that oak dining room set?"

"If I can squeeze it in." Sadie didn't like the store to look too cramped.

More customers came in, and she and Alice set to work. Between helping shoppers, they managed to situate the carved shelf unit and find display space for all the new items.

At last Alice went to the back room to make a pot of tea, and Sadie sat down behind the counter with her laptop. The first thing she did was to check her e-mail, and then she began an online search for George Watson. She liked to be as informed as possible about the items she stocked in her shop.

The bell on the door jingled once more, and her granddaughter, Sara, entered the shop. The fourteen-year-old had her strawberry-blonde hair in braids today, with beaded leather wraps ornamenting them. With her faded jeans, she wore a long-sleeved gray T-shirt with a black-and-white horse silhouette on the front.

Sadie grinned at her. "Well, hi! How're things?"

"Not too bad." Sara walked over to the counter. "Mom said you were going to an auction this morning."

"I sure did. Roz went with me, and I spent a little too much moolah."

Sara laughed. "I'll bet you got some goodies."

"I did indeed." Sadie laid a hand on the doctor's satchel, which rested beside her laptop. "Right now I'm trying to find out if the doctor who owned this was related to the major who owned that sword hanging over there." She pointed to the newly acquired Civil War piece, where she had hung it near the counter. She wanted to be able to keep an eye on that.

"Wow, Grandma. You made a haul."

"And there's more too. But I'll bet you came here to see your mom. She's out back."

Alice came to the doorway of the back room. Her face lit up when she saw her daughter. "Well, hi, sweetie. I thought I heard your voice."

"Mom, can I go riding?" Like a typical teenager, Sara didn't match the beaming affection of her mother, and instead got right to the point. "Daisy hasn't been ridden all week, and I want to take her out."

Alice frowned. "I guess so, but I don't like to have you go alone. Can Theo go with you?"

Sara scrunched up her face. "Maybe. I guess I can ask him."

"I'd really rather you did," Alice said. "There are all these rumors about someone skulking around in the woods lately."

"What, you believe those 'wild man' stories?" Sara shook her head, as though she was the most mature person in the room.

"I don't know if it's a wild man or not," Sadie said, "but I have to admit I was a little leery the other night when I took Hank out for a walk before bedtime. I heard something in the woods. I thought it was footsteps. Anyway, Hank started barking and growling to beat the band. He would have taken off after whatever it was if I hadn't called him back and made him go inside with me."

Sara laughed. "It was probably a raccoon."

"I don't know. It sounded bigger than that. A deer at least. Anyway, I made sure all the doors and windows were locked tight."

"Maybe we have a Bigfoot on our mountain," Sara said, still smiling.

"Well, you be careful," Alice told her. The teakettle began to whistle in the back room, and she hurried to take it off the burner.

"I will," Sara called. She waved at Sadie. "'Bye, Grandma."

"'Bye, honey."

Alice returned as Sadie was taking out her camera to snap a few pictures of the sword.

"Sara left already?"

Sadie nodded. "She'll be all right if Theo's with her."

"Oh, I know." Alice set two mugs of steaming tea on the counter and pulled up a stool. "I do worry about her."

"I know." Sadie smiled, remembering the heart traumas she had suffered when Alice was a teenager. She lifted the sword down and laid it carefully on top of an antique sideboard. No customers were in the store at the moment, and Sadie photographed the Civil War artifact and then went back to her e-mail program. She began a message to her customer in Denver, describing the sword as accurately as she could.

"It's not just these stories about a wild man," Alice said.

Sadie eyed her closely. "Is something wrong?"

"Not really, but Sara's had a bit of a hard time at school this week. There's a girl who seems to think Sara's after her boyfriend."

"Really? What does Sara say?"

Alice shrugged. "She likes this boy, but she says she's not chasing him, and she can't help it if he pays attention to her. But I guess it's made Tori, the other girl, upset. She's been bad-mouthing Sara to her friends."

"That can be hard to deal with," Sadie said.

"Yeah. We've talked about it a couple of times. I've encouraged Sara to stay friendly and not take what Tori says to heart, but I can tell it bothers her."

"Of course it does," Sadie said, her heart going out to her granddaughter.

"I just hope it doesn't turn ugly," Alice said.

"Do you think it could go too far?"

Alice's brow furrowed as she sipped her tea. "I honestly don't know, Mom. I wish I could be there and see it when they interact. I did mention it to Theo, and he said he doesn't know much about it. The guys his age don't pay much attention to the freshmen, I guess."

"Maybe having a ride with her brother will cheer her up." Sadie took the card out of her camera and plugged it into her computer to transfer the photos.

"I hope so," Alice said. "It's a gorgeous day out there, and the horses do need exercise."

A couple who shopped at the Antique Mine frequently came in, and Sadie and Alice greeted them.

"I'll help the McLeans, Mom," Alice said. "You can finish what you're doing."

Sadie finished sending her message to the Civil War collector and clicked on the bookmark for the *Chatterbox*, a blog in which an anonymous Silver Peak resident posted pithy comments about the goings-on in town. The latest post was short and to the point.

What's going on in Silver Peak? A rancher claims he saw a man with long, tangled hair trying to raid his vegetable garden at dusk last week, before the first frost hit. Others report sightings of the shadowy figure. Who is this wild man? Can you say, "Sasquatch"?

Sadie shook her head. The whole thing sounded outlandish. Someone probably saw a deer or a young bear and thought it was a person. She returned to her search for Major Watson and his family. If she heard back from her customer, it would be great to have more information on hand about the sword's owner.

Alice approached the counter, her eyes gleaming. "Mom, the McLeans are really interested in the Flow Blue China. Maybe you should come and close the deal."

Sadie rose. The stunning Flow Blue platters, serving dishes, and plates were some of the most valuable dishes in her inventory, and the most beautiful. The cobalt blue glaze blurred slightly, forming a hazy pattern that antique lovers and artistic souls drooled over. The coffeepot in the pagoda design was especially fine, and Sadie almost hated to part with it. On the other hand, she had recently found it necessary to replace the furnace that heated the Antique Mine and the apartments above it, and the credit card bill for that would come due the first of the month. If she sold a few of the porcelain pieces, she might be able to cover that bill all at once and avoid the finance charges.

She walked to the china display, smiling. "Find something you like?"

"All of it," the woman said. "But this platter especially caught my eye. How old is that?"

Sadie glanced at the flat, square platter decorated with palm trees in the bright cobalt blue glaze collectors coveted. "That's from about 1840. Isn't it gorgeous? I have four plates in that pattern as well."

An hour later, she began to tally up the day's sales, which included the platter, matching plates, pagoda coffeepot, and a teapot in a different Flow Blue pattern.

"This was a pretty good day for September," Alice noted as she straightened the small items on the counter.

"It sure was, considering the tourist season is about over and ski season's not yet in full swing. Now I don't have to worry about paying for the new furnace." Sadie smiled and took a deposit slip from beneath the cash register drawer.

"Did you find out anything about the doctor whose bag you bought?" Alice picked up a long-handled duster and swiped it over the leather bag.

"No, so I'm researching the Civil War officer. I figure the doctor may be a relative of his. Maybe a son-in-law, for instance. Some of those instruments are Civil War era, or even a little earlier."

"It would be neat if you found a connection to Silver Peak," Alice said.

"That would be icing on the cake, but anywhere in Colorado would be a plus. You know I can almost always sell items with a little local history. But I wasn't able to do much this afternoon—too many interruptions."

"But that's good," Alice said with a chuckle.

"Very good. I love the kind of interruptions we had today." Sadie stuck the checks and all but a few dollars of the cash from the till into the bank bag with her deposit slip. Most of her customers paid with credit cards these days, but a few still paid the old-fashioned way, including the couple who purchased the china.

The bell jingled, and Sadie looked up to see if they had a late customer. Closing time was only ten minutes away. Her grandson, Theo, walked in.

"Hey, Mom. Grandma." He grinned and walked over to lean on the counter.

"What's up?" Sadie asked.

"Nothing. Just came by to see if you needed any muscle around here before closing."

"Ha!" Alice said. "Did you have a good ride?"

"Ride?" Theo looked at her blankly.

"With Sara," Alice prompted. "I told her she could go horseback riding if you went with her."

Theo straightened, his expression a little flustered. "Oh, that. I didn't go. She pounced on me at the last minute, and I'd already promised some guys I'd play football with them this afternoon."

"Oh. So what did Sara do?" Alice asked.

Theo shrugged. "I don't know. Probably sat around texting her friends. She and Mia are always at it."

Alice frowned but began to gather her things. "Well, you can drive me home. I'm tired."

"Thanks for spending all day here," Sadie said, feeling a little guilty. She could have sent Alice home after she returned from the auction.

"I love helping you out." Alice leaned over to kiss Sadie's cheek. As she straightened, her cell phone rang. Alice fished it from the pocket of her jeans and looked at the display. She put the phone to her ear.

"Hey, Milo."

As she listened for a moment, Alice's face sobered.

"What time was that?"

Theo looked at Sadie, his eyes full of curiosity and concern. Milo Henderson was Sadie's closest neighbor, and he boarded horses at his ranch, including Sadie's, Alice's, and the children's mounts.

"I'll be right there," Alice said and closed the connection, her face gray.

"What is it?" A rush of fear clutched Sadie as she spoke.

"Milo says Sara took Daisy out three hours ago, and the horse just came back alone."

2

***

"WE'D BETTER GET OVER TO MILO'S," THEO SAID.

"Yes." Alice held out her car keys, her face stricken. "Mom, can you come with us?"

"Of course." Sadie reached for her phone. "But first I'm calling the sheriff."

Theo's eyes widened. "The sheriff?"

Sadie nodded as she pressed the buttons to bring up Sheriff Mac Slattery's number. "It'll be dark in a couple of hours, and Sara could be out on one of the trails needing help."

He answered on the second ring. "Sheriff Slattery."

"Mac, it's Sadie. Sara may be in trouble. She took her horse out from Milo Henderson's stable three hours ago, and Milo just told us her horse came back without her. I'm headed over there now with Alice. Could you meet us there?"

"I'll go right out to the ranch."

Sadie hung up a bit relieved. From the counter, she scooped up her purse and the stack of items she wanted to take home. "Come on. The sheriff will meet us there."

She ended up taking her own SUV, and Theo drove Alice in her Jeep. In less than ten minutes, they rolled into the barnyard at Milo's and parked in front of the stable. Milo walked out of the barn to meet them. The tall bearded man didn't give them his usual smile.

"I put Daisy in a stall inside, but I didn't untack her. I thought you'd want to see her the way she came in. You might see something I missed."

"Good," Sadie said. "Sheriff Slattery is on his way. Do you know what trails Sara took?"

Milo shook his head. The lines at the corners of his eyes seemed more pronounced than usual. "I went out and checked the nearest ones—made a quick loop up the high meadow trail and back through the pine woods, but I didn't see anything."

"You did that *after* you called me?" Alice's green eyes flashed.

Milo lifted his cowboy hat and settled it farther back on his head, avoiding her gaze. "Well, no. I—I went out before calling you, in case she was close by. I thought maybe Daisy had gotten away from her and she'd be walking in. I yelled and checked what I figured were obvious places. When Sara didn't turn up, I called you."

Alice's jaw clenched, and Sadie laid a hand on her shoulder. "That sounds like a reasonable thing to do, Milo. Thanks. But I'm glad you called when you did."

The sheriff's SUV rolled down the lane, and they all waited until Mac Slattery joined them. His solid form, wearing his official brown and beige uniform, lent a calming presence, but at the same time drove home to Sadie the seriousness of the situation.

Milo greeted Mac and repeated most of what he had told Alice.

"So which way did the horse come from?" the sheriff asked.

Milo stared at him blankly for a moment. "I don't know."

"You weren't out here when she came back?"

"No."

"Is there any possibility that Sara rode back here and left without you knowing it?"

Milo shook his head. "I don't think so. She wouldn't have gone off and left Daisy with her saddle and bridle on, and loose in my yard where she could get out into the road. The horse is inside now. Do you want to see her?"

The sheriff nodded, and they all followed Milo into the barn. He opened the Dutch door on one of the box stalls. Sara's bay filly stood inside, still saddled and bridled, her tail toward the door and her head drooping. She stood on three legs, with her right hind foot tipped up so only the toe rested on the floor. Sadie zeroed in on the hoof.

"Her hind shoe is loose."

"Yeah." Milo ran a hand down Daisy's leg. "Up, girl." He lifted her hoof and stretched Daisy's leg out toward them. Sadie and the sheriff moved closer. "It was that way when I found her."

Sadie noted that the shoe had separated slightly from the hoof wall in the back, and was attached by only four of the usual eight horseshoe nails. "She's lost a couple of nails, at least."

"I'd say she caught the heel of the shoe on something and pulled it loose," Milo said.

"So she probably stumbled." The sheriff arched his eyebrows at Milo for confirmation.

Milo set the hoof down gently. "I'd say so. Sara could have flown off over her head or to the side."

"She could be lying unconscious out there," Alice said, her voice unnaturally high.

The sheriff nodded soberly. "But where?"

"There's so many tracks around here, I couldn't tell where she came in," Milo said.

Sadie reached out and patted Daisy's flank. "She has burrs in her tail."

Milo moved around to look. Sadie reached out and separated a few of the long, black hairs from the rest of Daisy's tail and worked a couple of burdocks out of the clump.

"A lot of these grow up near the family silver mine." She turned to Alice. "Do you think Sara might have ridden up there?"

"It's possible," Alice said. "I don't like to think she'd go that far alone." She looked defensively at the sheriff. "I told her not to. I said she could go riding if Theo went along. But he didn't, and..."

"I'm sorry," Theo said. "I didn't think she'd go by herself."

Sadie walked over and squeezed his arm. "It's not your fault."

Theo's dark hair had flopped down over his forehead, and he shoved it back. His eyes misted. "I feel like it is."

Another car pulled in, and Sadie took heart. She had called Edwin Marshall just before leaving her parking spot at the Antique Mine, and she had known he would come. Edwin was always there for her. They had begun dating since he had moved back to Silver Peak, and Sadie cared deeply for him. As mayor of the little town, he would be helpful, but as someone who had become very close to her, he was irreplaceable.

"Hello," he said, glancing around at them all as he entered the barn.

"Mayor," said Sheriff Slattery.

"What's the word on Sara?"

"Nothing's changed since I called you," Sadie said.

The sheriff cleared his throat. "I'm thinking we'd better get as many people out looking for her as we can before dark."

"I've spoken to Roz and your cousin, Laura," Edwin said, looking at Sadie. "They're standing by to spread the word if needed. Shall I call them now? We could probably have twenty or thirty people out here in fifteen minutes."

Sadie nodded, though she hated the fact that they needed the whole town's help.

"Yes, let's do it," Alice said, her voice cracking. "Thank you, Edwin."

"Glad to help." Edwin stepped outside as he drew out his cell phone.

Milo walked across the barn alley and took a rasp and a pair of shoe pullers from his wooden toolbox. He walked back toward Daisy's stall.

"What are you doing?" the sheriff asked.

"I'm going to take that shoe off, before she hurts herself worse. She's already limping."

"All right." The sheriff turned to Alice. "What's your best guess on where your daughter would ride? Does she have favorite trails?"

"Anywhere, really."

"What about this trail to the mine? Do you think she'd go up there?"

"Maybe."

Alice's bleak expression prompted Sadie to speak up. "It takes about an hour to ride a horse up there at a leisurely pace, Sheriff. But we can drive up in less than half that. I think we should go there first and check it out, based on the burrs Daisy's carrying."

"Sounds good. Let's take my four-wheel drive." He looked at Alice. "Would you stay here? We can make this our command post. And send any new arrivals out to go over the nearby trails. Milo might have missed something."

Sadie tried not to think that Sara could be lying still and helpless within a few hundred yards of them, and they might ride or walk right past her.

"I want to go to the mine with you," Theo said.

"I'll take my Tahoe, and you can ride along."

"Mind if I tag along?" Edwin asked.

"No, I'd appreciate the help." Sadie turned to the sheriff. "It might be a good idea to drive a few people up there who know the trails and let them walk back over the paths Sara could have taken."

Sheriff Slattery nodded. "That might be about all we have time for before dark. Let's go."

"Wait," Alice said. She strode into the stall and worked at the saddle strings on the cantle of Daisy's saddle. A denim jean jacket was tied just behind the seat.

The star-shaped badge on Mac's chest glinted as he followed her.

"Sara took this jacket with her." Alice freed it from the saddle and clutched it to her chest.

"It'll be cold tonight," Milo said.

Alice looked at him and then at the sheriff. "Do you think we should bring in dogs? They could sniff it."

The sheriff frowned. "I doubt I could get a tracking dog in here tonight, but that's a good thought. Bag the jacket in case we need it. Don't let a lot of people handle it."

Alice nodded.

"I'll get you a sack," Milo said.

Sadie wished she had Hank with her. Her golden retriever knew Sara well, and he might be able to help, but she didn't want to take time to go home for him.

She looked at Alice. "Are you going to be all right?"

"Yes. Milo will be here with me, and I expect other people will come soon. I'm going to call Cliff."

"I think that's a good idea." Alice was on good terms with her ex-husband, and he would certainly want to know what was going on. Sadie gave her daughter a quick hug. "All right, Theo, let's roll."

The sheriff went outside with them and headed for his vehicle. Sadie, Edwin, and Theo got into the Tahoe. They passed a car and pickup as Sadie drove toward the road that wound up the mountain and would eventually take them to the Wright family's old silver mine. She recognized folks from town heading toward Milo's ranch, but didn't stop. Alice and Milo could fill them in and assign areas for them to search.

When they reached the mine, Sadie parked, and Sheriff Slattery pulled in behind her.

"There's a flashlight in the glove box," she told Theo, and he took it out.

They climbed out and walked toward the creek and the mine entrance.

"Sara," Sadie called. She and Theo strode without speaking toward the mine entrance. Sadie shone the light inside. "Sara? Can you hear me?"

Theo stepped into the entrance and shouted at the top of his lungs. "Sara, you in here?"

Only a faint echo answered.

They turned back toward the vehicles. Edwin was searching off to the side of the path to the mine entrance. The sheriff was bent over, walking slowly over the ground between the gravel road and the creek.

"See anything?" Sadie walked toward the sheriff as she called out.

Mac shook his head. "No hoofprints, so far as I can tell. It's been dry. I can't really tell if any horses have been up here lately or not."

"The burdocks grow over there." Sadie pointed and then walked toward a stand of the tall, dry weeds. Theo and the sheriff joined her and stood gazing at the open ground.

"I don't see any bent down," Mac noted.

"Me either."

He glanced up at the sky. The sun had already slipped over the mountain peak, and shadows were lengthening. "Why don't you look along the creek bank? I'll take a good look at this field before anyone else disturbs it. We ought to be able to tell if a horse or a person went through here today."

They had been searching for another ten minutes when a black pickup appeared on the road and pulled over in front of Sadie's Tahoe. Milo's brother, Wyatt, and his wife, Jenna, got out and hurried toward them.

"We heard," Wyatt said. "Did you find anything?"

"Nothing," Mac replied. "Do you feel like walking back along the trail that comes up here through the woods?"

"Sure," Wyatt said. "Jenna can take the truck back to Milo's and pick me up there."

"It's a long hike," Sadie warned him.

"I don't mind."

She nodded. "Do you have a flashlight? Take mine if you don't."

"Can I go with Mr. Henderson, Grandma?" Theo asked.

"Do you mind?" Sadie said to Wyatt.

"That would be good."

Sadie thought so too. Theo was feeling some misplaced guilt right now, and having a man to talk to might help him deal with his emotions. This stage in life was hard for a seventeen-year-old, especially one whose parents had separated.

They soon settled the details, and Jenna dashed back to their truck for a second flashlight.

"It'll be dark before you get back," Mac said. "Call out for Sara, and watch for fresh horse droppings on the trail."

Wyatt nodded. "If Sara or the horse left any sign, we'll find it."

He and Theo headed for the woods trail.

The sheriff let out a big sigh. "I'm sorry, Sadie. I guess we should go back to Milo's. Can't do much more tonight."

"I wish I'd brought my dog," Sadie said.

Edwin draped his arm lightly over her shoulders. "Would you like me to go to your house and get him? I could bring him to Milo's."

"It might be worthwhile, if he's a good sniffer," the sheriff said.

Sadie gave him a bleak smile. "I wouldn't say he's as good as a bloodhound, but he knows Sara."

"Why don't you two go get him?" Mac said. "We've tried the most obvious places. If she's tucked out of sight somewhere near Milo's, maybe your dog can find her."

Sadie agreed, and she and Edwin walked toward the Tahoe.

"If you want to drive, I won't say no." Sadie held out the keys, and Edwin took them.

"Sure."

"I'd like to call Alice and tell her what we're doing."

As soon as Edwin had turned the Tahoe around and headed back toward town, she keyed in Alice's number.

"Hello? Mom?" Alice said. Her voice sounded almost frantic.

"It's me, honey. Any word?"

"No."

"The sheriff is coming back there. Edwin and I are going to pick up Hank and bring him to the ranch. He can sniff around a little."

"What about Theo?" Alice asked. "Where is he?"

"I let him walk back with Wyatt. I hope you don't mind, but he wanted to go. I figured they might find something."

"Sure. That's okay. And Mom?"

Something in her voice told Sadie that Alice would not be easily calmed. "What is it?"

"I can't get hold of Cliff. I've tried about six times. It goes straight to voice mail, and I've left him three messages." Alice's voice broke. "I need him, Mom."

"I'm sure he'll call you soon," Sadie said. "Hang tight, honey. We'll be back soon with Hank." Sadie sighed as she put her phone in her pocket.

"Anything wrong?" Edwin asked. "I mean, anything besides Sara being missing?"

"Cliff isn't answering his phone, and she sounds a little panicky. That's not like her, but I can't blame her, with what's going on." Tears filled her eyes. "Edwin, what if we don't find her?"

He reached over and squeezed her hand. "I've been praying constantly since I heard, and I'm sure you have too."

She nodded.

"God knows where she is, Sadie."

"Yes," she whispered. "I need to remember that."

When they got to Milo's ranch with the dog in tow, Sadie was surprised at the number of vehicles parked in the barnyard. Her cousin, Laura Finch, ran to meet them as Edwin parked.

"Laura, thanks for coming." Sadie climbed out of the Tahoe.

"I couldn't stay away. Alice is in the barn, and Milo is heading up the volunteers who've been searching the grounds and the closest trails. I've been trying to help wherever I could."

"Thank you so much."

Edwin walked around the vehicle to join them. "A lot of people have turned out."

Laura nodded. "Roz and I called everyone we could think of. The sheriff came back a few minutes ago. He said when everyone who's out right now comes in, we'll have to quit until daylight." She eyed Sadie anxiously.

"It makes sense," Sadie said. With the sun behind the mountains farther west, dusk had settled over Silver Peak.

Edwin let out a sigh. "Unfortunately, I have to agree. The terrain is too rough to be traipsing over in the dark. Someone could easily get hurt."

Sadie opened the rear door and clipped the leash to Hank's collar. "Come on, boy."

Hank jumped down eagerly and sniffed about the ground near the Tahoe. Sadie tugged the leash and led him into the barn.

"Mom!" Alice hurried toward her. "I'm so glad you're back."

"Did you hear from Cliff yet?"

"No. I'm glad you brought Hank. Let me get the jacket."

Sadie spent the next twenty minutes leading Hank about the barnyard and driveway. He yipped and romped about, wagging his tail and greeting each of the people milling about in the driveway. After Sadie led him away from the distracting humans, he dutifully sniffed every weed and shrub along the lane, but to no avail. Edwin and Laura stayed with Sadie, illuminating her path with their flashlights.

"Hey," Sheriff Slattery yelled from near the barn, to call them back.

Sadie turned and squinted back at the barnyard. Milo had a floodlight mounted on a post outside the barn, and he stood in its glow with the sheriff, beckoning with big sweeps of his arm.

"Think they've found her?" Laura asked.

Sadie shook her head. "They'd have called my cell. Come on. I think Mac wants to call it a night."

They turned back, and when they reached the barnyard, she saw that Theo and Wyatt had arrived. Sadie arched her eyebrows at Theo as he walked toward her.

"Nothing," he said softly.

"We stuck to the trail," Wyatt said, "but there's a lot of country out there. If Sara got off the path and got lost…"

Theo touched Sadie's arm. "Grandma, you'd better talk to Mom. She's really upset."

Sadie handed him the leash and headed into the barn.

Inside, in the barn alley between the box stalls, Alice had squared off against Milo.

"How could you, Milo?"

3

MILO SPREAD HIS HANDS, PALMS UP. "I THOUGHT YOU KNEW SHE was going, Alice. I'm sorry, but I really don't think this is my fault."

"What's going on?" Sadie stepped forward and looked from Alice to Milo and back.

"Milo just told me he went to the feed store this afternoon— while Sara was out alone on the trail." Alice's chin held the stubborn set Sadie knew all too well.

Milo looked helplessly at Sadie and ran a hand through his black beard. "I assumed she had permission. If not, I certainly would have called to check with you. But I've never been under the impression that it's my job to watch these kids."

"Of course not," Sadie said, patting Alice's shoulder. "Sara's a good kid, and generally responsible. Nobody's blaming you, Milo."

Alice let out a deep breath, and tears filled her eyes. "Sorry. I'm upset, but I shouldn't have taken it out on you."

Milo looked slightly mollified, but he pulled off his hat and turned it in his hands. "Well, I did go get some feed about an hour after Sara took Daisy out." He puffed out a breath. "The horse was standing out by the corral when I got back. I guess I should have made that clear before."

Sadie considered what he had said. "So you didn't actually see Daisy come back."

"Nope. Nor where she came from. She was standing there by the corral fence when I drove in, with her head drooping. At first I thought Sara must have run into the barn for something, but she wasn't anywhere around."

"She could have come back here to the ranch, then," Alice said.

Sadie shook her head. "I don't think so. Hank isn't acting like he's found her scent, and as Milo said earlier, she wouldn't leave Daisy standing there all saddled and everything."

"I didn't think she would either." Milo scratched his chin. "I started to take off the bridle, and I realized that Sara wouldn't go off and leave her there like that. She's a good little horsewoman. So I led Daisy in here and left her while I went out to look around. I took my gelding out, thinking maybe Sara had been thrown. I expected to meet her walking in, but I didn't find any sign of her. That's when I knew I needed to alert you folks."

"Sounds like you did everything you could," Sadie said. She stared pointedly at Alice.

"I'm sorry, Milo." Alice's tears spilled over. "Really, I am. Mom's right. None of this was your fault. I'm just so frustrated right now, and so…scared."

Milo looked down at the floor and moved a wisp of hay with the toe of his boot. "Sure. I understand."

Sadie pulled her close. "It's okay, honey." She patted Alice's back and let her cry for a minute.

Mac stepped into the barn doorway and raised his voice so that people could hear him both inside and out. Sadie took a glance at her watch. It was nearly eight o'clock.

"Folks, I think we'd all better go home and get some rest," Mac said. "Sunrise is about six thirty, and I'll be here a half hour before that. I'll call Breckenridge and see if we can get a canine unit up here. Meanwhile, if anyone hears anything at all, keep me posted." He turned toward Alice and Sadie. "I'm sorry, ladies, but we can't have somebody out there breaking his neck in the dark. That wouldn't help Sara."

Alice sniffed and nodded. "I understand."

Sadie walked out to the yard with Alice. Hank barked and tried to haul Theo toward her, tugging on the leash.

"Put him in the back," Sadie called to Theo. She turned to Alice. "Do you want me to come to your house?"

Alice shook her head. "We'll be all right."

Sadie knew that wasn't true. None of them would be all right until they found out what had happened to Sara.

"I can come over. It's not a problem."

"No, you should take Hank home."

"Okay." Sadie hesitated. "Sleep if you can."

A little sob escaped Alice. Sadie put her arm around her daughter's waist.

"It's going to get cold, like Milo said," Alice sobbed.

"Not that bad. It won't freeze tonight."

"She left her jacket on the saddle."

Sadie had no answer for that. If Sara was lying on the ground somewhere tonight, she probably would be chilled. The thought made her want to stop the sheriff from leaving and send the searchers out again, no matter what the risk. She took a deep breath and exhaled slowly.

"We've got to keep our wits."

Alice nodded. "I know. I just…I never thought this would happen to me. You see people on the news pleading for help, but…Mom, it's Sara this time!"

"I know."

Theo shut the door of the Tahoe and came slowly toward them. "You okay, Mom?"

Alice nodded. "You drive. I'll fix you something to eat when we get home."

None of them had eaten supper. Sadie hadn't thought about it, but now her stomach clenched. She hoped Sara wasn't hungry, but she would be if she was conscious, and Sadie wouldn't wish it otherwise.

She would go home and eat and try to catch some sleep and be back here at dawn.

"Did anyone call Pastor Sweeting?" she asked.

"Laura did, just a little while ago. He offered to come out here, but I told him we'd have to give up the search soon. He said that if…" Alice cleared her throat. "If we didn't find her tonight, a lot of the church folks would come in the morning. He's sending the word around the prayer chain."

"Good."

"Mom, I still can't get ahold of Cliff. Where could he be?"

"I don't know."

Alice's face crumpled. "I am so furious at him. He should be here."

"He'll check in, sooner or later." Sadie leaned toward Theo and gave him a squeeze. "Take care of your mama, and call me if you need anything. Anything." She stepped back and held his gaze, and Theo nodded.

As she went to the door of her vehicle, Edwin stepped along-side her and pulled her into a hug.

"Anything more I can do?"

"Pray."

"I will. Call me if you need to talk, even if it's two o'clock in the morning."

"Thanks." She squeezed his hand and got into the Tahoe. In the back, Hank let out a whimper, and she was glad for the company on the lonely drive home.

———————

As she had expected, Sadie couldn't settle down that evening. She made herself eat a turkey sandwich, but she couldn't face getting ready for bed. She paced the main room, from the stone fireplace to the windows by the dining table. She pushed the curtain aside and looked out countless times.

Dear God, protect her.

Staying home went against all her instincts. She ought to be out there, calling Sara's name.

At ten minutes to eleven, she broke down and called Edwin's number. He answered on the first ring.

"Did I wake you?" she asked.

"No, I haven't gone to bed."

"This is awful, Edwin. I should be out there looking for her."

"You will be in a few hours."

Sadie sighed. "What if that's too late?"

"Sadie, dear, you can't think that way."

"I know. But I do. She could be hurting. And scared." She resumed her pacing, holding the cell phone to her ear.

"Easy, now." His deep, gentle voice calmed her. "If you can't sleep, think what you can do to help her."

"Well, I can pray, but I've been doing that nonstop."

"What else?"

Sadie stopped pacing. "If I knew… I guess I could make her favorite cookies."

"Yes, you could, if you want to. I know you, and doing something like that might help you feel a little better."

"The people who come to search can eat them. I'll keep some back, just for Sara."

"There you go," Edwin said. "I've been thinking about how to organize a more efficient search. I suppose the sheriff will see to that in the morning."

"He's done things like this before," Sadie said. "He'll probably have maps with grids laid out, and divide the searchers into teams."

"I expect so. And I've been away so long, I don't remember half the territory within an hour's ride on horseback."

"He should get Milo and his brother to help him set it up," Sadie said. "They've lived on this mountain all their lives."

"Good thought. Do you feel less helpless now?"

"I think I do. Thanks, Edwin."

"If you need someone to help mix the cookie dough…"

Sadie chuckled. "I'll do just fine. But thank you."

After they signed off, she went to the kitchen, took out a big stainless-steel mixing bowl, and set to work. At one thirty in the morning, she took the last sheet of crispy oatmeal-raisin cookies out of the oven. She had made a triple batch, and it looked like enough cookies to feed an army. She bagged a dozen, praying for Sara, and put the rest in large plastic containers to take to Milo's at sunup.

She was beginning to feel a little bit fatigued, so she went to her room and changed into her two-piece cotton pajamas. She had feared she wouldn't be able to sleep yet, but after a few minutes of intense prayer, she yawned and snuggled into her pillow. She shoved away thoughts of Sara lying somewhere on the cold ground, shivering. *Please, Lord, comfort her. Let us find her quickly in the morning.*

When she awoke, it was still dark. She rolled over and looked at the clock. Only five o'clock. She didn't bother trying to fall back to sleep, and instead showered and dressed in a flannel shirt, jeans, and hiking boots. She decided to leave Hank at home this time, since Mac hoped to have a police dog at hand.

It was still too early to leave. She got a container of blueberry yogurt from the refrigerator and ate it standing near the kitchen window. When she had finished, it was still too early to drive over to Milo's. She needed something to distract her, so that she wouldn't keep staring at the clock. She turned on her computer and forced herself to think about the owner of the Civil War sword.

On a well-documented genealogy site, she was able to locate the family of George Watson, who had risen to the rank of major during the war. Though George was born in Pennsylvania, he died in 1890 in Colorado. Sadie surveyed a family group sheet that showed George's wife and six children. The two girls had married eventually, but Sadie didn't see any in-laws with the initials on the doctor's bag she had purchased.

She got up and walked over to her bookshelves. The Colorado and local history volumes took up several rows. She took down two books about Silver Peak's history and one on the mining days in the surrounding mountains. Settling on the sofa, she browsed through them. One of the earliest accounts of medical treatment in the immediate area told of an influenza epidemic that swept through the mining camps in 1879.

On a whim, she went back to the computer and put in a search for the epidemic of 1879. The *Colorado Journal*, an early Denver newspaper, had run a short item saying no doctor was available, but the miners reported that a woman had come and tended to the sickest men. Her identity was not disclosed, but one of the prospectors referred to her as "an angel" who worked tirelessly among the ill.

Next, Sadie searched for the history of doctors in Silver Peak. She didn't expect the owner of the bag to connect with her town, but it wouldn't hurt to look. Someone knowledgeable might have posted something online that wasn't in her books.

Another item almost buried in local news and dated a few months later than the flu epidemic mentioned a mining accident. *A woman arrived on the scene clad in a voluminous black dress and cloak, and brandishing fearsome medical instruments. She claimed she could cure one Randall Pickens, a miner who had been crushed beneath a fall of stone and was clinging to life. The other miners drove her away, saying she could not help him. Some men said she looked like an angel of death and feared she would bring bad luck to the camp. Indeed, Pickens breathed his last soon after her dreadful appearance.*

Sadie frowned at that. She knew people were superstitious in the old days, and perhaps the all-black clothing might indicate that she was a widow. And a widow's mourning attire might make her look scary to men surrounded by chaos and death. But really, an angel of death? She checked the dates and found this event took place at a different mine from the one mentioned in the notice about the epidemic. Still, she felt there was a strong possibility they described the same woman.

Not many women had come to Silver Peak in the early days. Of course, the small item didn't say the "angel" actually lived here. She could have come from another nearby mining camp to offer her skills.

Sadie checked her watch. In a few more minutes, she could leave. She made notes of what she had found in the leather-covered journal she carried in her purse. Next she went to a site she considered the most reliable on Silver Peak history. As she had thought, Nell Andrews, one of the first women to move to Silver Peak, was the wife of a large mine owner. Could she have offered nursing to the injured and ill miners? Still, she hadn't arrived in town until 1880, coming with her husband from Virginia. That was after the epidemic and the mine accident Sadie had just read about. It was a puzzle, but probably had nothing to do with the doctor's bag, which carried the initials RMT.

Mildly disappointed, Sadie turned off the computer.

"Come on, Hank. Let's have a walk before I go."

Hank rose from his bed in the corner and stretched. As she took him outside into the murky predawn air, she shivered. Though not below freezing, the air had cooled enough during the night to make sleeping outside uncomfortable without proper bedding. She couldn't help thinking of Sara. As Hank bounded ahead of her, she lifted her petitions once more to God.

Help her to remember Your promises, Lord. And help us to find her.

4

As she left the house, Sadie stopped on the front steps, her heart lurching. She had suddenly remembered her hasty departure from the Antique Mine the previous evening. She'd had a sizable bank deposit prepared. What had she done with it? She hadn't stopped at the bank before driving to Milo's ranch.

She hurried back inside and searched her purse. The bank bag wasn't there. The few items she'd brought home from the shop were on her desk, but the bright blue zipper bag wasn't there. She looked on the floor all around and under the desk, with no luck.

She had to get to Milo's. Time to think about the money later. Even as she locked the front door, she knew this would nag at her all day, but she didn't want to take time to go to the shop and see if she'd left the deposit there on the counter. She quickly looked on the Tahoe's front seats, on the floor beneath them, and in the glove box, with no results.

As she buckled her seat belt, she made a decision and took out her phone. She called Julie, who answered sounding a bit sleepy.

"It's me," Sadie said. "Sorry to call so early."

"It's okay. I wanted to help with the search anyway. Is there any news?"

"No. But I wanted to ask you a favor."

"Sure," Julie said.

"Thanks. I can't find the bank deposit I got ready yesterday. I had the bag at the counter when Milo called about Sara, and we left right after that. I thought I had it with me, but now I can't find it. I don't think it's at my house or in the Tahoe. Could you please go over to the store and take a look?"

"Sure. Would it help if I come out to the ranch afterward?"

"That would be wonderful. Thank you!" Sadie clicked off and stuck the phone in her jacket pocket.

When she arrived at the ranch, Alice's Jeep was already there, and the sheriff drove in just behind her. Milo, Theo, and Alice stood inside the open barn door, talking. Sadie left her vehicle next to Alice's. Spike Harris stood nearby, ready to help with the search, and Sadie nodded as he caught her eye. As she left the Tahoe, Edwin and Wyatt arrived.

"Hello, Mac," Sadie said as the sheriff left his car.

"Hi." Mac walked toward the barn, and Sadie waited for Edwin and Wyatt.

"Did you sleep?" Edwin asked, taking her hand.

"Some."

"Morning, folks," Milo called to them as they approached the group in the barn's entrance. "Come on in."

"So far as I know, nothing's changed since last night," Mac said. He waited for a response, and Sadie nodded.

"No, nothing," Alice said. Her face looked gaunt, and dark circles rimmed her eyes. Theo didn't look much better.

The sheriff nodded. "We can't get a canine unit up here until tomorrow at the earliest. I'm praying we won't need it."

"We printed the pictures you asked for," Theo said. He stepped forward and handed the sheriff a stack of computer printouts.

Sheriff Slattery gazed at the top sheet for a moment and cleared his throat. Sadie could only imagine how difficult this was for Alice.

Other people were arriving to join the search, and Milo beckoned them to join the group. Soon a dozen people besides the family had gathered.

"These are pictures of Sara Macomb, the girl we're looking for," Mac said to the crowd. "Most of you folks know Sara, but if you don't, take a look at one of these. She's fourteen years old. She's out there somewhere, and it's up to us to find her." He handed Milo the pictures and held up a map. More vehicles drove in, and the people in them joined those gathered around the sheriff.

"I've brought some large-scale topo maps of this area, and I've marked them off into grids," Mac said. "Since Milo Henderson knows this ranch and the surrounding terrain better than anyone else, I've asked him to make the search assignments. Form teams of two to four people, and stay together while you're out there. Check with Milo for the grid you will search. He'll make assignments based on your ability and the severity of the terrain. Any questions?"

Wyatt stepped forward. "How do we report in if we find something?"

"Thanks. I meant to mention that." The sheriff gave his personal cell phone number, and Milo gave his so that the searchers could put them into their contacts.

"Call me if you find anything that looks promising," the sheriff said. "Call Milo if you need further instructions or have questions about the logistics of the search. I'll stay here until I'm needed elsewhere, so you know where to find me and can get through."

"There are places on this ranch where you can't use your cell phones," Milo said, gazing around at the grave faces. "If you get between rock formations or down over a ridge or something like that, you might not be able to call. You all know that reception can be sketchy up here. If that happens, try to get to a better location and call again."

The searchers nodded soberly.

"Make sure Milo has a phone number for at least one person in each team," the sheriff said. "And now, I see that Pastor Sweeting is here. Pastor Don, would you mind praying before we go out?"

Sadie turned, surprised at the announcement. Pastor Sweeting and his wife were standing nearby, and the tall African-American man nodded firmly. "Be glad to, Sheriff."

They all bowed their heads, and he offered a brief petition for Sara, and for their success and safety in searching for her.

When he finished, the volunteers queued up for their assignments. Laura had volunteered to list the phone numbers and make a directory for Milo and the sheriff, and Alice acted as Milo's secretary, writing down the names of the team members appointed to cover each numbered grid on the map.

"Do you want to be partners?" Edwin asked at Sadie's elbow.

"Thanks. I'd like that." The pastor and his wife walked close to them, and Sadie said, "Pastor Don. Jeanne. Thank you for coming."

The pastor gave her a sad smile and a nod. "I've canceled services this morning. We needed to be here, and I know most of the congregation is coming too." The care lines at the corners of his eyes were pronounced in his dark skin. Sadie thought that he, like the rest of them, hadn't slept much. But the retired Denver police captain-turned-pastor was an ideal volunteer for the search, she realized.

"Would you like to join Sadie and me as a search team?" Edwin asked.

Pastor Don glanced at Jeanne, and she nodded. "We'd be honored," he said. "If you want to get the assignment from Milo, I'd like to speak to Alice for a minute."

"Of course." Sadie and Edwin got in line behind others waiting to take instruction from Milo, while Jeanne went with her husband to express their sympathy to Alice.

Milo gave them a patch of open land on the mountainside, just off one of the closer trails, to search.

"There's some brush there," Milo said, pointing on the map. "This part is kind of steep. If it's too much for you..."

"We'll take it slow," Edwin said.

Milo nodded. "Okay. You'll get into some scrub pines over here. Nothing serious as far as cover goes. With four people, you should be able to thoroughly search this grid in an hour or so."

Sadie nodded. "We'll come back for another assignment, if needed, when we're through."

She and Edwin took note of the boundaries of their grid and stepped to one side to wait for the Sweetings. "I know that trail well," she told Edwin. "We can walk to the corner of our territory in about ten minutes." Her phone rang, and she pulled it out and frowned at the screen. Julie.

"Hey, Sadie," Julie said. "I've hunted all around the counter, in the register, through all the drawers, and on the floor between the counter and the door. I even took a look in the back room. Is there any way your bank bag could be someplace else in the store?"

Sadie let out a sigh, thinking. "No, I had it right there at the counter. I didn't take it anywhere before we left. Thanks for looking."

"No problem. I thought I'd come out to Milo's now and help with the search, if you don't want me to look for the bank bag anymore. Do they need more people out there?"

"We can use all the help we can get," Sadie said, looking around. It did look as though half the town had turned out, and more vehicles were still arriving. "And thanks for trying to find the bag."

"Problem?" Edwin asked as she pocketed her phone.

"Oh, I've misplaced my bank deposit. In the confusion last night, I must have stuck the bag someplace without thinking about it."

"Sorry."

She shrugged. This was not the time to worry about money. "It will turn up. Looks like Pastor and Jeanne are ready."

Sadie, Edwin, and the Sweetings hiked up one of the trails to their assigned area. The sun was rising, and the morning light splayed over the mountains in a breathtaking array of color. The leaves on the hardwoods had begun to turn to gold, with occasional splashes of orange and scarlet. If she'd been out for any other reason, Sadie would have stopped to take in the incredible views they encountered at every turn.

They spent the entire morning searching two squares on the grid, but turned up nothing to indicate Sara and Daisy had passed that way. At half past eleven, they headed back to Milo's for the second time.

"I admit, I'm tired," Jeanne said.

"I think we all are," Sadie told her. "I keep asking the Lord to give me more energy, so I can help Sara." She had to admit the rocky hillside they'd just gone over had drained her.

"I think a short rest and some lunch will do us all good," Pastor Don said.

About twenty people milled about the barnyard when they arrived, some getting sandwiches at a table set up by the staff of the Market, and others discussing their morning and where they would look next. Sadie waved to Theo, who stood talking with a cluster of teenagers.

"Looks like a lot of students came," Edwin said.

Sadie nodded. "Alice mentioned this morning that Sara's classmates wanted to help."

They trudged into the barn with the Sweetings, to report to Milo. At least forty squares on his grid were crossed off, working out from his home ranch. A few on the other side of the road had been searched as well.

"We're going to get something to eat," Edwin said. "Where do you want us to search after that?"

Milo frowned down at his map. "Most of the close areas have been done thoroughly. I could send you up here." He pointed to a wooded area at least half a mile from his house. "It's a hike up there though. Sadie, would you want to ride your horse up there?"

"Sure. Can you lend horses to the Sweetings? I'll ask Alice if Edwin can ride Rio."

Milo nodded. "I can, but I wondered if Pastor Don should maybe stay here this afternoon."

"For the family?" the pastor asked. "I'd be glad to."

"Yeah, for Alice, but also for the schoolkids. Some of them are having a hard time with this."

They all looked out the big, open doorway. Small groups of high school students stood talking, their shoulders drooping.

Alice came over to stand beside Sadie. "How are you doing, Mom?"

"I'm okay. A little tired," Sadie admitted. "How about you?"

"It's very tiring to be on the edge of expectation all the time. I've calmed down some." Alice pointed to one group of teenagers. "That's Tori Anderson, in the red hoodie."

Sadie zeroed in on the girl. "The one who's been hassling Sara?"

"Yeah."

Sadie noticed that Tori hadn't joined the group of kids around Theo, but was off near the corral, talking to a couple of other girls her age.

"Have you got a minute?" Alice asked.

"Sure." Sadie turned to Edwin. "Can I meet you outside?"

"Of course. Just come find me when you're ready to eat." Edwin walked outside and gravitated toward a group of men from the church. They had clustered close to the refreshment table, where the Market's staff and Luz Vidal had set up to serve sandwiches, pastries, and beverages to the search teams.

"What is it?" Sadie asked Alice.

"I found this in the pocket of Sara's jacket." Alice handed her a folded and crumpled sheet of notebook paper.

Sadie opened it and read the brief message. *Be careful at lunch. Tori has it in for you.* She frowned. "Who wrote this? Do you know what it means?"

"I'm pretty sure it's Mia Garza's handwriting. I think she passed it to Sara at school as a warning."

Sadie eyed her closely. "You said Tori was jealous of Sara."

"Yeah. I'm not sure what Mia meant by this, but I know one of Tori's friends bumped into Sara in the cafeteria the other day and made her spill her tray. She was mortified."

Sadie thought for a moment. "Maybe this note was written before that happened."

"Or maybe Sara got it Friday," Alice said.

"What? You can't think Tori has anything to do with Sara going missing."

Alice hesitated and then ran a hand over her eyes. "No, not really. Mom, I'm not saying anything like that, but—well, this is serious. Sara's *gone!* I just think we need to look at everything that could possibly have a bearing on the situation."

Sadie nodded slowly. "You're right, of course. Even being distracted by Tori's attitude could have made Sara lax when she was out riding. She could have been thinking about the ruckus at school, and when Daisy stumbled, she wasn't paying attention."

"Yes! That's more what I was thinking. Sara's a great rider. It would take a lot for her to get thrown. But if she was woolgathering, it could happen. Do you think I should tell the sheriff about this?"

"I don't know," Sadie said. "I hate to cause problems for the girl if it's not warranted."

"That's why I didn't want to say anything in front of Edwin, or anybody else, until I got your opinion."

Sadie frowned. As a teacher, Alice usually managed to keep an open mind when it came to disputes between students. But this was different. They were all too close to the situation to be objective.

Alice looked toward the barnyard and touched Sadie's arm. "There's Mia. Maybe we could ask her about it."

"That's a good idea." Sadie and Alice walked outside, but Sadie spotted a familiar face and paused. "Troy Haggarty's here."

"Word gets around." Alice frowned.

"Are you ready to speak to the press?" Sadie asked. Though their newspaper was small for a daily, Troy took his job as editor and chief reporter seriously. Naturally he would want to report on Sara's disappearance as a service to the community, not to mention as a lead story that would sell papers.

"I think I'll just refer him to the sheriff," Alice said, watching Troy bleakly.

"Okay, but sooner or later, you'll probably have to talk to him."

"To tell them we've found Sara, I hope."

Sadie squeezed her shoulder. "Come on. Mia's talking to her parents. Let's go have a word with her."

The crowd in the barnyard shifted constantly as teams who had eaten went out to continue the search and new volunteers arrived. Deep gratitude welled up in Sadie's heart as she saw all the people who had given up their plans for the day in order to help. Dear friends, casual acquaintances, and complete strangers reported to the command center in the barn for assignments.

The Garza family stood together near their car. Ramon, Gloria, and their two teenage daughters, Mia and Elena, appeared to be preparing to go out as a team. Mia was pulling on a sweatshirt as they approached, and Gloria said, "Now, you girls have your phones turned on, yes?"

Mia nodded, and Elena said, "Yes, Mom."

"Hi," Sadie said.

The Garzas all turned toward her and Alice.

"Oh, Alice, I'm so sorry about this!" Gloria gave Alice a quick hug.

"We came to see if we could help," Ramon said to Sadie. "Milo gave us a section to search."

"Thank you all," Sadie said.

"We are praying for Sara too," Gloria added.

Alice smiled, and tears pooled in her eyes. "Thank you. We wondered if we could ask Mia about something."

Mia looked surprised, but she nodded. "Sure, Mrs. Macomb."

Alice held out the note. "This was in the pocket of Sara's denim jacket. I found the jacket on her saddle, when her horse came back yesterday."

Mia took the sheet of paper and unfolded it. She looked up at Alice. "I wrote this to her. She wore that jacket to school Friday, and she must have stuck it in her pocket."

"What's that all about?" Alice asked.

"It's stupid, really. Tori is jealous of Sara. See, she likes this guy, Hunter. But lately, he seems to like Sara better—or at least that's what Tori thinks. Sara's not trying to steal him away or anything."

"So what did you mean when you wrote that note?" Sadie asked. "Did Tori make trouble for Sara on Friday?"

"Not really. She made a few snide comments when we were standing in line in the cafeteria, but a couple of friends and I stuck with Sara to make sure nothing happened."

"Thanks," Sadie said. "You're a good friend."

Mia's eyes misted. "I just want her to come back! Mrs. Macomb, have you heard anything? I feel so horrible. She might have fallen off a cliff or something!"

"Oh, honey." Alice shook her head and dashed a tear from her cheek.

"We're going to find her," Sadie said. "She has to be out there somewhere. With all these people helping, we'll find her."

"That's right," Ramon said. "Come on, girls. Let's go do our part. We might find something."

5

As the Garzas headed across the pasture, Alice said to Sadie, "Edwin's waiting for you. You'd better go eat now."

Sadie spotted him, still talking to his friends from church, but Edwin's gaze did stray her way, and he gave her a little wave. "Okay," Sadie said. "Would you mind if Edwin rode Rio? Milo gave us a section that's a ways out, and he thought we'd do best if we took horses up there."

"I should have thought of that. Theo could take Bronco too."

Sadie looked around for her tall grandson. "If he hasn't already gone out with another group, I'll ask him to go with us."

She found Theo with his friends, and he was eager to accept.

"Great. I'm going to get a sandwich," Sadie said. "Edwin and I will meet you in the barn in ten minutes."

She hated to take the time to eat. She had already spent about twenty precious minutes talking to people. Time was against them—against Sara. Edwin understood her urgency, and they ate quickly.

When they got to the stalls in the barn, Theo had all three horses saddled. The three of them led the horses outside, mounted, and rode up a steep trail toward the section they planned to search.

On the way they saw other teams walking slowly over the rugged hillside and looking behind every rock and into every thicket.

When they reached the edge of their new area, they sat on their horses for a moment and looked around. The mountain vista was heart-wrenchingly beautiful, and so deceptively peaceful.

"Fabulous view," Edwin said. "It's been years since I was up here last. Decades."

Sadie exhaled heavily. "I have to keep reminding myself of why we're doing this. But I don't want to think about it."

Theo pivoted Bronco around and brought the black gelding over next to Sadie's chestnut, Scout. "Most of this part is woods. Should we tie the horses here and go on foot?"

"I think so," Sadie said. "Once you get off the trail, the footing can be pretty bad. If we're on foot, we can spread out about five yards apart and go through the woods slowly."

They followed the plan, making a swath along one end of their section. Sadie's fatigue set in long before they had finished going back and forth over the rough ground, dodging tree roots and rocks. In several places, they had to hunt for a way down a steep drop, and then work their way back up on their return sweep.

"I'm not sure this is a good use of our time," Sadie said when they were about half done. "What would Sara be doing out here, anyway?"

"I know," Theo said. "Even if she got dumped off Daisy and was lost, why would she even think of coming through here?"

Edwin looked around at the rough terrain. "That's true, but we've searched the obvious places. Milo is sending people out, one section at a time, from closest to the ranch on out. We need to search every square foot of this mountain until Sara's found."

Sadie sighed. "She could have been unconscious for a few hours and woken up after dark, disoriented. I guess you're right, Edwin."

After another hour of poking through brush and examining boulders, they hiked back toward their horses.

"Well, we know she's not out there in that patch of woods or that piece of mountainside," Edwin said. "We can be confident of that much."

"Right. I expect our next assignment will be above the tree line." Sadie sharpened her gaze as movement near their waiting horses caught her attention. "Who's that up there?"

Edwin and Theo looked ahead.

"I don't know," Theo said.

Edwin shook his head.

They quickened their steps. Although Sadie was tired, her interest was piqued. As they approached, the young man she had noticed sauntered out to meet them. He wore black jeans and a faded camouflage jacket. His long hair was tied back in a ponytail, and his chin was scruffy with stubble. He had a drab backpack slung over his shoulder, and the long limb of a wooden bow stuck up from behind him.

"Hey! Are you looking for that girl?" he asked.

"Yes, we are," Sadie said. "Are you?"

"I just heard about it from some people going up the trail," he replied.

"Have you been out here long?" Edwin asked.

"I hiked over the crest yesterday and camped beside a stream near the summit." He stepped forward and extended his hand. "My name's Lane Pomeroy."

"I'm Sadie Speers." Sadie shook his hand. "This is my grandson, Theo, and Edwin Marshall."

Lane's eyes narrowed as he shook Edwin's hand. "I've heard that name. Aren't you the mayor of Silver Peak?"

"That's right," Edwin said. "Do you live in town?"

"No, I'm from Breckenridge. I come up here to rough it." Lane gave them a lopsided grin. "Guess you could say I'm a survivalist."

"What's that?" Theo asked.

"Oh, you know. Where you go out and live in the wilderness and see if you can make it without modern technology. I've been out four days this time."

"Your skills might be useful here," Edwin said.

Lane nodded. "I'd be glad to help."

"Assignments are being made down at the Henderson ranch," Edwin told him. "We're about to ask for a new area to search."

The wind ruffled Sadie's hair, and the fluttering of a small item hanging from one of Lane's buttons caught her eye. She reached out to touch it but stayed her hand.

"That feather ornament. Where did you get it?"

"What, this?" Lane looked down at his chest and fingered the small brown feather that hung from a leather thong with two red beads. "I found it."

"Where?" Sadie asked.

"Let's see, it was back up the mountain a ways." Lane turned and gazed behind him, up the trail. "I noticed it beside the path when I left my campsite this morning."

"Sadie?" Edwin eyed her closely.

"It looks like one of Sara's hair ornaments. She was wearing them when she came into the store yesterday."

Lane stared at her. "You mean it belongs to the lost girl?"

"Theo, what do you think?" Sadie asked.

Theo leaned closer, and Lane removed the trinket from his button, so Theo could examine it better.

"I don't know," Theo said. "I'd have to ask Mom to be sure."

"I think we'd better tell Sheriff Slattery." Edwin took out his phone. "If we can't reach him by phone from here, I'll ride down and tell him." He looked at his screen and then walked out onto the trail. He held the phone higher.

"Grandma, Bronco and I could make it down there in fifteen minutes," Theo said. "Maybe ten."

"I wouldn't want you endangering life and limb," Sadie said, knowing he would have to push it to accomplish that feat on this steep trail. "Just wait a bit."

Edwin walked away from them, toward an outcropping of rock that stood between the trail and a drop-off.

"Hey, Theo, can you climb up there?" he called.

Theo ran to him, and Sadie and Lane followed at a more leisurely pace.

Edwin handed Theo his phone. "There's hardly any signal here, but I thought maybe up on top of that rock…"

Theo shoved the phone in his pocket and climbed nimbly up the jagged rock face. Ten feet above them, he stood and took out the phone.

"Two bars."

"Give it a try," Edwin said.

After some fumbling, Theo put the phone to his ear. "Hello? Can you hear me? This is Theo Macomb."

He paused for a moment, and Sadie realized she was holding her breath, not a good idea up here in the thin air. She inhaled slowly and deeply.

"Milo?" Theo said. "Is that you? We may have found something. We need the sheriff." He looked down at them.

"Need me to come up there?" Edwin asked.

"I don't think so. Milo's gone to get the sheriff." A few seconds later, he spoke into the phone again. "Hi. We're on the trail next to the section Milo gave us, and we met a guy who found something that could be Sara's." He paused, listening. "Yeah, okay. Can you bring my mom up here? We'll wait right beside the trail. Thanks."

Sadie couldn't wait for him to climb down. "What did he say?"

"He's going to bring Mom up. If they can do it in the Jeep, they will. Otherwise they'll have to saddle horses."

"I think they can drive up here if they're careful," Edwin said as Theo clambered down.

"Might as well take a break." Sadie walked toward Scout. "You guys want some cookies? I've got two water bottles."

"I brought my own water," Theo said.

"So did I," Lane told her, "but a cookie sounds good."

Sadie chuckled. "I guess you never know what you can forage in the wilderness, eh?" Her nerves were wound tight, but she managed not to show it too badly. She got out the small plastic container of cookies she'd put in the saddlebag and handed it to Theo. "Share that around." She handed Edwin her extra bottle of water.

They all sat down in the shade of the rock formation and sipped their water slowly. Sadie made her two cookies last as long as she could. She had just finished the second one when they heard an engine. Theo stood and scrambled up the rock.

"It's Mom's Jeep."

Sadie stood close to Edwin as the blue Cherokee moved up the trail, raising a cloud of dust in its wake. Meanwhile, Lane fiddled with the ornament in his hand. Alice downshifted for the steep grade and at last came level with them. She stopped the Jeep at the base of the rock formation, set the parking brake, and got out. Sheriff Slattery opened the passenger door and climbed out.

"What have you got?" Alice asked as she strode toward them.

Sadie looked at Lane. "This is my daughter, Alice Macomb. She's Sara's mother. And this is Sheriff Slattery." She nodded at the sheriff. "Lane Pomeroy. He's been hiking in the area."

"Did you find something?" the sheriff asked Lane.

"Yes, sir." Lane held out his hand and opened it. The feathered thong lay in his palm.

Alice caught her breath and reached for it. Lane surrendered it, and she held it up. Sadie started to comment, but decided to let Alice reach her own conclusions.

After a long moment, Alice nodded and held it out to Sheriff Slattery.

"This is Sara's. It was on one of her leather hair wraps, and she was wearing them yesterday."

6

"WHERE DID YOU FIND THIS?" THE SHERIFF ASKED.

Lane turned toward the trail above them. "A ways up there. I came onto this trail off another one. I had camped last night by a stream."

"I think I know the place," Sadie said. She seldom ventured that high anymore, but when she was younger she had roved all over the mountains on foot and on horseback. The path she was thinking of was a rugged one, accessible only on foot.

"If he's talking about the place I think he means, it's a ways from here," Sadie said. "I doubt anyone has searched that far out yet."

The sheriff gazed up the trail. "Can we drive there?"

"I doubt it," Lane said. "But you could get a lot closer than this. Maybe a mile. Where the smaller trail goes off, you'd have to walk. Horses might get in, I suppose." He glanced toward the tethered mounts on the other side of the trail.

"All right," Slattery said. "Alice, are you willing to drive up there?"

"Of course."

The sheriff turned to Lane. "I want you to go with us and show me exactly where you found this."

"Yes, sir. I can do that."

"May I come, Mac?" Sadie asked.

"I guess so. Climb in."

"Can we take the horses up?" Theo asked, eyeing the sheriff hopefully.

"Don't see why not. The ladies could use them when we go off-road."

Edwin nodded. "Go ahead with Alice, Sadie. I'll ride Rio and lead Scout up there."

Sadie squeezed his hand. "Thanks. I'll see you in a few minutes."

Edwin and Theo headed for the horses while the sheriff installed Lane, with his backpack and bow, in the back of Alice's Jeep. Sadie envied him his litheness as she clambered in beside him.

She waved to Edwin and Theo as the Jeep passed them. Theo had taken the lead rope from her saddlebag and clipped it to Scout's cheek strap. She knew this trail, and they would have to take it slowly—probably much slower than Theo would like.

As Alice downshifted for the grade, Sadie looked over at Lane. How long had this young man really been out here? The tales of a wild man in the woods raised more questions in her mind. Could Lane Pomeroy be the one people had seen flitting about Silver Peak in the shadows? Even more serious, could he be somehow connected to Sara's disappearance?

He was openly wearing the hair ornament. Did that support his innocence? Or was it brashness on the part of a disturbed young man? Had he really found the bead-and-feather thong by the trail, or had he come by it in a less innocent manner?

So far, she had considered only an accident as the thing that kept Sara from returning home. But could something more sinister have happened?

Lane met her gaze, and Sadie looked away.

Lord, I want to be fair to this young man, but I don't want to overlook any possibilities either. Help us all to see clearly and to reserve judgment.

"We're almost there," Lane said. "See that path?"

Alice parked the Jeep, and they all got out.

"How far in to the stream?" Sheriff Slattery asked.

"Not too far," Lane said, "but I found that doodad partway along the path."

The sheriff crouched and looked at the earth where the path veered off from the main trail. Sadie walked over to stand just behind him.

"Do you see something?"

"No."

"I'd be surprised if Sara came all the way up here," Alice said, a catch in her voice. "Especially alone."

"Me too." Sadie looked around. They were above the tree line, and the terrain had given over mostly to rocks and low-growing shrubs. "Still, you never know. If she was distracted, thinking about something else..."

"Yes, like that mean girl at school."

"Now, Alice." Sadie straightened.

"Something I should know?" Sheriff Slattery asked.

"It's nothing, really," Alice said. "Just a schoolgirl tiff. I'm sorry I even mentioned it. I guess I'm still trying to find someone to blame."

Sadie went to her and put her arm around Alice. "This is a hard day. Nobody's upset with you. We need to follow up on this clue that Lane found."

Alice gazed at Lane. "Show us the spot, will you, please?"

"Do you want to wait for the horses?" the sheriff asked.

"No. Let's go."

He waved toward the trail. "Mr. Pomeroy, would you lead the way, please?"

Lane set off down the narrow track, and Alice followed. Sadie fell in behind Alice, with the sheriff bringing up the rear. A few minutes later, Lane stopped and looked around uncertainly.

"It was right along here somewhere."

They stood on a bluff, with the mountainside falling away just a few feet off the path. Sadie looked out over the valley. A silvery stream cut down from near the summit, and from here she could see across to the next mountain, but even with the broad vista she enjoyed, she couldn't see any houses or roads from this spot.

"I camped down there," Lane said, pointing. "The path is a little tricky, but I think it's only a few yards to where I found the beads and feather."

He walked a few more steps and stopped. "Yeah, this is it."

The sheriff came closer, and he and Sadie and Alice all examined the ground. Some dried grass and other low plants grew between the gnarled krummholz shrubs on the rocky slope. The sheriff's keen eyes scanned the ground in all directions.

Lane stooped and touched a low-growing juniper bush beside the path. "I saw the red beads here, and then the feather."

Alice hugged herself and shivered. "Why would she be way up here?"

No one had an answer. Sheriff Slattery moved slowly over the ground, searching. Sadie and the others stayed put, waiting. While they watched, Theo and Edwin joined them.

"We left the horses out near the Jeep," Theo said to Alice. She nodded and sidled closer to him. Theo put his arm around his mother.

After about ten minutes, Sheriff Slattery came back to them. "I don't see anything. No hoofprints. There are a few scuff marks on the trail, but Mr. Pomeroy could have made those when he hiked down this morning."

"I'm sorry if I messed anything up," Lane said.

"So now what?" Alice asked.

The sheriff glanced at his watch. "I'd like to send Wyatt Henderson and a couple of other folks who are used to rugged terrain up here." He looked sharply at Lane. "You say this path goes down to your campsite?"

"Eventually, yeah. It was a tough hike coming up. Going down is probably more dangerous."

The sheriff nodded. "You didn't see any other sign of hikers or campers?"

Lane shook his head.

"Hear anything last night?" Sheriff Slattery asked.

He shrugged. "Some coyotes, but they weren't close. Wind. Nothing much."

"Okay." The sheriff took out his phone and looked at it. "Let's go back out to the main trail. I'll call the ranch when we can get a signal."

They all tramped out to where the horses and the Jeep waited. As soon as they reached the Jeep, the sheriff tried the phone again.

"Well, what do you know?" He punched a few buttons. "Milo? Is your brother down there?" For the next minute or two, the sheriff stood frowning and listening, with an occasional, "Uh-huh" or "I see." Finally he said, "Hold on."

Sheriff Slattery looked around at the small group. "Somebody's found something on a grid section two over from the last one Sadie and Edwin searched."

Alice grabbed Sadie's arm, squeezing tightly. "What is it?"

"Maybe nothing," the sheriff said, "but Milo advises we should take a look."

"Let's go," Theo said. He went to Bronco and untied his reins.

"But what about this path?" Alice asked. "Sara's hair tie…"

"Let's see what they've got," Sheriff Slattery said. "We can come back here."

"Okay." Alice got into the driver's seat.

"Do you want me to come?" Lane asked.

"I want you where I can see you," the sheriff said.

Lane opened his mouth as if to speak, then closed it and climbed into the back of the Jeep.

Sadie was surprised at Mac's words, but she was glad too. Until they were sure Lane Pomeroy didn't have anything to do with Sara's disappearance, she wanted someone to keep an eye on him.

"I'll ride Scout down," she said. They would get there nearly as fast as the others, and her riding the horse would make things easier for Edwin and Theo.

They started out before Alice had turned the Jeep around, and it didn't take them long to find the place beside the trail where Wyatt, Jenna, and the Garza family waited for them at the head of another path that led into a stand of small pines.

Sadie dismounted and ground-tied Scout just off the trail. Edwin and Theo found spots to leave Rio and Bronco. Mac and Alice were just getting out of the Jeep, and Lane slowly followed them.

"What have you got?" Mac asked Wyatt.

Wyatt led him onto the side trail and stopped about fifty yards into the trees. "Right here."

The sheriff bent down and studied the ground. After a half minute, he straightened. "Sadie, come here."

She walked to his side.

"What do you make of that?" The sheriff nodded to a bare spot near the base of a pine bole.

Sadie caught her breath and went to her knees to look closer. "It looks like a hoofprint, only like the horse slid or..." She looked up and met Slattery's eyes. "Do you think this could be where Daisy snagged her shoe?"

"Could be."

Wyatt scratched the back of his neck and shifted his hat. "I was thinking that. So far as we know, no one else has been up here lately on horseback, and that root is in a bad spot."

Sadie stood slowly. "But if Daisy stumbled here and Sara fell off, how did her hair wrap get up to that other trail?"

"What's that?" Wyatt asked.

Mac explained about Lane's find, and showed the ornament to Wyatt and the others, who had gathered around.

"Sara wears those all the time," Mia said. Tears streamed down her cheeks, and her mom hugged her close.

Sheriff Slattery put his large hand on Wyatt's shoulder. "I know your brother's doing a great job down at headquarters, but I wonder if you could get him to come up here. I want a search team that knows the terrain to hike the trail this young man came up this morning. And check down below the bluffs it follows too."

Wyatt nodded. "Milo and I can do it."

"I want to go," Theo said.

Alice opened her mouth and closed it again.

"All right, son," Mac told him. "I'll call Milo now. We'll have him get a few supplies for you—a rope and some water and flares."

"I don't know if Milo has any flares," Wyatt said.

"I've got some in my vehicle. After you show him this spot, if he thinks it's reasonable, the two of you head on up the mountain to that other trail. Theo can guide you. I'll put some more people on this grid."

"What about him?" Wyatt nodded toward Lane.

"He'll stay with me," Sheriff Slattery said. "You weren't on a schedule today, were you, Pomeroy?"

Lane shook his head. Sadie almost felt sorry for him. He hadn't known what he was getting into today. Or had he?

"Okay," Slattery said to Wyatt. "Don't let anyone mess up this scuff mark. We'll spiral out a search from here. If there's anything else to be found, we'll find it."

"You'll want people who understand how to look carefully before they step," Wyatt said.

Slattery nodded. "This country's not as dangerous as where you're going. Other people who are experienced hikers can handle this part. Just concentrate on that ridge trail, the campsite, and what's below the ridge."

Sadie shivered. She wondered where she would be of the most use. She crouched and traced one hoof mark with her finger. How could they possibly know what horse had made that print? Or how long it had been there?

She rose and walked a few yards along the trail, searching the ground for more marks.

"Will I be in the way if I come along?" Edwin asked, close behind her.

She turned and smiled. "No. I'm not going far. Just look carefully before putting your feet down."

After a few more steps, she stopped. Another hoofprint. She knelt in the path and picked up a small object—a horseshoe nail.

She fingered the checkering on one side of the square-shaped head. That texture helped the blacksmith feel which side of the nail was which, and that told him how to position it when he drove it into the horse's hoof. The nails were designed to curve outward as they made their way through the horn, so that the procedure was painless for the horse. The blacksmith then clipped off the end of the nail and clinched the stub down against the outside of the hoof, so that it couldn't pull out or hurt anyone. This nail had been used, shortened, and bent over. The clinched end had probably damaged the horse's hoof when it was yanked out.

Holding up the nail, she said to Edwin, "Please tell the sheriff and Wyatt that I've got something."

A moment later, Mac was at her side. "What is it?"

"And all for the want of a horseshoe nail," she quoted the old nursery rhyme, placing it in his hand.

7

MAC EXAMINED THE NAIL SADIE HAD FOUND. "THE SHAFT IS shiny. It hasn't lain out here very long."

"I agree. And there's a distinct hoofprint here with only four nail heads showing." She indicated the spot, and Slattery and Wyatt hunched over it.

"Do you think it's Daisy's print?" the sheriff asked Wyatt.

"Nearly certain. It's a back hoofprint. See how it's a little narrower at the toe? The front hooves are a bit more rounded. Why don't you ask Milo to bring up that shoe he took off Daisy? If it fits this impression, it'd be a pretty strong indication that this is where she had trouble."

"Good idea." The sheriff took out his phone and walked toward the open area near the main trail.

A short time later, Milo arrived with the worn horseshoe. He held it to the print Sadie had found on the trail.

"I'd call that a match."

Wyatt nodded. "Same here."

"Okay," Sheriff Slattery said. "We now know Daisy was here, and she probably snagged her shoe back there where we found the scuff marks. Sara may have fallen off the horse back there, or somewhere between these two marks. Somewhere on this trail, Daisy turned around or made a loop and ended up at the ranch without Sara."

Alice stepped up to him. "Thank you, Sheriff. I feel as though we have some real clues now."

"We'll find her," he said. "Sara's out here, Alice. Now, I want you to go down to the ranch and stay with Laura Finch. She's working the assignments now, and we'll call you or Laura if we find anything. Tell her to send the best of the volunteers up here to me. Adults who have experience hiking these mountains or in doing search and rescue. Meanwhile, I'm putting the Henderson brothers on that other trail with Theo."

Alice nodded, her lower lip trembling. "All right."

Sadie could see that her daughter was near her breaking point. "I'll go with you, Alice."

"Thanks, Mom," Alice whispered. Sadie walked between her and Edwin back toward the Jeep.

"What about the horses?" Edwin asked.

Sadie frowned. "Are you coming down with us?"

"I'm good for another round of searching. Maybe I should stay here with Mac."

"All right." Sadie looked at Alice. "Shall we offer our horses to Wyatt and Milo? Theo can ride with them to the trailhead."

"Sure."

Sadie settled the details with Theo and hurried back to the Jeep. Alice had opened the passenger door. "Would you drive?" she asked. "I'm a little shaky."

"Sure." Sadie climbed in behind the wheel.

She drove carefully down the mountain. As soon as they reached the barnyard, Laura ran out to the Jeep.

"Did you find something up there, Sadie?"

"Maybe. We met a hiker who had found a little ornament by the trail. It looked like one of Sara's hair ties."

"And Wyatt and Jenna found a place where it looked as though a horse had stumbled," Alice added. "The only thing is, those two spots were pretty far apart."

"How far?"

"Not really *that* far," Sadie said. "A mile or so. Less than two miles. The sheriff wants you to send the very best, most experienced searchers up there to him." She put her arm around Alice. "Do you want a sandwich?"

"No, but I'd love some coffee."

"I've got some chairs in the barn now," Laura said. "Bring it in there if you want. It's more private."

Sadie gazed around the yard. At least fifty people were clustered in small groups, talking. She noted three, including Troy Haggarty, who seemed to be interviewing searchers. One man was roaming about with a video camera rolling. Two police cars besides the sheriff's vehicle sat near the corral fence.

She watched Alice and Laura dodge between people and into the barn. Sadie turned toward the table where Arbuckle's Coffee had set up.

Luz Vidal smiled at her. "How is it going?" While she spoke, Luz reached for a cup and began filling it with fragrant coffee.

"Not as well as I'd like, obviously, but they do have a couple of leads to follow now."

Luz handed her the cup. "It's on the house for people who are actually searching. I make the reporters pay."

"Yes, the press is out in force," Sadie noted.

"It sure is. Our paper, Breckenridge, and one other." Luz nodded toward a graying man who wrote in a notebook as he stood talking to some of the high school kids. "I'm not sure where he's from."

"Huh." Sadie turned her back to the reporters. She didn't feel like talking to them. "Could I have one for Alice, please?"

"Certainly. I will give you her favorite. Please tell her our thoughts are with her."

A moment later, Luz put the second cup in her hand.

"Thanks a lot. You have no idea how much you're helping today."

Luz smiled. "I'm glad we can do something."

Sadie walked carefully to the barn, where Laura was back at work, assisted by Roz.

"Did more officers come to help?" she asked them.

"Yeah, Breckenridge and Aspen both sent a couple of men," Laura said.

Roz nodded. "We sent two of them out with some of the locals to search the grids just beyond where Milo found the hoof marks, and the other two to Sheriff Slattery."

"That's encouraging," Sadie said.

"Oh, and Julie's been here," Laura added. "She went out with a search group about an hour ago."

"Thanks," Sadie said.

Alice sat to one side in a lawn chair, staring off into space. Sadie walked over and handed her the special coffee.

"Luz sends this and her love."

"Thanks." Alice took a cautious sip. "Oh, that hits the spot."

Sadie pulled over another chair and sat down. "Maybe you should go home and rest, honey."

"No, I'm okay. And they might be close to finding her. I can't leave now."

Sadie nodded. "All right." She took a drink and closed her eyes for a moment. Even such a little thing as perfect coffee could mean so much. *Thank You, Lord. Please let them find her!*

"Mom?"

She opened her eyes. Alice was leaning toward her.

"While you were getting the coffee, I tried to call Cliff again."

"You still haven't been able to reach him?"

"No. And now his voice mailbox is full. It's after four o'clock. Where could he be?"

"I suppose you called the office, as well as his cell?"

"Yes," Alice said. "I didn't expect him to be at the office on Sunday, but I figured anything was worth a try." She let out a deep sigh. Why do you suppose Sara's hair tie was so far from where Daisy fell?"

"I don't know," Sadie said, thinking carefully. "I don't want to upset you, but it's possible that trinket Lane Pomeroy found wasn't Sara's after all."

"It is," Alice said firmly.

"Okay."

"Do you think Sara went way up there after she fell off the horse?"

"Anything could have happened," Sadie said. "It seems pretty certain that the hoofprints where I found the nail were made by Daisy. But a bird could have come along and picked up those bright red beads thinking they were berries and carried the thong up to where Lane found it."

Alice held up a hand to stop her. "You're right. I'm not being objective. It just seems so odd, that Sara would get thrown in one spot and hike up the mountain to the second spot, instead of down it, toward Milo's and home. And yeah, I know she might not have been thinking straight, but it's hard to think she'd do that."

"Maybe she rode up to the higher trail first, where Lane found the hair tie, gave up on it because it's so rough and narrow, and went back down to the other trail, where Daisy stumbled."

"Was there time for her to get that far, before Daisy came back?"

"I don't know." Sadie's mind whirled. Alice's suggestion about the timing troubled her. No one really knew what time Daisy had returned to the barnyard. There was at least an hour during Milo's trip to town when no one was at the ranch. Daisy could have been standing by the fence for an hour—or two minutes—when Milo returned.

Sally Henderson came into the barn with a tray of dough-nuts and went around to the workers, offering them a snack. She was Milo and Wyatt's mother, owner of the Alpine Hair Salon. When she came to where Sadie and Alice were sitting, she smiled sympathetically.

"How are you holding up, Alice?"

"Not too well, I'm afraid. It's hard to stay hopeful, when I know every hour that goes by makes it less likely we'll have a good outcome."

"Oh, honey. I'm so, so sorry. If I wasn't holding this tray, I'd give you a big hug."

Alice managed a weak smile. "Thanks. Your boys are up the mountain, looking for Sara. They're my angels today. You too, Sally. All of you who came to minister to us."

"I'm not doing much," Sally said. "Just passing out a little sugar, and I hope, a little encouragement. Your Sara is a strong girl. From what I hear, she may have had a rough fall, but Sheriff Slattery and the boys will find her."

"Thanks."

Sally smiled. "Now, how about a doughnut? I'm sure you didn't eat much today."

Alice sighed. "You're right. I suppose an infusion of carbs would help."

"It might boost your brain a little," Sadie said. "Personally, I'm done in. I don't think I can do any more searching today."

"Then you'd better eat a doughnut too," Sally said.

Sadie chose one and took it on a paper napkin. "Thanks so much. Listen, Sally, this is a little off topic, but maybe we can use a distraction right now. Alice mentioned angels, and that reminded me of a little historical puzzle I'm working on. Have you ever heard of a woman in the old days ministering as a nurse to the miners of Silver Peak? I'm talking way back, maybe when it was just a tent city, or in the early days of the town."

"*Hmm.* Yeah, actually, I think so." Sally's forehead furrowed. "Seems like there was a woman who opened a dance hall in Silver Peak when it was just a mining camp."

Sadie sat up a little straighter. "Did she endear herself to the men of Silver Peak and become known as the 'angel'?"

"I have no idea. But you could ask Harry Polmiller. He might have some stories from his family in the good old days."

"That's a great idea," Sadie said. This would be something to make note of. Harry was the oldest member of the congregation at Campfire Chapel. At ninety-four, he still got around and tended his garden, not to mention keeping friends entertained with tales of yesteryear. "I'll ask him about it the next time I see him."

"Okay. Well, you ladies enjoy the doughnuts. I'm going to go and see if I can peddle the rest of these."

Alice set her coffee and doughnut aside and took out her cell phone as Sally walked away. She pushed a couple of buttons and put the phone to her ear. After about ten seconds, she closed it. Tears spilled over her eyelids and ran down her cheeks.

"I don't get this, Mom. Where is he?"

Sadie knew she was talking about Cliff. She studied Alice's face. Her daughter wasn't just angry with her ex-husband, she was frightened.

"I'm sure there's some explanation."

Alice's face contorted and she met Sadie's gaze. "Do you think it's possible he picked up Sara without telling me?"

"You mean…?"

"I don't know what I mean." Alice dashed the tears away with her sleeve. "Nothing makes sense, Mom." Sadie sighed. "Okay, let's think about this. Cliff doesn't have a horse. None of the other horses looked as though they'd been ridden, or Milo would have noticed. We have the evidence of Daisy's mishap. She came home limping and with one shoe loose. We found the scuff marks and Sara's hair ornament. Cliff wouldn't be way up there on the trail in the places where we think Sara went."

"No, he wouldn't," Alice agreed. "But just suppose he came while Milo was at the feed store. He drives in, and no one's around.

A couple of minutes later, Sara walks in, leading Daisy. Cliff could convince her to leave the horse where Milo could tend her and take Sara away with him."

"He would have called you," Sadie said.

"You'd think so, wouldn't you?"

"Yes, I would. He's never done anything like that before, and you two have never squabbled about custody."

"I know." Alice's tears flowed freely now.

Sadie ate the last bite of her doughnut and handed Alice her napkin. "Here. It's probably a little sugary."

Alice sniffed and wiped her eyes with the napkin. "Thanks. I know it's not logical, but at this point, I'm open to anything."

"Then consider this," Sadie said. "How would Cliff have known Sara was over here riding Daisy? You didn't tell him, and if he had contacted Theo, or if Theo knew he had talked to Sara, he'd have told us."

"Yeah, you're right."

"So there's no way Cliff could have known where she was."

Alice nodded slowly. "Unless Sara told him. He could have called Sara on her cell phone and decided to come up to Silver Peak, but when he got to our house, he found it empty. Or what if she told him she was going riding, and he came straight here to get her?"

Sadie didn't like to think something like that had happened, but she couldn't totally discount it. "I still say he would have called you, or even come by the store to ask me where you all were. And I doubt he called Sara while she was out on Daisy. You know how hard it is to get cell service on the trails. It's hindered the search all day."

"Yeah. But I can't think of anything else. And the fact remains that I've called and texted him and Sara several times, and neither of them is answering."

Sadie reached over and patted her hand. "Honey, I have no answer for that. But there are still a lot of square miles out there we haven't covered. Let's pray."

8

———

Sadie and Alice finished their coffee and went over to Laura and Roz's makeshift desk for an update.

"What do you hear from the searchers?" Sadie asked.

Laura glanced up from the lists she pored over, spread out on a sheet of plywood that rested atop a barrel. "We haven't heard from Milo and Wyatt for the last twenty minutes. I'm assuming they're out of cell range. Sheriff Slattery called in ten minutes ago and said they haven't got anything new, but they're working outward from the hoofprints, if you know where that is."

"We do," Sadie said.

"Well, he said they're being very thorough, but it's a wooded area, and there are lots of places to look."

Sadie nodded. "If Sara was disoriented, she might have walked away from the ranch instead of toward it."

"Do you think she might have holed up to sleep last night?" Alice asked.

"Could be," Roz said. "Maybe in a thicket, or under a rock overhang. If she took shelter, she could be out there now, sleeping."

"Or too weak to walk," Alice said grimly.

Sadie put an arm around her. "I think it's more likely she got lost in the dark. When she woke up this morning, she probably chose the wrong direction, that's all. They'll find her, honey."

Alice let out a shaky breath but said nothing.

"Come on," Sadie told her. "Let's go out and get some fresh air. Clear our heads."

The man Sadie had noticed earlier and pegged as a journalist was coming into the barn. He eyed Sadie and Alice and walked toward them, his notebook in hand.

"Are you members of the girl's family?"

Sally stepped up, her empty tray snug against her side. "I'm Sally Henderson, and this is my son's ranch. May I help you?"

"Excuse us," Sadie said. Sally was the perfect person to run interference with reporters. She propelled Alice past him into the sunlit barnyard.

"How much daylight is left?" Alice asked.

"Three hours or so. The sun won't set until after seven, and they can keep going for a half hour or so after sunset."

"They'll need that time to get down the mountain. So. Less than three hours left to find her today." Alice stopped walking. "Mom, I don't think I can take another night with her out there."

Sadie pulled her into her embrace, and they stood holding each other for a minute. Another vehicle pulled into the yard, and Sadie squinted at the logo on the driver's door.

"Come on, honey. Let's make ourselves scarce. The TV station's news crew just arrived."

"Oh no. I can't talk to them." Alice pulled up the hood on her zip-front sweatshirt.

"You don't have to. Anyone with good sense will direct them to Laura and Roz, and they'll tell them to wait and talk to Mac."

"Maybe we should tell them to alert the sheriff."

"Good thinking," Sadie said. "They could call him and ask if he can come talk to all the reporters for a minute. Give them some sound bites for the evening broadcast."

"They'll want pictures," Alice said.

"You don't have to unless you want to," Sadie repeated.

"I mean of Sara." Alice shuddered. "I e-mailed the ones we printed out to the sheriff last night."

"Maybe he can give them those. Don't watch the news tonight, Alice."

"What if they get something wrong?"

"A hundred other people from Silver Peak will call in to protest if they do. And they won't have a scrap of information that you don't already know." She eyed Alice sternly.

Alice nodded. She looked around the yard and focused on a small group of teenagers who seemed to be just returning from one of the search grids. "I know that girl—the one in the green jacket. She's in Sara's class."

"Let's talk to her," Sadie said. "She may give us some perspective on how things are going at school."

They ambled over to meet the teens, who glanced at them and kept talking as they walked.

"Hi," Alice said. "I'm Sara's mom. I wanted to thank you all for coming today."

"Hi." The girl in the green jacket stopped, and her friends flanked her. "I'm Hailey. This is Mallory and Jason."

"And I'm Sara's grandmother," Sadie said.

Mallory and Jason nodded and murmured, "Hi."

"We're awfully sorry about Sara," Mallory said. "Has anyone found any clues to what happened?"

"Not really," Alice told her. "We know her horse slipped or stumbled and pulled a shoe loose. We're guessing Sara fell off at that point."

"Funny nobody's found her yet," Jason said. "How far away could she have been from here?"

"The place we think she fell is less than two miles from here," Sadie told him. "And we don't know which direction to look in. Some of the terrain on this mountain is thick with brush, and some is so rocky it makes it hard to search."

Hailey nodded. "Tell me about it. We spent the last three hours climbing over a place like that."

"I wish we had found something," Jason said, "but there was nothing out there. We were just talking about whether we should ask for a new assignment."

"That would be very generous of you to put in more time on this," Alice said.

"It is late in the day though," Sadie put in. "If you do go out now, you might consider going with an adult. At least have some-one who is an experienced hiker go with you, and make sure you have flashlights, in case it gets dark before you come in."

"I think I should call my mom and ask her if it's okay," Mallory said. She took out a cell phone and wandered a few feet away.

"Hailey," Sadie said gently, "Mrs. Macomb and I wondered how things were going for Sara at school. We've heard she had some friction with another girl."

Hailey rolled her eyes. "You mean Tori Anderson, I guess."

"Yes," Alice said. "Do you know her?"

"Everyone knows Tori. She's a drama queen."

Jason grimaced. "Yeah, the universe revolves around Tori."

"She's not that bad," Hailey said. "But she does get upset easily, and she thought her boyfriend..."

"He's not her boyfriend," Jason said.

"Okay, the boy she likes." Hailey shook her head. "She thought this guy paid too much attention to Sara."

"She was here earlier," Alice told her.

"Yeah, I talked to her." Hailey's face went sober. "She was pretty upset. In fact, she started crying."

"Why crying?" Sadie asked.

Hailey huffed out a deep breath. "Tori wasn't very nice to Sara at school, but today she said she'd be devastated if something bad happened to her and she didn't have a chance to say she was sorry."

"So you think she *was* sorry?" Alice said.

Hailey nodded. "Big time. This has really jolted her. Made her think about how she's been acting."

"What about the boy, Hunter?" Sadie asked. "Has he been around today?"

Hailey frowned. "I think he and his parents went away this weekend. I'm not sure."

"He told me they were going to Colorado Springs right after his football practice on Friday," Jason said.

"What kinds of things has Tori been saying to Sara?" Sadie asked.

"Some name-calling," Jason said. "Like, slimeball and..." He broke off and glanced at Alice. "Well, she wasn't very nice."

"Friday, someone put a note in the crack of Sara's locker door."
Hailey grimaced. "It said, 'Go back to Denver, you sleaze.'"

Sadie looked at Alice. "That's hurtful."

"Yes, but I don't think Sara would fall apart over it." Alice
arched her eyebrows and looked at the kids.

"She crumpled it up and threw it away," Hailey said. "I told her
she ought to tell the principal, or at least her homeroom teacher,
but I don't think she did."

"Thanks," Sadie said. "And thank you again for joining the
search."

"I hope they find her soon," Hailey said.

Mallory came jogging toward them. "My mom said I can stay
until dark."

"I'm going out again." Jason looked at Hailey. "You coming?"

"Yeah. Let's get a drink and go back out." Hailey turned back
to Alice. "That's Tori's parents, over there, by that minivan."

"Thanks," Alice said.

As the teens walked away, Sadie asked, "Do you want to talk
to the Andersons?"

Alice nodded. "I don't think Tori is directly involved in this,
but it wouldn't hurt to cover all the bases."

They walked over and introduced themselves to the couple.

"I'm so sorry," Mrs. Anderson said to Alice. "This must be
terrible for you."

"It is," Alice admitted. "It's an encouragement to see so many
people come out to help. The kids have really been pitching in."

"Our Tori insisted on coming today," Mr. Anderson said.

His wife nodded. "We're usually in church Sunday morning,
but we let Tori skip today, and we came after the services let out."

"We hoped you'd have good news by the time we got here," Mr. Anderson said.

"We thought we would," Sadie said. "It's a real puzzle where Sara is. I understand Tori is a classmate of hers."

"Yes," said Mrs. Anderson. "Last night, we came home from a shopping trip in Breckenridge, and a friend of Tori's called and told her Sara was missing. Tori told me that they haven't gotten along well, and I could see she felt bad about it."

"That's really why we let her come this morning," her husband said. "She wanted to do something, and we thought maybe that would help her sort out her feelings."

"I appreciate that," Alice said. "And Tori's efforts."

"Yes, the young people are a big help," Sadie said. "I wish I had half their energy."

They parted cordially, and Sadie and Alice walked back toward the barn.

Alice kicked at a pebble in the driveway. "At least we know Tori was nowhere near here or the trails yesterday, when Sara went out to ride."

Sadie nodded. She hadn't really thought so, but Alice seemed relieved to have proof that the teenager had been with her parents the day before and wasn't involved in Sara's mishap.

"Oh, look. Mac's going to hold a press conference." Sadie pointed, and Alice looked toward where several reporters had clustered around him.

"Two TV stations now," Alice said.

"Yes. And where is that other man from?" Sadie asked, eyeing the middle-aged man with iron-gray hair.

"I don't recognize him," Alice said. "I see Lane Pomeroy is still glued to the sheriff's shirttail."

Sadie saw the young man then, standing to one side, a couple of yards from the sheriff. He didn't look happy, and his backpack and bow rested on the ground.

"Looks as though Mac hasn't cleared him yet. I know Lane says he only picked up that hair ornament by the path, but..." She swiveled to look at Alice.

"I know," Alice said. "I hate to be suspicious of people who probably are perfectly innocent, but right now I'm suspicious of anyone and everyone. I'll admit I'm glad Mac hasn't let him go."

Inwardly, Sadie had to agree. If Lane had anything to do with this, letting him go back into the wilderness could be a big mistake.

The thirty or forty people who had gathered quieted as the sheriff began to speak.

"Thanks for coming out, folks. The girl we are looking for is Sara Macomb. She is fourteen years old. My office has made photographs available to area news agencies. We have a promise of a K-9 unit being brought here by 7:00 AM, if we still need it. At this point, we have some leads we're following up on, but we haven't found anything conclusive. It's our belief that Sara is out there in the wilderness area surrounding this ranch and Silver Peak. Personally, I don't think she's all that far away, but we haven't found her. When she was last seen, she was wearing jeans and a gray, long-sleeved shirt with a horse on it. Her hair was in braids."

He paused, and several people in the crowd threw questions at him. Sheriff Slattery held up a hand. "One at a time please." He pointed at Troy. "Mr. Haggarty?"

Sadie smiled. It was nice of the sheriff to give the *Silver Peak Sentinel*'s editor the first question.

"Sheriff, I understand you think Sara is injured. Could you tell us what evidence you have of that?"

"Nothing conclusive, but the fact that we believe she had a cell phone with her tells us she either can't use it now, she is in an area where there's no service, or she's separated from the phone. The horse she left on returned limping, with a loose shoe, and we've found a place where we think they may have had a mishap, but we're not certain."

Several hands shot up, and he pointed to a young woman who was one of the TV reporters and had a cameraman capturing the entire exchange.

"Sir, do you think this girl could possibly be a runaway?"

"I don't think so. I know the family, and she's not the type. For one thing, she's very considerate of animals. If she did want to run away, I don't think she'd do it at her horse's expense. And I don't think Sara would willingly put her mother and her brother through this."

The sheriff's eyes roved over the onlookers, but the reporter called, "Follow-up question! Is it possible she's been abducted?"

A gasp went up from several people in the crowd, and Alice grabbed Sadie's wrist. She looked at Sadie with fear in her eyes.

9

SADIE PATTED ALICE'S ARM. "EASY NOW. THEY ASK ALL SORTS OF questions, you know, fishing for something juicy."

Sheriff Slattery leveled his gaze at the woman from the TV station. "We have no indication that anything like that happened, but of course anything's possible. Right now, we have to assume she was injured in a fall from the saddle. She's been out there twenty-four hours, and time could be critical. If we don't find any more evidence of her being nearby, we'll have to expand the search, of course."

His eyes scanned the group, and the gray-haired man with the notebook stuck his hand up.

"Yes, sir?" Mac said.

"I heard you've found an article of Sara's clothing."

The sheriff's face stayed neutral. "That's not quite true. A hiker did find a small item that could possibly be part of an ornament Sara wore. We've got searchers in that area as well—experienced locals who know how to navigate this terrain safely. But I've got to say, that spot was quite a ways from where we found the hoofprints."

He pointed to another man.

"Were these clues you found close to the trails, or off the track?"

"The hoofprints were actually on one of the trails, and if Sara was seriously injured there, we should have found her. We have people in the woods and rocky areas nearby, in case she got disoriented and left the trail. The ornamental item was found on a hiking path on the other side of the mountain. It's hard to believe a seriously injured person would go that far."

Hands shot up, and Mac called on a man whom Sadie thought was from the Breckenridge paper.

"Can't you track the girl's cell phone?"

"The state police are working on that for us," Mac said, "but so far we don't have anything. We're thinking her phone was shut off, but we don't know why. It could be she's saving her battery. Sara's a savvy kid. She's smart. If she couldn't get service and saw that her phone was searching for it and running down the battery, it's possible she would shut it off for a while, to save what juice she's got. Troy, you have another question?"

"Yes," Troy said. "Thank you. Have you considered using a helicopter in the search?"

"Yeah, I've talked to the National Guard, and if nothing is changed by morning, they may be able to send a chopper out from Denver, but that's not a done deal yet."

The sheriff looked over the crowd and ignored the hands waving at him. "Folks, time is short. I know you have deadlines, but we want to get as much ground covered as we can before dark. Any newcomers wanting to help search should speak to Laura Finch or Roz Putnam at the desk in the barn. That's it for now. Excuse me." He turned and walked toward the barn. As he passed Lane, he jerked his head slightly, and Lane followed him.

Alice's face was pale.

"Are you okay?" Sadie asked.

"Let's get some juice. And don't let those reporters near me, not even Troy."

Sally walked over to them. "Alice, honey, why don't you go into the house and stretch out on the couch? I'd ask Milo if he were here, but I'm sure he wouldn't mind."

"Oh, I don't know," Alice said.

Sally smiled. "Hey, I'm his mother. I'm telling you it's okay. Come on, I'll take you in the back door."

"It might be a good idea," Sadie said. "You'll be out of the reporters' sight. I'll go and get you a bottle of juice."

Sally put her arm around Alice. "That's it, come on. You can rest a little, and when the boys come down the mountain, they can tell you in private if they've found anything."

Alice went with her, and Sadie hurried to the refreshment tables.

"Sadie!"

She turned to find Roz hurrying toward her.

"Where's Alice?" Roz asked.

"Sally took her in the house to rest."

"Oh, good. We just wanted her to know Milo and Wyatt called in. They followed that trail down to the campsite by the creek and halfway around the mountain, but they didn't find anything."

Sadie exhaled, realizing her expectations had risen, just from seeing Roz moving a little faster than normal.

"I'm sorry," Roz said, touching her shoulder. "Jenna's gone to pick them up at the bottom of the trail on the Sterling Road. They should be back in half an hour or so. Oh, and the sheriff sent some deputies to bring the horses down from the trailhead where the guys left them."

"Thanks," Sadie said. "I'll tell Alice. I know she was hoping they'd turn up something new."

"We all were." Roz scrunched up her face. "Oh, Sadie, I feel so helpless."

"You? You're doing a lot. And we all appreciate it."

"Thanks, but it feels so futile when we get news like this. I really wish I could go to Alice with something tangible and see her face light up, you know?"

"I sure do."

Sadie got a bottle of juice and a cup of coffee from Luz and let Maggie Price, from the Market, talk her into adding a pair of chicken sandwiches to her load. She carried the cups and a bag holding the sandwiches toward Milo's house. Halfway there, she met Sheriff Slattery.

"Hi," she said. "Anything I don't know already?"

"I've been thinking about that silver mine," Mac said. "I know we went up there and didn't see any sign Sara had been there, but since we're at a loss for new clues, I thought maybe it was time we thoroughly searched it."

"I guess it makes sense. When you've eliminated so many other places…"

"Exactly. There are a couple of other mines within five miles, and I've got Laura calling the owners to see if they'll take a look and just make sure nobody's been in there lately. How long do you think it would take to search the Wright family mine? Can we do it before nightfall?"

"Probably. It's not that big. In fact, if I can get on a laptop, I can get you a diagram. I gave one to the historical society, and they posted it in their Web site archives."

"That sounds like a big help. Laura's got a laptop in the barn."

"Just let me take this to Alice. I'll be right there." Sadie quickened her steps and hurried into Milo's house through the back door. She barely glanced at the spartan kitchen, but went on through to the living room.

Alice was stretched out on the couch, and Sally slouched in a recliner nearby. Both sat up when Sadie entered.

"Here's your juice and a couple of chicken-asiago sandwiches," Sadie said. "Sally, I got myself some coffee, but if you'd like it…"

"No, dear, I'm fine," Sally said.

Sadie handed Alice the small bottle and set the sandwiches on the coffee table. She took a sip from her cup. "I was going to stay, but Mac wants to search the mine. I'm going to the barn to pull up the map of it on Laura's laptop."

"I thought you went to the mine last night." Alice frowned as she twisted off the bottle top.

"We did, but we didn't search it," Sadie said. "Theo and I just yelled into it from the entrance. Now the sheriff wants to get some people in there and look in every cranny."

"I guess that's logical, though I doubt Sara would stay in there."

"If she was hurt…" Sadie winced and gave a little shrug. "We just don't know where else to look, Alice. Milo and the boys didn't find anything on that trail where Lane found the hair tie."

"There's still a lot of woods out there," Sally said.

"I know." Sadie sighed. "It's just hard to imagine her being so badly hurt she couldn't get home or call us, and yet walking that far. I think we've covered every square inch of ground within two miles at least once."

"Maybe." Sally's brow furrowed. "There's a cave on Ben Trainer's place."

"That's four or five miles from here," Alice said.

"Yeah. I'm just saying, it's a possibility. And there may be others we haven't considered."

"I'll mention Ben's cave to the sheriff." Sadie took another swallow of coffee and set down her cup.

"You know, if I had Sara's password, I could look at her e-mail," Alice said.

"Her e-mail?" Sally looked blankly at Alice. "Would that do any good?"

"We could rule out her having planned this."

Sadie stared at her. "You can't think… Oh, Alice, honey, no. This couldn't possibly have been planned. Sara wanted Theo to go with her."

"I know. I'm just so confused. Nothing makes sense."

"Do you know her password?" Sadie asked.

Alice shook her head. "I'll bet Theo does though. Or he might be able to guess it."

"You think so?" Sadie hesitated. "Just hold that thought, okay? I'll mention it to the sheriff. If he thinks it's an avenue we ought to pursue, we can send someone to get Sara's laptop."

She went out through the kitchen and hurried to the barn. It took her only a minute to find the diagram of the mine using Laura's computer.

"Thanks," Sheriff Slattery said. "I've got a team of officers and locals who will head right up there."

Sadie told him what Alice had said about Sara's e-mail.

"You know, that's not a bad idea," the sheriff said. "It may seem far-fetched, but it would give Alice peace of mind if we ruled out the possibility."

"Should I go get Sara's computer?" Sadie asked.

"*Hmm.* Jenna Henderson just picked up Theo, Milo, and Wyatt. They could swing by there and get it on their way here."

Laura had been listening to the conversation with interest. "I can call them for you, Sheriff."

"Good. You do that."

Sadie went back to the house. Milo's place could use a woman's touch, she noted as she crossed the kitchen again. The scuffed, brick-pattern linoleum looked as though it had been there for thirty years, and the one window over the sink was curtainless. Of course, the view of the mountains was worth seeing unhindered.

Alice snapped her cell phone shut as Sadie walked into the living room.

"Mom!"

"What?" Sadie asked.

"I just talked to Theo. They're out on the road, and he had a signal, so he called me."

"He's a good boy," Sadie said.

"Yes, he is. And he said Laura asked them to stop at the house for Sara's laptop."

Sadie nodded. "Sheriff Slattery thought it wouldn't hurt."

"I asked him if he knew the password to Sara's e-mail account."

"Does he?"

"Yes. At least, he's pretty sure he does." Alice stood and walked over to the window. She looked out at the people in the barnyard and twisted her hands together. "I wouldn't snoop ordinarily, but every minute counts now."

"We know that, honey." Sadie went to the end table and picked up her cooling coffee. "I'll stay with you until he gets here."

"If you ladies are comfortable, I'll go out and see if I can help with anything else," Sally said.

"Sure," Sadie told her. "And thanks a lot, Sally."

"Yes, it's nice to get away from all the buzz," Alice said, sinking into the recliner. After Sally had gone out, she said bleakly, "The sun goes down in an hour."

Sadie nodded. "The sheriff is sending a search party up to the mine anyway. It won't matter if it's daylight or not when they search in there."

They waited in tense silence for several minutes, until a knock came on the front door. Sadie and Alice looked at each other, and Sadie walked over to the door. She opened it, and the gray-haired reporter stood on the porch.

"Mrs. Speers?"

Sadie met his gaze. "Yes?"

"I'm Chris Willard. I wondered if you or Mrs. Macomb would give me a few minutes."

"I'm afraid not," Sadie said.

"Please, I don't want to sensationalize this tragedy. I just want to make sure my report is accurate."

Sadie looked over her shoulder. Alice had shrunk down in the recliner and was shaking her head vehemently.

"My daughter doesn't want to talk to any reporters," Sadie said. "And there's no tragedy to speak of. Sara will be found." Sadie's tone carried more confidence than she felt, but there was no way she was willing to use the word *tragedy*. Yet.

"Mrs. Speers, I only want to see the girl found. If my article can help..."

"Please be considerate of the family," Sadie said. "My daughter has stated that she can't do interviews today, and I don't want to either."

"Then perhaps you would..."

"The sheriff can tell you the status of the search. I don't have anything else for you." Sadie closed the door firmly.

"I wonder who told him we were in here," Alice said. "I really don't want to open tomorrow's paper and see accounts of the distraught mother telling what a bright, cheerful girl her daughter is."

Sadie walked briskly to the large front window and pulled the drapes. "Are you hungry?" She tried to keep her voice level, but she understood Alice's feelings. If they didn't find something soon, she would be at her wits' end too.

"No," Alice said.

Sadie wanted to tell her she should eat, but she let it go. There would be time for that later. All night long, if Sara wasn't found. She was sure they would both be awake again tonight.

Every couple of minutes, she went to the window and peeked out the crack where the drapes met. Finally Wyatt's pickup drove in. Jenna and Wyatt got out of the cab, while Milo and Theo climbed out of the back.

"Theo's here," she said to Alice. "Looks like he's got the laptop."

"Get him in here, okay?" Alice sat up eagerly.

Sadie went out the front door and hurried across the yard. Even so, Mac beat her to the pickup.

"Got it right here." Theo held up the laptop case so the sheriff couldn't miss it.

"Alice wants you to bring it into the house," Sadie said. "Milo, I hope you don't mind, but your mom said we could..."

"Absolutely," Milo said. He looked tired, and his eyes were grim. He turned and walked to the house, went in through the front door, and left it open behind him.

"We'll go check in with Laura," Wyatt said. He and Jenna headed for the barn.

Sadie, Theo, and the sheriff followed Milo into the house.

Milo sat on the couch, facing Alice.

"I'm really sorry," he said. "I wish I had better news for you." His voice cracked a little, and Sadie realized the terrific strain this day had put on him.

"I'm sorry, Milo." Alice sniffed. "I don't blame you. Really, I don't. That was my fear talking last night."

Milo exhaled slowly and nodded. "I will keep on looking until we find her, Alice. I promise."

Alice reached out and squeezed his hand. "I know you will. Thank you."

Sheriff Slattery closed the door and cleared his throat. "Let's get this laptop set up, shall we?"

"We can use the kitchen table," Milo said.

Alice stood and went to Theo. "Thank you so much. It's a big relief, knowing she's not out there at the bottom of those bluffs." She hugged Theo and clung to him for a moment. When they separated, Theo's eyes were as misty as his mother's.

Alice took the laptop and carried it into the kitchen, where Milo turned on the lights and pulled out a chair for her. She opened the case and turned on the computer.

"Theo, can you bring up the e-mail server and put in Sara's password?" she said.

Theo took her place in the chair. Sadie, Alice, Sheriff Slattery, and Milo gathered close around him. Milo helped him log on to the house's wireless network, and then a minute later, they all stared at the list of messages that had come in for Sara.

"I don't see anything from Cliff," Alice said, as Theo scrolled down the page. "Oh, wait!"

"You've got something?" Sadie leaned in closer.

Alice pointed on the screen. "It's two weeks old, but ..."

Theo clicked on the message, and it opened. "It says, 'I can't come this weekend, honey, but I'll try to soon. I'll call you. Don't tell your mom about you-know-what.'"

"I wonder what's that's about," Alice said. "Don't tell your mom." She turned and stared at Sadie. "You know what I'm thinking."

"I could probably guess," Sadie said, "but why don't you tell us?"

"Okay. I'm wondering if Cliff called Sara without my knowledge and made arrangements to pick her up yesterday."

"Oh, honey!"

"Think about it, Mom. Neither of them is answering calls or texts. Cliff could have suggested Sara leave the horse there for Milo to find."

"And pulled Daisy's shoe half off? And not put her away before they left?" Sadie shook her head. "It doesn't make sense."

"No, Mom," Theo said gruffly but firmly. "Dad wouldn't do that. And even if he did, Sara would tell me if he suggested anything odd like that."

"Then what's this 'don't tell your mom' business?"

"I don't know, but I can't imagine it's anything bad." Theo's eyes glistened, and Sadie laid her hand on his shoulder.

Alice began to pace and run her hand through her hair. "Okay, how about this? Sara fell off Daisy but came back, leading the horse. Cliff was waiting here and convinced her to just get in the car and go with him."

"No," Sadie said. "I can't believe that. Cliff wouldn't do something like that, and neither would Sara."

"She wouldn't," Theo agreed. "She would think about how upset you'd be. Whatever Dad was referring to in this e-mail isn't something that would hurt you. I won't believe that. And Sara would have at least put Daisy in a stall, not left her loose out there."

"Maybe Cliff told her he'd talked to me and gotten my permission." Alice whirled to face them. "That would work."

Heaviness settled on Sadie's heart. "No, I don't think so. Sara would still have called you last night, wouldn't she? Just to let you know she was okay. And she wouldn't ignore the calls and texts we've tried to send her."

"Unless Cliff told her something," Alice said.

Theo scowled. "You mean Dad might have told her some lie to keep her from calling you?"

Sadie shook her head. "No. Listen to yourself."

"Or she lost her phone," Alice persisted.

"Then she'd use Dad's phone," Theo said.

Sadie didn't like the way this was going. Alice seemed to be losing control of her thoughts. *Lord, show me what to do. She's so scared!*

Sadie put her arms around Alice. "Please stop thinking that way, honey."

Alice collapsed against her, sobbing. "Mom, I'm so confused. God is supposed to be in control. Where is He now?"

Sadie held her close. "He's here, honey. And He's where Sara is too."

10

"TELL ME ABOUT YOUR HUSBAND'S RELATIONSHIP TO SARA," Sheriff Slattery said.

Sadie whirled on him. "Oh no. You're not taking what Alice said seriously?"

Mac eyed her coolly. "Settle down, Sadie. We have to look at every possibility. Now, I don't know Cliff Macomb. I have no idea if he would pull something like this or not. So convince me. Why are you so sure he wouldn't?"

Sadie huffed out an exasperated breath. "He and Alice have never fought over the kids. And if he asked her to let Sara visit him, or even take a trip with him, Alice would say yes."

"Would you?" Mac asked Alice.

"Probably. If she wouldn't miss school."

"*Hmm.*" He looked over at Theo. "Can you open her sent messages for that same period?"

"Sure." Theo clicked a button.

"At least she hasn't cleaned out her mailbox for a while," Sadie said when the long stream of messages came up.

"True," said Mac. "That makes me think Sara had nothing to hide. Kids who plan to run away usually delete their messages and their browsing history—or take the laptop with them."

Theo looked up from the screen. "Here's a message Sara sent to Dad the same day that other one came in."

"Let's see it." Mac moved in and leaned over his shoulder. "Huh. 'Okay, but I hope you make it soon. School is going okay, but I miss having time with you. Can you come up to Silver Peak next week? I want you to see my rabbit.' Does that mean anything to you?" He turned and looked sharply at Alice.

"She had found a little bunny that seemed to be motherless."

"A wild one?" Mac asked.

"I don't think so," Alice replied. "It didn't act afraid. I figured it was a tame one that had escaped his cage. We asked around the neighborhood, but nobody had lost a bunny recently, so I let Sara keep it in the backyard."

Mac nodded and glanced back at the screen. "It does seem odd that you can't get ahold of your ex-husband. How often do you speak to him?"

"Maybe once a week. But I've never had trouble reaching him like this before."

"Has he started a new relationship?"

"You mean—no, not that I'm aware of," Alice said. "He was dating someone briefly, but I think that fizzled out."

"Is there anyone else you could call?" Slattery asked. "A friend of his, maybe?"

Alice frowned. "I don't have many of his friends' numbers in my directory." She took out her phone, opened it, and scrolled through her contacts. "Hey, I've got his receptionist's home phone."

"From the dental office?" Sadie asked.

"Yeah. She offered me a recipe once—long story, but she gave me her number. She lives in Denver."

"Maybe she could tell you something," Sadie suggested, and Mac nodded.

"I'll try her." Alice punched buttons, and Sadie leaned back against the counter. Milo was puttering around. He got a can of coffee down from the cupboard beside his coffeemaker.

"Hello, Nancy?" Alice said into her phone. "This is Alice Macomb. Hi." After a short pause, she went on, "I'm sorry to bother you at home, but I've been trying to reach Cliff since yesterday, and I can't get hold of him." She paused. "Oh, I see. Do you know when he's coming back? Because I've tried his cell phone multiple times." After another short pause, Alice said, obviously relieved, "Would you? I'd appreciate that so much! Thanks."

She closed the connection.

"So?" Sadie asked.

"She said he's at a two-day conference in Chicago. Nancy has no explanation for why he isn't answering his phone, but she offered to call his hotel and have him paged."

"That should ease your mind," Sadie said.

"Not until I hear from him personally."

There was that stubborn streak, but Sadie really couldn't blame her. A conference in another state might be the convenient explanation for a lot of things. She didn't want to think bad thoughts about her former son-in-law, but the fact that Mac Slattery seemed ready to cast him as a villain made her waver.

Alice turned to Theo. "Did your dad tell you he was going to this conference?"

"No, but he doesn't always mention things like that if it's not our weekend with him. Mom, I know he'll call," Theo said staunchly, and Sadie's heart ached.

She walked over to him and patted his shoulder. "I'm sure he will."

"You let me know the minute he does," the sheriff said. "Right now, I think it's time for me to talk a little more with Lane Pomeroy, find out what he's been up to. Especially his life in the past two days."

"Would it be all right if I came along?" Sadie asked.

"I guess so." Mac turned toward the door.

"I think I'll stay here," Alice said. "That is, if Milo doesn't mind. It's quiet here."

"I don't mind." Milo put a filter in his coffeemaker. "Theo can stay too, if he wants to."

"I'm pretty tired," Theo admitted. "I wouldn't mind sitting down until we hear from the people searching the mine."

"There are a couple of Maggie's sandwiches on the coffee table," Sadie said. "You boys can have them if Alice doesn't want hers."

"I'll share with Mom," Theo said.

Sadie hurried to catch up with Mac. He was entering the barn when she started across the yard. The vehicles had thinned out a little, and the people serving refreshments were packing up their things. Sadie wondered if Lane had eaten all day. She walked over to the table and asked Lou and Maggie Price, "Do you have any sandwiches left?"

Maggie smiled at her. "Hi, Sadie. How's it going?"

"About the same, unfortunately."

"I've still got some chicken salad on ice. How many sand-wiches do you want?"

"Two would be great. Thanks."

Lou laid two small bags of organic potato crisps on the table in front of her. "If you hurry, you can probably still get drinks from Luz."

A couple of minutes later, Sadie entered the barn with the sandwiches, chips, and a bottle of water. She walked over to the makeshift desk Laura and Roz were using.

"Hi. Where's the sheriff?"

"He's got that young man, Lane, in the tack room," Laura said.

"Thanks. I wondered if Lane was hungry."

"I haven't seen him eat anything," Roz said. "When the sheriff left him here to go and talk to Alice, he told him not to set foot outside the barn until he got back."

"Is he, like, a suspect or something?" Laura asked.

"I'm not sure," Sadie said, "but the poor kid is probably nervous. Mac Slattery can be intimidating when he wants to be."

She went to the door of the tack room. On a bench between the saddle racks and the bridles and tools hanging on the walls, Lane was taking things out of his backpack, one item at a time. Sheriff Slattery picked up each piece of clothing or camping equipment and examined it before setting it aside.

He glanced up and nodded. "Sadie."

"I wondered if Lane had eaten."

The sheriff looked at the young man. Lane's gaze shifted from the food she was holding to Slattery's face, his blue eyes filled with anxiety.

"When we're done here," the sheriff said.

That seemed to motivate Lane to move a little faster in emptying the backpack. Sadie saw nothing unusual in the growing pile that held extra socks, a steel mess kit, a compass, a topographical map, a trowel, and granola bars. The sheriff opened a small plastic container to reveal matches, a fishhook, and several adhesive bandages.

"That's it," Lane said.

Slattery took the backpack from him, tipped it upside down, and shook it. Something thudded on the floor and skittered a couple of feet away.

"What's that?" the sheriff asked.

Lane stooped and picked it up. "Oh, it's a pebble I picked up in the creek. It looked like it might have a little fossil in it." He handed it to Slattery.

The sheriff examined the rock and then set it on the bench with the other things. He looked at the backpack again and undid a zipper on a small side compartment.

"I guess you forgot about this." He pulled out a plastic zipper bag with a few small items in it. Holding them up closer to the light, he examined them. "Arrowheads?"

"Yes, sir. I collect them. Sorry about that."

The sheriff laid the bag on the bench. "Okay, now your pockets."

Lane stood and took out his wallet, a pocketknife, and a crumpled bandanna.

"Nothing else?" the sheriff asked.

Lane shook his head.

"Do you carry a phone?"

"I didn't for this trip. I sent my route to my dad in advance, but if you take along a cell phone, it kind of defeats the purpose of going out into the wild, don't you think?"

"*Hmm.*"

Lane glanced at Sadie, as if hoping she would support him.

"It's hard to get cell service anyway, in a lot of the places you say you were hiking," she said.

Mac picked up the topo map. "Can you show me exactly where you were yesterday, and give me times for each place?"

"*Uh*...sure." Lane took the map and studied it for a moment. "I hiked up this trail from the base in the afternoon."

"What time?"

Lane glanced off to the side. "I guess I started up about noon."

"And how did you get to the trailhead?"

"I walked. I had camped in another place the night before."

"What other place?"

Lane looked down at the map. "It's not on here." He pointed to a road. "It was a few miles in this direction. I camped off the road, in the woods."

"And that's all you did yesterday afternoon, was walk?"

"Well, I took breaks."

"Anybody see you?"

Lane shrugged. "Maybe. Some vehicles passed me between my campsite and the trailhead. But I didn't meet anyone on the trail, once I got off the road."

The sheriff frowned, perusing the map.

"That's near Ben Trainer's place," Sadie said. "His property borders the road there, opposite the trailhead."

"He the one with the cave?" Sheriff Slattery asked.

"Yes," Sadie replied.

"You didn't go explore the cave, did you?" He eyed Lane keenly.

Lane hesitated. "No. I haven't been in any caves."

"So you started up the trail around noon. What time did you get to the spot on the creek, where you camped last night?" Sheriff Slattery traced the trail with his finger and pointed to the place Lane had told him about earlier.

"Maybe five thirty or six."

"Seems like you took a long time getting up there."

Lane swallowed hard. "Yes, sir. It's a rugged trail."

Sadie's mind raced. Five to six hours was a *very* long time for that trail. Had Lane stopped along the way to look for fossils and artifacts? On a hunch, she excused herself and stepped out into the barn alley.

At the desk, she asked Roz, "I don't suppose you've got a phone directory handy?"

"As a matter of fact, we do. Sally brought Milo's out for us." Roz handed the phone book to Sadie. "What's up?"

"I just want to check something." Sadie found Ben Trainer's number and carried her phone out into the yard and around the corner of the barn.

"Ben? This is Sadie Speers."

"Well, hello," the rancher said. "I heard about your granddaughter. Have they found her yet?"

"No, we're still looking," Sadie said.

"That's terrible. I'd have come over today, but the vet was coming to vaccinate my herd. I sent up a few prayers for your family."

"Thanks," Sadie said. "Ben, I wondered if you saw a young man walking past your place yesterday, or maybe even poking around."

Ben's voice sharpened. "What, you mean poking around as in stealing artifacts? Digging on my property without permission?"

"Well...could be," Sadie said.

"*Hmpf!* I was out near my pasture after lunch, and I saw this fella near the road, down on the ground. I thought maybe he'd stopped to eat his sack lunch, and I didn't say anything. But an hour later, he was still at it, so I walked over, and the no-good kid was digging along the edge of the creek that runs through my pasture, where my stock get water. He was cleaning off an arrowhead."

"What did you do?" Sadie asked.

"I said, 'Thanks for finding me a nice artifact on my land,' and then I reached out and took it right out of his hand," Ben said. "He was a little put out, but I told him he was trespassin'. He apologized, sort of, and said he'd be on his way. I asked him if he'd found any other things before I got there. He said he didn't, but there's no telling what he had in his pockets, or that knapsack of his."

"Did you let him go?"

"Had to. Oh, I suppose I could have called the sheriff, but then I'd have had to hold him there until Slattery came, and it didn't seem worth it. I just wanted him out of there."

"Can you describe him?" Sadie asked.

"Sure can," Ben said. "Young fella, ponytail, blue eyes. He was wearin' a camo jacket, and he had a bow slung on his shoulder with his pack. Had a bedroll too. One of those lightweight sleeping bags."

"And what time did he leave your pasture?"

"Must have been two thirty or three by then. Why?"

"Thanks, Ben. I think we've got the same young man here at Milo's now."

"Well, my kids and I like to dig for Indian items around the ranch, and I don't like other people doing it without asking."

"This young man has a few arrowheads and such in his pack," Sadie told him. "Do you want to come and look at them?"

Ben sighed. "I wouldn't be able to say for sure if he took them from my place."

"I'll have the sheriff ask him, if you like."

"Why not? Thanks, Sadie. And I hope you find your granddaughter. And soon. If they don't find her tonight, could I help if I came over tomorrow?"

"We need every able-bodied, rational person we can get," Sadie said.

Teams were straggling in from their grids on the mountain, and the sun threw bands of purple and pink against the clouds in the west. Sadie went to the tack room door and asked Mac to join her for a moment.

"You stay put," the sheriff told Lane.

"Could he have these now?" Sadie held out the food.

"Sure, why not?"

"Thanks, Mrs. Speers." Lane looked extremely grateful as he took the food from her.

Sadie led Mac to the quiet corner where she and Alice had talked earlier. "I just called Ben Trainer. He says Lane Pomeroy didn't start up the Blue Fork Trail at noon. Ben says he was digging for arrowheads on his land until two thirty or later. Ben didn't like it, and he ran him off."

"*Hmm.*" Sheriff Slattery pursed his lips. "Pomeroy's got some arrowheads."

"I told Ben, but he said he wouldn't be able to tell where they came from. He wasn't happy with Lane trespassing on his land, though, and especially removing artifacts."

Slattery nodded. "Seems unlikely he could start up the trail that late and be up on the mountain by the time Sara rode up there. But I'll ask him a few more questions."

"You won't arrest him, will you?"

"Not unless I find more cause than a trespassing claim. Thanks, Sadie. I may go around and talk to Ben when this is over, but right now my priority is Sara."

Sadie touched the sleeve of his uniform. "Thank you. We appreciate that, and all the work you've put in on this."

Mac glanced at his watch. "I suppose we'll have to call in the searchers soon. I'm sorry it didn't go better today, Sadie."

"I know." Sadie sighed and looked toward the doorway, thinking of Alice. "It's going to be another long night."

"You know, people have mentioned to me seeing someone hanging around at night, or at dusk. Some folks have had small items and food go missing."

"The so-called wild man," Sadie said.

Mac eyed her thoughtfully. "How do you like Lane Pomeroy for that role?"

"Could be, if he lied about more than the arrowheads. It would mean he has hung around this mountain for two or three weeks, not just this weekend."

"I think I'll do some more checking up on Pomeroy," the sheriff said. "We'll see if he can prove where he's been."

"You're letting him off the hook on Sara?"

"I don't see how he could have been where the horse stumbled. Now, if Sara got up disoriented and went up the mountain instead of down, she could have met him on that Blue Fork Trail, where he found the hair tie. I want to know where to find him until this is over."

"So you're arresting him?"

"No," Sheriff Slattery said. "Not yet, anyway. Hate to let him go though. He's into this survival stuff. He could disappear into the woods and we might not be able to find him. I'll put a deputy on checking background on him. Maybe we can talk to his family."

"He *was* trespassing," Sadie said.

"Yes, he seems to think 'finders, keepers' means he can pick up anything he wants and walk off with it, even if it's on someone else's property. The thing is, if he has nothing to do with Sara's disappearance, that's small potatoes. I don't want to get so sidetracked on this that I miss something pertinent."

Sadie had to agree. "Finding Sara is the vital thing right now."

The sheriff put a hand on her shoulder. "I know this is tough on you. We're going to find her."

"Maybe not today." Sadie's eyes filled with tears. Could she get through another night not knowing where Sara was?

"Sheriff," Laura called from near the desk, holding out her phone. "It's Edwin Marshall. He's with the search team that went to the mine."

Mac hurried toward Laura. Sadie stepped closer. She hadn't thought much about Edwin for the past few hours, but he had stayed out there, searching for Sara.

"Hello, mayor," the sheriff said.

Laura and Roz stood still, obviously craving news, and Sadie joined them.

"Okay," Mac said. "Might as well come on in. Most of the other teams have checked in." He raised his eyebrows at Laura for confirmation, and she nodded.

Sadie glanced toward the big barn door. Darkness had descended quickly on the mountain. There would be no more searching tonight.

11

SADIE WENT TO THE HOUSE AND FOUND ALICE AND THEO SITTING listlessly in the living room.

"Come on," she said. "I'm taking you two home and making sure you eat something. You could use a nice hot bath, Alice."

"Oh, Mom, you're as wrung out as I am." Alice gripped the arms of her chair and stood. "My mind keeps whirling 'round and 'round."

"You need some sleep." Sadie glanced at Theo. "You too."

"I don't know if I can sleep, Grandma," Theo said. His face was haggard.

"You're young," Sadie said. "Nature will take over for you." She wasn't so sure about Alice. "Are you up to driving?" she asked Theo.

"I'll drive," Alice said. "He's been out hiking all day, and I've been sitting still."

Sadie poked her head into the kitchen, but it was empty.

"Where's Milo?" she asked Alice.

"I think he was going over to help them lay out grids for the search tomorrow. He hopes the sheriff will send the canine team right up to where they found the hoofprints."

"That might be a good idea." Sadie handed Alice her sweat-shirt and guided her toward the door. They stepped out into the chilly night air. Most of the volunteers had left, though the lights were still on in the barn. She could see the sheriff, Laura, Milo, and a few other people in there. Edwin's vehicle was still in the parking area, and she wondered where he was.

"Mrs. Speers?"

"Yes?" Sadie turned toward the voice.

A teenage girl walked toward her. "I'm Tori Anderson. I just wanted to tell you and Mrs. Macomb how sorry I am about Sara."

Tori had pulled up the hood of her sweatshirt, and she looked almost elfin standing there in the moonlight.

"Thank you," Sadie said. "It means a lot to the family that you came out to help today."

"I hope it goes better tomorrow." Tori sobbed and swiped at her cheek with her sleeve. "Do you still want people to come tomorrow? Because I heard they may cancel school."

Alice stepped closer to her. "That's very generous of you to offer. Come only if you really want to, Tori."

"I want to." Tori's voice broke. "I said some mean things to Sara, and I wish I hadn't."

Theo shifted his feet on the gravel driveway. Sadie glanced at him and saw that his eyes were misty too.

"This is a very emotional time for everyone," Sadie said, "but it's good to take stock of things. Honey, I hope you'll have a chance to make up with Sara."

Tori nodded, her mouth skewed in a grimace. "I was feeling hurt because Hunter seemed to forget all about me after Sara came to our school. But that wasn't really Sara's fault. If she comes home, I'll just step out of the picture. She can have Hunter, for all I care."

Sadie couldn't help smiling. "Why don't you just leave that up to Hunter? He should be the one to decide if he prefers you or Sara."

"Oh, I know." Tori wiped her eyes on her sweatshirt cuff. "I know he'll do whatever he wants. I just meant I won't be mad at her anymore. I don't want her to be...to be lost."

Theo said nothing, but jerked his head away. Sadie wondered if Tori's tears had moved him, or if he thought she was putting on a performance.

Alice patted Tori's shoulder. "Please don't agonize over what happened between you and Sara. When she comes back"—Alice hauled in a deep breath—"I hope you two girls can be friends."

"I'll try," Tori said. She looked over at Sadie. "You know, I think I really would have liked Sara if Hunter hadn't come between us."

Sadie couldn't help thinking that Tori and Sara were awfully young to be so worried about boys.

"As odd as it may seem," she said, "it's possible for a boy to be friends with more than one girl at a time. There's plenty of time to have fun together."

Tori nodded soberly.

"Your family goes to church, right?" Sadie asked.

"Yeah."

"Then pray for Sara."

"I will," Tori promised.

Sadie nodded. "Friends are a gift from God. You're being a friend to Sara by helping to look for her."

"I wish I had been the one to find her." Tori's lip trembled. "I prayed the whole time we were out there. But we didn't find a single thing. I felt like we had wasted our time."

"That's not true," Theo said. "Every square inch that we searched today, we now know she's not there."

"Yes," Sadie said. "Ruling out a lot of places will help the sheriff plan where we should look next."

Tori nodded solemnly. "I'll be back here at sunup."

"Thank you," Alice said.

Tori turned away and trudged over to join two other girls waiting near a compact car.

"Let's go, before I drop right here," Alice said. She and Theo got into her Jeep.

As Sadie unlocked the door to her Tahoe, a vehicle came slowly up the driveway. When it parked, Edwin and two other men got out. Sadie walked swiftly toward him.

Edwin stretched and smiled sadly. "Hi. Nothing at the mine, I'm sorry to say."

"You look exhausted," Sadie said.

"A bit tired."

"Well, I'm glad you went. I know you did a thorough job of it. With anyone else, I'd probably wonder."

Edwin put his arm around her shoulders and walked her to her SUV. "How's Alice doing?"

"Not real well, although she did manage to be gracious to Sara's classmate just now. I'm going over to her house to draw her a bath and cook an omelet or something. She and Theo aren't taking care of themselves."

"Make sure you take care of yourself too, Sadie." His blue eyes were sober as he gazed at her.

"I will."

He squeezed her gently and dropped a kiss on her forehead. "I guess I'll see you in the morning. I wish it were for other reasons."

"Thanks. Good night."

Alice had driven out, and Sadie drove to the house on Grubstake Road. Alice and Theo were just going inside. Sadie parked behind Alice's Cherokee and hurried up onto the front porch.

"Come on in, Mom," Alice said.

"Thanks. I'm going to draw you a bath. Do you have eggs in the fridge?"

"I think so," Alice said.

"Theo, how does an omelet sound?" Sadie asked.

"Real good, Grandma. I think I'll hit the shower while you make it, if you don't mind."

Alice's phone rang, and she yanked it from her jacket pocket. When she glanced at the screen, she caught her breath and hit the speaker button so the others could hear.

"Cliff? Where are you?"

"I'm in Chicago. What's up? Nancy said you wanted to talk to me."

"I sure do."

"I'm sorry about the phone thing. I didn't realize it until I got to the airport, but I went off and left my cell phone charging at home. I've been kicking myself all…"

"Cliff, Sara's missing."

For a moment, they were all silent, then Cliff regained momentum.

"What happened? When? Where…"

"She went out horseback riding at Milo's yesterday, and Daisy came back alone."

"You're joking."

Alice scowled and stamped her foot in frustration. "Would I joke about something like that?"

"But…you haven't found her yet?"

"No, we have not." Alice's voice caught, and she sobbed. "Cliff, we need you. Come home!"

"I will. I'll catch the first plane."

Alice sniffed.

"Dad, do you want me to meet you at the airport?" Theo asked.

"No. I left my car in long-term parking. What's going on? What are you doing to find her?"

As Theo began a rundown of all that Sheriff Slattery and the search teams had done, Sadie slipped upstairs to Alice's bathroom and started the hot water running. A bottle of lilac bubble bath sat on the edge of the tub, and she poured a capful under the cascade of water. She laid out two fluffy bath towels and a clean washcloth.

Alice appeared in the doorway. "Cliff will call when he lands in Denver."

"Good," Sadie said. "Now, undress and climb in there. I'll be in the kitchen."

"Mom, you're so sweet. You should be at home."

"I will be soon. Get in that tub, or you'll make me mad."

Alice laughed for the first time in thirty hours. "I love you."

Sadie hugged her tightly, and their tears mingled. "Alice, my dear, dear girl. I don't know what I would have done if this had happened when you were Sara's age."

"Don't even think about it," Alice said. "Just pray for Sara."

"Always. And Cliff will be here in the morning."

Alice sighed as she pulled away. "I'm glad we got ahold of him, and that he's coming. But I would rather he could have told me where Sara is."

"One thing at a time," Sadie said.

She went downstairs and into the kitchen. She loved what Alice had done with the 1940s house. Many of her decorative items had come from the Antique Mine. The kitchen needed a makeover, but that probably wouldn't happen for a while.

Sadie tied on an apron her mother had made for Alice years ago and set about cooking a light supper. She wished she had the energy to make it special, but she dragged around the kitchen, and when she opened the refrigerator to get the eggs, she found herself leaning on the door and staring inside without seeing the contents.

"Lord, give me a little spurt of energy," she whispered. She spotted some refrigerator sweet rolls and grabbed the container. "Just the thing."

Theo entered a few minutes later, as she was flipping the first omelet out onto a plate. He wore clean jeans and a T-shirt, and his hair was still wet.

"Smells good in here," he said.

"You're just in time." Sadie handed him the plate. "Onions, cheese, and bacon bits okay?"

"It's great. Mom won't want the onions in hers though."

"Thanks for the warning." Sadie glanced at the oven timer. "Sweet rolls coming in three minutes."

"I could eat about six." Theo opened the refrigerator and took out a jug of orange juice.

Neither of them mentioned Sara. Theo sat down at the small kitchen table with his omelet and juice, and Sadie started another omelet. When it was done, Alice hadn't come down, so she put it on a plate for herself and cracked two more eggs into her mixing bowl.

The timer went off, and she took the tray of sweet rolls from the oven.

"Here." She set it on a trivet on the table near Theo and handed him the small container of glaze. "If you ice them, you can eat your six."

He laughed. "Well, maybe not quite that many. I'll leave you and Mom a few."

The doorbell rang.

"I'll get it." Sadie laid down her oven mitt and walked quickly out through the dining room to the entry and opened the door. Pastor Don and Jeanne Sweeting stood on the porch.

"Come on in," Sadie said, swinging the door wide.

"Thanks," the pastor said, letting Jeanne precede him. "We wondered how Alice and Theo are doing, but if you're here…"

"I'm not staying," Sadie said. "I need to get home and walk Hank. But I had the same mind you did, I guess. Wanted to make sure Alice took care of herself."

"We didn't want to call, in case she'd gone to bed." Jeanne smiled apologetically.

"I think she's still in the tub. But come on in the kitchen. We've got sweet rolls and omelets to order."

Sadie brought them plates, and the pastor asked for a brief blessing. "And Lord," he added, "You know where Sara is. You know what she needs right now. We ask that You would keep her safe in Your loving arms and bring her back to us soon."

The others added their amens to Pastor Don's, and looked up to find Alice sobbing quietly in the doorway.

"Alice." Sadie moved quickly toward her. "I didn't hear you come down."

Alice came into the room, tears streaking her cheeks. She wore her plush blue housecoat and slippers. "I just keep thinking how comfortable we all are." She sank into a straight chair between Theo and Jeanne. "And Sara's out there somewhere..." Her voice broke, and she shook her head helplessly.

"There now." Jeanne put an arm around her, and Theo passed the tissue box.

"You need something in your stomach," Sadie said. "I've got the eggs all ready to cook up, and I baked the rolls you had in the fridge."

Sadie prepared her omelet, while the pastor spoke to Alice gently. Then she placed the dirty dishes in the dishwasher and put away the egg carton and other food items.

Alice had eaten her omelet and half a sweet roll. Sadie decided her mission had ended.

"I'm going to get home and feed Hank now. I'll see everybody in the morning."

Theo and the pastor stood.

"Thanks for everything, Mom," Alice said.

Sadie leaned over and kissed her forehead. "Love you all." She waggled her fingers at Theo and went out to her Tahoe.

"Things will be better tomorrow," she said as she opened the driver's door.

"I just want Sara to be safe." Theo's voice broke, and Sadie pulled him into a brief hug before she got into the Tahoe.

When she got home, the house was dark. Hank met her at the door with a little whine. Sadie decided he was more interested in getting out than into food, and she released him into the yard. She let him run at liberty about the property and leaned against a porch pillar, watching him in the moonlight. A cold breeze wafted its way around the mountain, and she shivered.

Don't let her be cold tonight, Lord.

Sara never left Sadie's thoughts, even though she was severely fatigued. She knew the agonizing possibilities Alice was turning over in her mind.

Give Alice peace. And Theo—settle him, Lord, and don't let him blame himself.

That thought brought Milo to mind, and she added him to her prayers, then Sheriff Slattery and all of the searchers. She even prayed for Lane Pomeroy, though she wasn't sure what he needed.

Hank's low growl jerked her back to the present. He stood facing the tree line at the edge of Sadie's lawn, about thirty yards away. She squinted into the darkness, trying to see what Hank saw. He growled again, deep and menacing.

12

"Hello?" Sadie called, but only the rustle of the wind in the branches answered.

Hank barked, one sharp, quick woof, and bounded toward the trees. Sadie had only a fleeting impression of a figure darting into the trees. A figure larger than Hank. Not a deer either. It had looked like a man. Or had it?

"Hank!" She hurried down off the porch and took a few steps toward the woods. Suddenly she didn't want to get too far from the light that spilled out of the windows. "Hank!"

Branches rustled, and then the dog leaped out of the tree line and raced toward her.

"Good dog!" She patted him and looked toward the woods again, but she couldn't see anything there now. "Come on, boy."

She took him with her to the Tahoe, where she retrieved her flashlight. Together, they walked to the tree line.

"Anyone there?" she shouted.

Nothing.

She panned the flashlight's beam over the nearest trees and undergrowth. Something fluttered on a twig, at the spot where she thought the figure had entered the woods. Sadie stepped closer and studied the low branch. A few hairs clung to it. She worked them loose and held them carefully, pinched between her thumb and forefinger.

"Come, Hank."

He followed her back to the house, and they walked up onto the porch. Inside, Sadie closed and locked the door. She went straight to the kitchen and got out a plastic sandwich bag and placed the hairs in it. They were brown, about four or five inches long. They couldn't be hers.

She set the bag aside. "Okay, Hank. Are you hungry?"

She filled his food and water dishes. While he dove in to his supper, she sat down on a stool nearby and watched him. Hank didn't like to be petted while he ate, so she didn't touch him, but she kept thinking about what had happened outside.

"What did you see, boy? Was it the wild man?" She chuckled, but somehow the joke didn't seem funny. She picked up the bag and peered through the plastic at the hairs. They certainly looked human, and they definitely had been too high up to belong to a dog. They weren't coarse enough for a horse's mane or tail, and a deer's hair would be shorter. Considering the shadowy shape she had observed, she would have been shocked if the hairs hadn't appeared to be human. But who had left them?

She supposed it could have been one of the searchers, still out looking for Sara, but then why hadn't the person spoken to her? Why had he run away?

And was it a he? A sudden doubt entered her mind. The person hadn't impressed her as being tall. Could it possibly have been a woman she saw? Or a teenager? The hairs might have broken off short, but they were still longer than many men wore theirs. Of course, some men had long hair. Lane Pomeroy, with his ponytail, came to mind. Had Sheriff Slattery released him? And if so, where had he gone for the night?

"Oh, Hank. If only you could talk."

He lifted his golden head from his dish and turned to look at her. He made a little chirp in his throat and turned back to his supper.

Sadie looked at the clock. It was too late to call anyone, but she wished she could talk to the people who had claimed to see the wild man. She turned on her computer and went to the *Chatterbox* site. To her surprise, the newest post was about Sara.

The town of Silver Peak turned out in force today to support the Macomb family and search for young Sara, who was reported missing Saturday evening.

Sadie tore her gaze away from the words. She didn't want to remind herself of her grief right now. She clicked on "Archives," and scrolled through the posts of the last month, looking for mentions of wild man sightings. Except for a note of congratulations for a local couple's anniversary, the previous entry she had read about the wild man was the last post. She frowned over the sentence: *A rancher claims he saw a man with long, tangled hair trying to raid his vegetable garden at dusk last week, before the first frost hit.*

The rancher wasn't named. Was it someone on this side of Silver Peak? It couldn't have been Milo, or he would surely have mentioned it to her in connection with the search. What about Ben Trainer? She sighed. More than a dozen ranchers held property inside the bounds of Blake County, of which Silver Peak was the county seat. Who were the *Chatterbox*'s sources for these reports?

If she knew that, she could talk to the people who had supplied the information.

But for that matter, who was the *Chatterbox* writer? That little mystery remained unsolved. Sadie had never seriously tried to unmask the blogger. Not knowing was fun in a way, and the writer seemed harmless. She wouldn't want to spoil his or her fun.

She was sure she had read another report about the wild man, though, or heard something. When had this all started?

She scrolled through the archives and found one, posted nearly two weeks earlier. *Emma Roundy saw someone in her backyard last night. She shouted, and the person yelped and ran into the woods. She described the intruder as a short man, wearing a hat or a hood, and carrying what looked like a gunnysack.*

Emma Roundy. Sadie knew the old woman. Her husband, Lionel, had died ten years ago, but Emma still lived in their old home on the south edge of town. She got her journal out of her purse and made a note to call Emma sometime soon. After Sara was found, of course.

She yawned. Maybe she would be able to sleep tonight. She hoped so. If she could just keep her thoughts from drifting to Sara's plight!

Something Sally had said came back to her. A woman had opened a dance hall in Silver Peak. That was something Sadie could look into, and a short stint of research might relax her and help her not to dwell on Sara. She went to the bookcase and took down two volumes that had sections on the early mining communities.

The first one mentioned Pearl Holliman as the founder of a dance hall shortly after the first strikes in Silver Peak, but it gave few details. Sadie checked the index of the second volume. Pearl was listed by name, and she turned to the page.

"Pearl Holliman's Pearl of the Mountain Dance Hall," the section heading read. Sadie sat down in her recliner and delved into the account. It took only a few minutes to read how the feisty woman had arrived in town with a large tent and a fiddle player in tow. Pearl of the Mountain had soon been remodeled into a frame building, and somewhere Pearl had found a concertina player to join the fiddler. Evenings were filled with music and lively dancing with a few girls Pearl had persuaded to make the trek to the new boomtown.

Sadie's hopes were dashed when she read an account of trouble at the dance hall. One night two customers got into a fight, and a brawl ensued. A man was shot, and Pearl ran out into the street, screaming for the sheriff. If she had been the angel of mercy, wouldn't she have been trying to help the wounded man? Somehow Sadie couldn't quite cast Pearl Holliman as the woman who had ministered to the ill and injured.

She browsed the next page and saw a mention of the mine owner's wife she had read about before. Unfortunately, it seemed that woman had died the year after she moved to Silver Peak, and rumors of the "angel" persisted over a longer span, so she couldn't be the one who inspired the stories either.

Sadie flipped back to the index, looked under "Doctors," and found an entry for "first female physician in Colorado." She turned to the page and scanned it. A female doctor had come to Denver during the approximate time period of Silver Peak's early boom. Could she possibly have made her way up here? Sadie determined to follow up on that later. Maybe the newly discovered doctor was the person she was looking for.

Her cell phone rang, and she jumped. It was nearly eleven o'clock. Who would call this late? She pulled it out. Edwin, of course. She smiled as she answered.

"Hi."

"Did I wake you?"

"Nope, you're batting a thousand. But I was thinking of heading off to bed."

"I spoke to Pastor Don earlier," Edwin said, "so I knew you'd gone to Alice's for a while."

"How are *you* doing?" Sadie asked. "You put in a long day."

"I'm all right. A few sore muscles. I rode more today than I have in a long time."

"Did you hear that Alice finally reached Cliff, and he's coming home?"

"Yes, the pastor told me. Oh, and did you ever find your bank deposit?"

Sadie started. She'd all but forgotten about it. "No. Julie called me earlier and said she went back to the store and hunted for it again, but she didn't find anything."

"Is that going to be a hardship for you?"

"I'll miss the money, but it won't put me in the poorhouse."

He chuckled. "I'm glad you can joke about it. Listen, the same offer stands tonight. Call anytime. I'm turning in now, but I won't mind if you need to talk in the wee hours."

"Thanks. That's good to know. And I'm here for you, anytime you need me."

"I know. Thanks. That means a lot." After they hung up, Sadie put her books away and went upstairs. She nestled down under her cozy patchwork quilt with a last prayer for Sara sent from her heart.

She awoke to the ringtone of her cell phone and groped for it on her nightstand. Was Edwin calling again? A quick glance at the digital clock told her she had slept for two hours.

"Hello?"

"Grandma?"

Sadie's heart seemed to stall and then race. She clutched the phone to her ear.

"Sara?"

"It's me, Grandma. I'm lost."

13

"Sara!" Sadie struggled to sit up and turned on the lamp. "Are you all right?"

"Not really. My ankle hurts awfully bad, and my head aches."

"And you don't know where you are?" Sadie stood up. "Sara? Sara?" For an agonizing moment, she thought the call had been dropped, but as she walked toward the window, the plaintive voice faded back in.

"...and I saw Quandary Peak. At least I'm pretty sure it was Quandary. And I know you can see it from your upstairs back windows."

"Yes! I can see that, honey. What else do you see?"

"I'm kind of in the woods, but I crossed a stream a while ago. It was more open there, and that's when I saw Quandary Peak. The phone wouldn't work there, so I tried to figure out which way to go and walked for a long time uphill. I think I'm closer to you than to Mom, and that's why I called you first, but I just don't know."

"Sara, listen." Sadie grabbed a sweatshirt as she spoke and tossed it on her bed. "I'm going to get dressed and go outside. Hold on, honey. Don't hang up, okay? If you get where you can see Quandary again, tell me."

"Well, it's all trees now. Grandma, I'm scared. I keep hearing things. I don't know if it's animals or if someone's chasing me."

Sadie hauled in a deep breath. "Okay. Listen to me. No one's going to hurt you. Can you hear water running, or anything like that?"

After a moment, Sara said, "No, but you're breaking up, Grandma."

"I'm sorry." Sadie went back to the window. "How about now?"

"That's better. But all I hear now is the wind."

Sadie looked out her window. The moonlight streamed down on her front yard, clearly revealing her flower beds and the Tahoe parked in the driveway. "Can you see the moon?"

"Not right now."

"Well, there's a three-quarter moon tonight, and it's giving lots of light. If you can get out of the woods again, you might be able to orient yourself." Her thoughts raced. Sara was below the tree line. "Honey, keep walking uphill."

"I'm afraid my phone will die. Grandma, don't hang up on me."

"I tell you what," Sadie said. "I'm getting dressed. Let me get my jeans and boots on, and I'll come outside and try to find you. You know Silver Peak is high on the mountain. You must be quite a ways down if there's a big patch of woods."

"That's what I was thinking."

"Keep coming uphill. I'll call you right back when I get out-side. Two minutes. I promise."

"What if my phone won't work again?" Sara's voice quivered.

"All right, I'll stay on with you, but I need my boots! And if we lose the connection, I'll keep trying to get you. Let me call. Save your battery."

"Okay."

Sadie dropped the phone on her bed and whipped on her jeans and sweatshirt. She shoved her feet into her boots, not taking time to find clean socks. She might regret that later, but she couldn't stop for socks.

She snatched up her phone. "Sara?"

There was no answer.

Sadie grabbed her flashlight and ran down the stairs and out the back door. She raced across her backyard and stopped. With shaking hands, she punched the contact button and brought up Sara's number. She bungled on her first try and hit the wrong name.

Lord, help me!

It occurred to her that perhaps she should call Sheriff Slattery or Alice first. But no, she needed to focus on Sara. She hit Sara's number again, and this time it rang. She waited, holding her breath.

"Grandma?" Sara sounded panicky now.

"Yes, it's me. I'm sorry I lost you. I'm in my backyard now. Honey, are you still in the woods?"

"Yes, but I think I see light up ahead. Yeah, I'm...I'm coming out into the open now."

Sadie exhaled. *Thank You, Lord.* "Can you see Quandary Peak?"

"N-no. The trees are kind of blocking my view now." Sara's breathing was labored.

"Sara, I think the signal is better now. You must be getting closer."

"My ankle hurts, Grandma."

"I'm sorry. Don't give up now. Do *not* give up."

"I won't." Sara sounded small and vulnerable.

Sadie tried to infuse her voice with confident cheer. "It won't be long now. Tell me again about when you saw Quandary Peak."

"Well...I had sloshed through a stream. My sneakers are wet. But it was off to my right."

"Did you see the moon then?" Sadie had read up on moon phases and knew that a full moon was visible during the approximate hours between sunset and sunrise, and the half moon roughly from midnight to noon the next day. The waning three-quarter moon had come up before she walked Hank at ten thirty. It should be visible for the rest of this night's dark hours.

"Yeah," Sara said. "It was kind of near the mountain. To the left of it when I faced that way."

Sadie did some quick east-west calculations in her mind. "Then what did you do?"

"I walked uphill."

"And Quandary Peak was still on your right?"

"Yes. Maybe a little behind me. But I couldn't see it anymore after I got in the woods."

"Okay. I think you did exactly the right thing. Sara, are you still walking?"

"Yeah, but I'm slow, Grandma."

"Listen to me. I don't know how far you are from me, but I've got my flashlight. I'm going to shine it down the mountainside. You tell me if you can see it."

She turned on the light and shone it down the slope, then made a slow arc across the mountainside. "Anything?"

"No. Grandma, I'm scared."

"Don't be. I'll find you. What if I send Hank out to find you? Can you yell for him?"

"Yes. But what if I'm too far away for him to hear me?"

"Honey, I think I should call Sheriff Slattery on my landline. He might be able to have someone get a signal from your cell phone now and track it."

"Don't leave me, Grandma!" Sara's breath was coming in gasps.

"Easy. I'm right here." Sadie thought for a moment. "I need to get Hank. I hope I won't lose the signal when I go back to the house. If I do, just hang up and wait. I'll call right back."

"Okay."

Sadie jogged the twenty yards to her back door and opened it. "Hank!" She whistled sharply into the kitchen. The dog woofed and bounded to her. Sadie stroked his glossy head. "Okay, boy, I'm counting on you. Go find Sara."

Hank looked up at her and whined.

Sadie held the phone to her ear. "Sara?"

"Yeah?"

"Speak to Hank. Tell him to come to you." She put the phone to Hank's ear.

Faintly, she heard Sara say, "Hi, Hank. Come on, buddy. Come find me."

Hank woofed.

Sadie touched his nose. "Go find Sara."

Hank eyed her quizzically.

"Oh, why didn't I choose a bloodhound?" Sadie jogged across the yard again, and Hank loped beside her. Where the ground sloped away, she stopped and pointed downhill.

"Go get Sara, boy."

Hank gave one sharp bark and rocketed off down the moonlit mountainside. Sadie stood for a moment watching him, wondering if he had even the tiniest idea of what she wanted him to do.

She put the phone to her ear. "Sara, honey?"

"Yeah."

"He's out here, looking for you. Yell. Now. As loud as you can."

She heard Hank bark in the distance.

"He's barking, honey. Can you hear him bark?"

There was silence for a moment, and then Sara said, "I do! I hear it. Hank!"

Sadie lowered her phone and listened. She heard a couple more yips, but they were farther away, and she couldn't hear Sara's voice. She turned on the flashlight and directed the beam toward where Hank had gone.

"Grandma! Grandma! I've got him. Or he's got me!" Sara's laugh was the most wonderful music Sadie had ever heard.

"Oh, ouch! *Uh!*"

"Sara?" Sadie asked, her heart thumping.

"I... I fell down. Oh, it hurts. My ankle."

Sadie began walking carefully down the hill, illuminating her steps with the flashlight. "I'm coming toward you. Keep talking to me."

"Okay, I'll try. But Hank's running away. Hank!"

Sadie heard the dog bark.

"It's okay, Sara. I think he's coming back to me. Maybe he can help me find you."

She swung the flashlight across the slope before her. The dog burst into her view, and she turned the beam aside so she wouldn't blind him.

"Come here, boy!" Hank ran to her, and she petted him. "Good, good dog. Now, let's go get Sara." Into the phone, she said, "Sara, he's with me. We're not far from you. I'm coming!"

Even so, it was farther than she had expected, and the terrain was rough going in places. Hank didn't think about looking for the easiest path.

A few minutes later, Sara cried in her ear, "I see your light! Grandma, I see it!"

Hank leaped back and forth between them, barking and prancing.

"Oh, what a good dog!" Sadie ran the last few yards. Sara was sprawled on her stomach, holding her phone to her ear. "I'm here, sweetie!"

They sat on the ground, hugging and getting dog kisses.

"You're so warm," Sara sobbed.

"Here. Take my sweatshirt." Sadie peeled it off and pulled it over Sara's head, then hugged her close again.

"I love you, Grandma."

"I love you too. So much." Letting out a deep breath, Sadie sat back. "Now we have to get you home. But first, I'm going to call your mother."

"Is she worried about me?" Sara asked.

Sadie laughed. "Honey, you have no idea! The whole town is worried about you. I'll bet we had a hundred people out at Milo's ranch today—no, yesterday—looking for you. Your mother's beside herself." Sadie punched in the numbers for Alice's home phone. The extension on Alice's nightstand would ring, and she wouldn't care that it was two o'clock in the morning.

"Hello?" Alice sounded groggy and a little wary.

"Alice, it's Mom. I've got Sara with me."

"*What?*"

"You heard me right. Sara's at my place. Well, down the hill from my place. We're going to work our way up to the house. Her ankle's hurt, but we'll make it. Call the sheriff and Dr. Conroy, and then get over to my house. Bring Theo too."

"Can I talk to her?" Alice pleaded.

"Sure." Sadie passed her phone to Sara. "Your mom wants to hear your voice."

Sara sniffed and raised it to her ear. "Mom? I'm okay. Grandma and Hank found me." After a few seconds, she said brokenly, "I love you too," and handed the phone back to Sadie.

"Where were you?" Alice was saying, and without waiting for an answer, "What happened?"

"Alice," Sadie said firmly. "Calm down. We'll talk about all that when you get here. Now, call Mac Slattery and the doctor."

"Okay," Alice said meekly.

"All right. We'll see you soon." Sadie closed her phone and shoved it into her pocket. "You ready?"

Sara sniffed and nodded.

"I'm so proud of you!" Sadie stood and held out both hands. "Grab on, and I'll pull you up."

Sara gasped as she pushed upward and then stood trembling. Sadie put an arm around her. "I'm so sorry. Should we wait and get some EMTs to come down here with a stretcher?"

"No! I can do it." Sara put her arm around Sadie's waist.

"All right," Sadie said, "but I don't want you to make your ankle worse."

Sara leaned into her.

"That's it," Sadie said. "Put your weight on me. If I thought I could do it, I'd carry you."

Sara barked a little laugh. "Don't think of it, Grandma. We can do it."

One step at a time, they hobbled up the mountainside. Hank ran ahead, then doubled back, barking encouragement.

"I'll bet you're starved," Sadie said when they paused for breath.

"Kinda. I guess it could be worse," Sara said. "She *did* feed me."

Sadie stared at her. "She? She who?"

"The crazy lady."

Sadie's heart lurched, but she made herself remain calm. "Well. I see there's more to this story than I was aware of. Probably best to save your breath now and tell it all when the sheriff gets here."

"Okay." Sara adjusted her weight and lifted her right foot off the ground. "One, two, three." She swung forward on her left foot, and they resumed their painful progress.

A chilly breeze teased them, and Sadie consciously tried not to shiver. She didn't want Sara to worry about her, though with just a T-shirt, she did feel the wind's bite. But that was nothing compared to what Sara had endured.

They had just reached the edge of the backyard when headlights washed over the house, and right behind came flashing blue strobes.

"I'm glad he didn't put the siren on and wake all the neighbors," Sadie said. "Come on."

Hank ran barking around to the front of the house. Sadie and Sara kept steadily on until they heard several car doors slam.

"Out here," she yelled. "Alice! Mac! We're out back!"

"Mom!" Sara called.

A moment later, Alice, Theo, and Mac appeared at the corner of the house. The sheriff beamed a powerful flashlight at them, and Theo sprinted toward them.

"Sara!" Theo gathered her into a bear hug.

"*Oof!* Take it easy." Sara didn't really sound annoyed.

"Can you carry her into the house?" Sadie asked. "Her ankle is hurt."

"Sure." Theo swung her up into his arms as if she weighed mere ounces.

Alice reached them. "Sara, baby!"

"Mom!" Sara leaned over to accept her kiss.

"Let Theo take her inside," Sadie said. "Come on, right through the kitchen door."

She opened it and stood aside. Alice hurried in and turned on the lights. Theo, carrying Sara, followed.

Mac met Sadie's gaze. "I guess you've got a story to tell."

"I'll make the coffee and hot chocolate. But I think Sara's the one with the story."

14

"ARE YOU UP TO TELLING US WHAT HAPPENED, SARA?" SHERIFF
Slattery asked as he took a seat in the armchair opposite the couch
where Sara lay propped up on pillows sipping orange juice.

"Yes, but then I want a bath, please."

Alice laughed. "Sweetie, you can have anything you want
tonight." She spread a crocheted afghan over Sara's legs.

Sara grasped her hand. "I'm just so glad to be back here." Her
eyes filled with tears.

"We're thankful you're safe," Sadie said. "I've put the coffeepot
on, and I'll make hot chocolate for you kids."

Mac took a small notebook and pen from his pocket, and
Theo and Sadie found seats. Alice squeezed in on the edge of the
couch, unwilling to leave Sara's side.

"Why don't you start at the beginning, if you don't mind," the
sheriff said gently.

"Well, I went over to Milo's." Sara looked over at her mother.
"I'm sorry. I knew I shouldn't go by myself, but I really wanted
to ride. And I was mad at Theo. I wanted to prove I could go
alone and be all right." Her face crumpled. "Guess I proved
the opposite."

Alice stroked her hand. "There now. Nobody's angry with you. Just tell us what happened with Daisy."

Sara swallowed hard. "Well, we went up the main trail from the pasture, and everything was going well. It was warm, so I didn't wear my jacket. It was tied to my saddle."

"We found it," Alice said.

"I sure wished I had it later." Sara shivered. "Anyway, I let Daisy run up one of the side trails. She was rarin' to go. I didn't expect any trouble. I mean, we'd been there a hundred times." She glared at Theo, as if daring him to contradict her.

Theo only gave a slight nod and sat watching her, anxiety etched on his face.

"And then she tripped," Sara said. "I don't know what she stumbled over, but I pitched over her head so fast! I couldn't stop myself. I must have landed on my foot. That and my head. Is that possible? Because I've got a goose egg." She put her hand to her head, high on the side nearest Alice.

Alice leaned over and gently ran her fingers over Sara's skull. She frowned. "You sure do. Were you unconscious?"

"I must have been," Sara said. "I don't remember really, but when I looked around, I couldn't see Daisy. I tried to get up, and my foot hurt so bad, I just lay there and cried for a while."

Headlights flashed on the wall, and Sadie turned toward the door. "That must be Dr. Conroy."

She hurried across the room and opened the door. The silver-haired doctor was getting out of his car. Sadie stepped out onto the porch. "Hello, Doc. I'm sorry to get you out in the middle of the night."

"For this happy occasion, no problem."

Sadie showed him into the living room, where he greeted Mac and the Macombs.

"Well, young lady, how are you feeling?" He sat down in the chair the sheriff set for him near Sara.

"My ankle hurts, and I have a bump on my head."

Doc nodded. "If you don't mind, I'll give you a quick once-over, and we'll see what's what."

"I think the coffee's about ready," Sadie said. "Theo, could you help me in the kitchen?"

"Sure, Grandma." Theo pushed his lanky form up off his chair.

Alice stayed with Sara, but Mac followed Sadie and Theo to the kitchen.

"Would you like coffee or hot chocolate, Theo?" Sadie asked.

"Chocolate, thanks. But I can make it."

Sadie took a canister of cocoa mix out of the cupboard. "Would you mind microwaving a cup for Sara too? I gave her that glass of juice because it was quick and sweet. The poor dear is probably dehydrated." She smiled at Mac and handed him a mug. "Here you go, Mac. Cream or sugar?"

"Thanks. I've been trying to do without the sugar lately." He poured the mug full from the coffee carafe.

Sadie filled her favorite mug with black coffee and sat down at the small table.

"Got any marshmallows, Grandma?" Theo asked.

"I sure do. In the cupboard to your left."

Mac sat down opposite Sadie. "What else do you know that I don't?"

Sadie sighed and lowered her voice. "I think Sara was just getting to the good part. She mentioned a crazy woman while we were coming back to the house."

Mac held her gaze for a long moment. "A crazy woman?"

Sadie nodded. "She said someone fed her while she was out there."

"Sounds like I have a lot of questions to ask her."

Theo came over, stirring his mug of hot chocolate. "She really said that, Grandma?"

"Yes, she did. I didn't press her. I thought I'd let her tell it her way, and I wanted the sheriff to hear it when she did, so we just concentrated on getting home."

"I appreciate that," Mac said. "You did an outstanding job of finding her, and I want to hear more details about that later, after Sara's cared for."

"Wow." Theo was still staring at her. "Do you think there's really a crazy woman? I mean, Sara couldn't be delirious, could she?"

"To be honest, I don't know," Sadie said. "Dr. Conroy will make that call. But Sara seemed to be lucid. She was frightened when I got to her, but I don't think she imagined things."

"Wow." The bell on the microwave went off, and Theo went to put the second cup of water in.

Sadie propped her chin on her hand, thinking back over the last hour. "I wondered if I should call for an ambulance and let them carry her up from where I found her. But she didn't want me to leave her, and they never would have found us if I didn't come up to show them the way."

"I'm sure you did what was best," Mac said.

"That's all we can do, isn't it?" Sadie smiled at him. "In the moment, we do what seems best."

Alice came to the doorway. "Dr. Conroy thinks Sara should go to the hospital for observation and to have her ankle X-rayed."

"Does he think it's broken?" Sadie pushed back her chair and stood.

"He's not sure, but he's hoping it's just a bad sprain. He's concerned about the head injury too. He said she could have a slight concussion, and she doesn't know how long she was out."

"I'd like to ask her a few more questions before you take her in," Sheriff Slattery said.

"I think that would be okay," Alice said. "Doc is giving her some Tylenol, and he said to keep putting the fluids into her."

"Got it right here." Theo headed for the living room with Sara's cup of hot chocolate.

The others followed him. Doc Conroy was closing his medical bag. "I've wrapped the ankle, just to stabilize it during transport. Mrs. Macomb, do you want an ambulance?"

"Oh no, I'll take her," Alice said. "There's no need for the EMTs to come all the way up here. But is it all right if she finishes telling her story to the sheriff first?"

"I don't see why not," Dr. Conroy said. "If you don't mind, I'd like to hear it myself."

They all took seats, and Sheriff Slattery resumed his spot near Sara.

"So, young lady, you were telling me that you fell off the horse, and you suspect you may have blacked out for a while."

Sara nodded, frowning. "It couldn't have been too long. When I realized I was on the ground, it was still daylight. But Daisy was nowhere in sight."

"So what did you do?" the sheriff asked.

"I tried to get up, but my ankle hurt so bad, I couldn't. I just lay there for a while, trying to get up my nerve to try again. I cried some, and I prayed a lot. I told myself Daisy had gone back to the stable, and Milo would come find me."

"What about your cell phone?" Alice asked.

"I tried it, but I didn't have a signal."

Alice sighed but said no more. Sadie knew that Alice looked upon the kids' cell phones as a safety net, for just such emergencies. But the peaks and valleys of the area, as well as the vastness of the space, made reliable cellular service a near impossibility in many places.

"I tried it a few times, and then I was afraid my battery would die, so I shut it off. And then I heard something in the woods. I was really scared. I thought maybe it was a bear."

"Oh, honey." Alice patted her arm.

Theo leaned forward. "Was it the..."

Sadie quickly touched his arm. "Let her tell it, Theo."

He clamped his lips together and nodded.

Sara sipped her hot chocolate and handed the mug to her mother. "Well, like I said, I was petrified. I looked all around, and after a bit I saw this...this woman come out from behind a tree."

"A woman?" Alice's eyes widened.

"Yeah. I thought at first it was a man, but right away I knew I was wrong. She was wearing camouflage clothes and boots, and she had her hair up under her cap. As soon as I realized she was a woman, I wasn't so scared. She came over and asked me if I was hurt. I told her about my ankle, and she said, 'I can help you.' Just like that. I was so relieved. I thought she'd take me back to the ranch, you know?"

"But she didn't," the sheriff said.

Sara shook her head and winced. "*Ooh.*" She put her hand to her temple.

"Take it easy," Dr. Conroy said. "Does your head still hurt?"

"Not as bad now," Sara said. "So, anyway, she helped me get up, but I couldn't put any weight on my foot. She had me lean on her, and we hopped along for a long ways. Then I realized we were going the wrong way."

"Did you tell her?" Alice asked.

"Well, yeah. I told her I wanted to go home, but she said she had stuff for my ankle at her place, and that it wasn't far." Sara scowled, and tears filled her eyes again. "She lied. It was a long ways."

"We saw a place where we thought Daisy might have stumbled," Sheriff Slattery said. "It was on a trail just off the main one. Did she take you up that trail?"

"If it's the one I'm thinking of, yeah, for a ways. But then we went off on a path through the woods that was really overgrown. I don't know if even a horse could do it. It came out on a part of the mountain I didn't know, and it went along a ledge with a sheer drop on the side."

They all sat in silence for a moment, and Sheriff Slattery wrote notes on his pad. "I'll tell Milo about that. He may know the place you're describing."

"I don't recognize it," Sadie said, "unless she means that part of the Blue Fork Trail beyond the place where Lane found the hair ornament."

Sara turned toward her questioningly. "What do you mean?"

"One of the searchers found a bead and feather ornament on a little leather thong," Sadie said. "We thought it might have been one of your hair ties, honey."

Sara put a hand up to her matted hair. "My braid wrap. It caught on something, and I lost part of it." Her face scrunched up like a squeezed lemon. "Dad got me those when we went to Arizona. I must have left them behind."

"Don't worry, honey," Alice said. "We'll get you some more. Where did the lady take you?"

Sara lay back on the pillows with a sigh. "She had a kind of a hut. A little cabin, I guess you could say, but it was pretty rough, like it'd been thrown together by whatever she could find."

"You must have been outside the area we searched," the sheriff said, "and we searched a lot of ground. But we never saw anything like that."

"It was a long ways, and I thought I would collapse before we got there. It was dark when we finally did. We were going slow, and she even picked me up and carried me a couple of times, but she couldn't keep that up. I made her let me rest once, but mostly she just kept me moving. I knew we were getting farther and farther from home, but my head hurt, and by then I didn't think I could find my way back alone." Tears filled Sara's eyes as she gazed at Alice. "I really botched it, didn't I, Mom?"

15

ALICE PULLED SARA CLOSER AND HUGGED HER. "NO, YOU DIDN'T botch anything, honey. You did great."

Theo handed Sara a tissue, and she settled back on the couch and wiped her eyes.

"What did the woman do once she got you to the hut?" the sheriff asked.

"She had me lie down on some blankets, and she brought me a drink. Some kind of tea that tasted like grass. Then she mashed up some leaves and put them on my ankle."

"Do you know what kind of leaves?" Sadie asked.

"No. But she told me to sleep. I wasn't scared of her by then. I was more mad at myself for going with her and not making her take me home. But I was so tired, and after she gave me that tea, I really was sleepy. I guess I slept for a while. When I woke up, it was dark outside. I turned on my phone, but I didn't have a signal yet. The lady had a fire going right outside the hut. I guess she heard me moving around a little, because she came in and told me to go back to sleep."

"What then?" Theo asked.

"She said I couldn't walk anymore on my ankle until it was better. And she gave me some kind of cereal."

Alice blinked at her. "Cereal?"

Sara frowned. "It wasn't oatmeal, or Cream of Wheat. Corn-meal mush, maybe? She had cooked it over the fire in a little pot. And she gave me more of that tea. She said it would help the pain go away. And I slept some more."

Alice faced Sheriff Slattery, her eyes wide. "Do you think Sara was drugged?"

"I don't know. Maybe. Or maybe it was just aspirin or some natural painkiller that would have that effect."

"Did you think that tea she gave you made you sleepy?" Alice asked Sara.

"Not at first. I didn't think about it. But now I guess I do. She didn't want me to try to leave."

"Why would she want to keep you there?" Theo asked.

"She said it was so I wouldn't hurt my ankle worse."

"Oh, sure," Theo said sarcastically. "After she dragged you miles across the mountain on it."

Dr. Conroy leveled his gaze at Alice. "We'll do some blood work and see if there's any trace of narcotics in her system."

"Thank you." Alice's voice choked on the words.

"You think she gave me something really bad?" Sara asked.

"Probably not," Doc said, "but we want to make sure. The fact that you were able to escape tonight tells me you weren't too heavily sedated. You may have just been exhausted that first night."

"I hope so."

"Did you have any odd dreams?" Doc asked.

"Not that I remember." A flash of fear crossed Sara's features. "Then when I woke up in the daytime, she still wouldn't let me go. I told her I wanted to go home, but she said not yet." She turned to her mother, obviously agitated. "I didn't tell her I had my phone in my pocket because I was afraid she would take it away. But I tried to call you while she was outside, Mom. I couldn't get through. There just wasn't any signal."

Sara's tears flowed freely now, and Sadie got up and took her the box of tissues. "Here, honey. It's all right now. You're home. You did a great job getting away from there."

"Well, she wasn't there tonight. I'd been sleeping again, and when I woke up, the sun was low. I hobbled outside the hut, but she was gone. So I just took off. I figured if she didn't catch me, I'd just walk until I could get a phone signal. And then I found a stream, and I saw what I thought was Quandary Peak, and so I thought I must be near Grandma's house."

"Oh, baby." Alice pulled her into her arms.

"I guess I'd better let you get her to the hospital," Mac said. "Sara, I'd like to bring Milo and Wyatt to see you in the morning and have you tell them as much as you can remember about that hut and how you got to it. That might help us find that woman. I'd like to talk to her and ask her why she took you there. Can you help us with that?"

"I'll try," Sara said.

"Thank you."

Sara glanced at Theo and smiled wryly. "It was better than that hut we made at Grandma's one summer. Remember that?"

Theo nodded, smiling. "I sure hope it was better than that."

Alice stood. "Will you arrest that woman?"

"I might," Mac said. "If I can find her."

"She kidnapped my daughter."

The sheriff nodded. "Sounds like it. But she may have had good intentions."

"How can you say that?" Alice said adamantly. "She wouldn't let Sara leave."

"But it's true Sara was injured."

"She didn't try to get word to us."

Sadie stepped over to Alice and put an arm around her. "You know, this may sound a little off the wall, but I think she may have come around here last night."

"What are you talking about?" Theo asked.

"When I came home, after I went to your house, Alice, I took Hank out for his nightly run. He'd been cooped up all day, and he was anxious to get out. He started barking at something—or someone. I saw it go into the woods. I had the impression it was a person, but I wasn't a hundred percent sure. I called Hank back and made him come inside."

"Why would she poke around here, when she had Sara?" Alice asked.

"Yeah," Theo said. "I thought she was watching Sara to make sure she wouldn't get away."

"Maybe she thought Sara would sleep for a long time and went out to get some food," Sadie said.

"Or maybe it wasn't her at all," the sheriff added, tucking his notebook in his pocket.

Sadie nodded. "I pulled a few hairs off a bush and saved them for you." She hurried to the kitchen and got the plastic bag she had put away earlier. When she returned to the living room, she placed it in the sheriff's hand.

"Well, she did give me an orange yesterday," Sara said. "I wondered where she got it from. I didn't get the impression she goes into stores very often."

"*Hmm.*" Sadie frowned. "I don't think I've had any oranges in the house this week."

"That wild man stole from people's gardens," Theo said.

They all stared at him.

"Do you think she was the wild man?" Sara's voice trembled.

"Maybe," Alice said. "If people didn't see her clearly, they might think she was a man."

Dr. Conroy nodded slowly. "That would explain some things. But let's not think about that right now. It's after three o'clock, and I'm sure Sadie would like to get to bed. Alice, do you want to follow me in your vehicle?"

"Sure. Theo, do you want to come with us?"

"Of course." He stood and zipped his jacket.

"Let me get a coat Sara can wear," Sadie said.

A few minutes later, Theo carried Sara out to the Jeep. Dr. Conroy set out down the driveway, and Alice and the kids followed.

Mac lingered for a moment next to his SUV. "Sadie, this is the first time in a long time that I've been happy to be awakened in the middle of the night."

"I'll call Milo and Laura and Roz around five," Sadie said. "It'll be great to tell them Sara's been found."

"Yes, but I may get up a search party later, to try to find that woman. I think I'll only take the experienced mountaineers though."

"I'll leave that up to you, sheriff."

Sadie planned her arrival at the hospital to coincide with the start of visiting hours—10:00 AM. When she entered the cheerful second-floor room, she found not only Sara, looking clean and refreshed, but Milo and Mac sitting nearby and talking to Sara earnestly. The sheriff still had a fatigued, careworn look, with fine lines pronounced at the corners of his eyes.

"Grandma!" Sara wriggled more upright in the bed when she saw Sadie and grinned at her. Her strawberry-blonde hair lay in gleaming waves about her shoulders, and her smile reached all the way to her bright hazel eyes.

Milo stood, and the sheriff started to rise, but Sadie waved them back into their seats. "Don't get up, boys."

"I understand you're the rescuer and woman of the hour," Milo said.

"No, this is the woman of the hour." Sadie pointed at Sara. "She rescued herself. I just reeled her in the last quarter mile."

"Well, that's the truth," Mac said.

Sadie walked around the bed and gave Sara a big hug. "Don't you look fine this morning?"

"Thanks. The nurse helped me get a shower. They put a plastic bag over my foot, so I wouldn't get the bandages wet."

"What's the verdict on the ankle?"

"Bad sprain, just like Doc thought."

Sadie nodded in satisfaction. "Are you going home today?"

"I sure hope so." Sara rolled her eyes. "Dr. Conroy wanted to keep me a full twenty-four hours, but he and Mom compromised. If she would go home and sleep, he would release me this afternoon, provided nothing bad shows up."

Sadie nodded, translating "nothing bad" into "complications from the head injury." She looked over at Milo and Mac. "Sorry to interrupt. I'm guessing you're here on business. Just pretend I'm not here."

"Oh, and Dad's coming," Sara said eagerly. "He called Mom right before she left and said he'd landed in Denver. He's on the way now."

"Wonderful." Sadie squeezed in on the edge of the bed next to Sara. It was probably against hospital rules, but Sara didn't seem to mind. She used the bed rail as leverage and scooted over to make more room.

"All right then," Sheriff Slattery said. "Milo and his brother and a couple of deputies will get right out there and see if they can locate this hut in the woods. Judging from your injury, I don't think you managed more than a mile or so an hour last night, Sara. I'm guessing that hut is within six miles of where your grandmother found you, and maybe within four."

"It was an awful long way," Sara insisted.

"Yes, but, honey, you called me about one thirty. If you left the hut at sundown, you couldn't have been out there more than five or six hours. A lot of the time you were going uphill."

"I found a stick," Sara said, frowning. "I used that for a while. But I lost it." She blinked several times, and tears pooled in her eyes.

Sadie put her arm around her. "It's all right, honey. Take your time."

Sara drew in a deep, shaky breath. "I was scared she would never let me go. It was creepy, and I felt like I had to do something."

"You did just right," the sheriff said.

"Thanks. That was the first time I woke up and she wasn't in the hut or nearby. And after I left, I was afraid she'd come after me and find me. I walked a long ways, until I couldn't go any farther, and then I hid for a while in a thicket to rest. That was before the stream."

Milo was listening carefully to every word she said.

"I might have slept for a little while," Sara admitted. "I woke up, and it was really cold. I figured I'd better keep moving, but it was hard to stand up and get going again. I didn't want to, but I made myself. Oh, and I tried my phone again then." She looked over at Sadie. "I was afraid I'd never get home. Grandma, it was awful."

Sadie held her and stroked her hair, and the sheriff placed the tissue box on Sara's lap. After a moment she sat up, sniffed, and took a tissue to mop her blotchy face.

"Sorry."

"Don't be sorry, Sara," the sheriff said gently. "You had every right to be frightened. We're going to find this woman and ask her what she was doing, and why she didn't try to get you some help, or at least tell your family where you were."

"Do you think she really went to Grandma's house last night?" Sara asked.

"I don't know. I had another call early this morning. One of your grandma's neighbors had some meat go missing out of their freezer last night. That supports the theory that this wild woman of yours is helping herself to other people's groceries. Foraging, at other folks' expense."

"Do you think that's how she's living?" Sara asked.

He shrugged. "Maybe having you for a houseguest drove her to find more food quickly than if she was on her own. If she thought whatever she gave you in that tea would knock you out for a few hours, she might have come into town to make the rounds of people's pantries. We've had reports of half a dozen petty thefts over the last two or three weeks, and most of them involved food items."

"Did you tell this woman you wanted to go home?" Milo asked.

"Only about a gazillion times," Sara said. "She wouldn't let me. She kept saying, 'No, you have to heal first.' And she kept giving me that awful tea. The last time, I dumped it out on the floor, since it was a dirt floor. I waited till she wasn't looking and spilled it near the wall and then wadded up my blanket over it, so she wouldn't see the wet spot."

"That may be why you woke up when she was gone," Mac said. "If she'd been drugging you, she figured she knew how long she had to go and forage and still get back before you woke up."

Sara's lower lip trembled. "I didn't think about it having something like that in it. I just knew it tasted bad, and I was sick of it. I hope she didn't give me bad drugs." She looked anxiously to Sadie. "They took some of my blood last night, and again this morning. They're checking for things like that, right?"

"Yes, and we'll ask Dr. Conroy as soon as he comes in," Sadie said quickly, "but I don't think you need to worry too much about that. Your thinking seems as clear as ever."

Sara sighed and snuggled against her. "Thanks, Grandma."

"Can you tell us more about this hut?" Milo asked. "What was it made out of?"

"Poles, I think. Small tree trunks, maybe. And it had a tarp or something over it, and I think she put branches on top of that to hide it, but I could see the tarp from underneath. Green."

"That would help camouflage it if any part of it showed through the branches," Milo said. "How big was it? Could I stand up inside?"

"Yeah." Sara looked around for reference. "It wasn't half as big as this room. Maybe a quarter. It seemed pretty sturdy. When I lay on the blankets and looked up, I could see where the logs or tree limbs or whatever they were came together. They were tied with twine in some spots. And in between was the green tarp. Oh, and she used some evergreen branches on top. It smelled good in there."

"What about the outside?" Milo leaned forward. "When you got there, or when you left, did you notice what the outside of it looked like?"

Sara frowned. "It was dark when we got there. I thought it was a little cabin. Oh, I know. One wall was up against a rock or a cliff. It was rock inside. One whole wall."

"That helps," Milo said. "We can look at the base of cliffs and rock faces. Anything else?"

"Well...I was kind of in a hurry when I left. I did look back a couple of times. But I didn't take her path, the way we came. I was afraid I'd meet her, so I dove into the woods. And I didn't get very far at all before I couldn't see it anymore."

"So the woods were thick there," Milo said.

"Yeah."

"What kind of trees?"

"Um...pines and aspen for sure. Maybe some spruce or fir. Oh, and oak. Little scrub oaks, I think. Where I hid in the thicket, there were little acorns on the ground."

Milo nodded almost grimly.

"Not much help?" the sheriff asked.

"I wish it was more specific," Milo said, "but there aren't many places where you'll find just one or two kinds of trees."

Sadie raised her chin. "Well, I think Sara has done wonderfully, noticing all of that. She kept her wits, and she was able to navigate in the dark, when she was in a lot of pain."

"That's true," Mac said. "Sara, we're all proud of you."

"Yeah." Milo smiled at Sara. "I only meant it would be more helpful for us as searchers if the place had been more unusual."

"Like if I saw a palm tree or something?" Sara asked with a teasing gleam in her eye.

They all laughed.

"Something like that," Milo said. "Was there a stream near the hut? Do you know where she got her water?"

Sara shook her head. "I didn't think about it while I was there, but it couldn't have been too far. I saw her bring in a jug of water once. She had a green plastic jug that she carried it in."

"I'm guessing the source wasn't far away," Milo said.

"I didn't see water when I left. Not until later, when I crossed that one stream and saw Quandary Peak."

"It's okay," Milo said. "You weren't thinking about water at that point, just getting out of there."

"Exactly." Sara sighed. "Sorry I'm not more help."

"It's all right. You've given us some great details." Milo stood. "I'll get the boys together and get out there. Sheriff, I'll call in with a report by two o'clock—sooner if we find something."

"Where will you start?" Sadie asked.

"At my house with topo maps. We'll mark likely places and then drive as close as we can and hike in. Secluded, wooded areas below rock faces, within a half mile of water."

"There's only a few thousand of those out there," Mac said with a grim chuckle. He stood and set his chair back against the wall. "Thank you, Sara. I hope you feel well and are allowed to go home today. And if you remember anything else that could help us find this woman or her hideout, let me know."

After Milo and the sheriff had left, Sadie squeezed Sara. "Good job. I assume they asked you to describe the woman before I got here?"

Sara nodded. "I did the best I could. Long brown hair, dark eyebrows, brown eyes, camouflage clothes. I think she was taller than me, but not much. And heavier. Kind of muscular, but not fat."

"They'll find her," Sadie said, but she wondered. Now that her prisoner had vanished, would the woman panic and move to a new location?

16

"Do you want to rest now?" Sadie asked Sara.

"No. I want to go home." Sara gave her a mischievous grin. The expression was so typical of her that Sadie was encouraged. Her granddaughter was well on her way to healing.

Sadie took the chair Milo had vacated. "A lot of kids came out yesterday to help look for you, and I think half the people from Campfire Chapel were out there."

"What did everyone do all day?" Sara asked.

"We beat the bushes from Milo's barnyard out in all directions, but especially on the riding trails and the woods near there. And where there's open ground, we tramped all over it, looking behind rocks and under bushes, in case you'd crawled somewhere for shelter and passed out."

"Oh, Grandma, you're exaggerating."

"No. I'm not. We were very scared for you." Sadie took her hand and gave it a gentle squeeze. "I cannot tell you how glad we are that you're back. We sent up an awful lot of prayers, and God has answered them in the nicest possible way."

"Hey there, kiddo!"

They both looked toward the door, where Cliff Macomb stood, wearing a rather rumpled suit and carrying a blue plush teddy bear.

"Dad!" Sara's whole face lit up.

Cliff walked over to the bed and gave her a hug. "Your mom told me you were here, so I came straight from the airport. Hi, Sadie." He gave her a cordial hug, then looked around. "Where's Alice? I thought she took today off."

"The doctor sent her home to rest," Sadie said.

"She'll be back in a while," Sara told him. "She's going to take me home later. Sit down, Dad."

Sadie hopped up and brought the second straight chair closer to the bed. "Here you go, Cliff."

"Thanks." He held out the teddy bear to Sara. "The gift shop was limited in its selection."

Sara laughed. "I love it. Thanks!" She cuddled the toy in the curve of her arm.

Cliff settled into his chair. "So what exactly happened? Alice said you fell off the horse and some deranged woman kidnapped you?"

"Well, sort of. I guess." Sara sighed and stroked the teddy bear's electric blue fur. "I suppose I have to tell it all over again."

"I suppose you do," Cliff said. "I want to hear every detail."

Sadie listened closely as Sara went through the recital again, hoping some new memory would come out.

"...and then I heard Hank barking, and within minutes he and Grandma were with me, helping me get up to Gram's house," she concluded.

"Wow. So have they found the woman?" Cliff asked both Sara and Sadie.

"Not yet," Sara said. "The sheriff has some people out looking for her now."

They talked for a few more minutes, and Dr. Conroy walked in. "Hello, folks. Sara, how are you feeling?"

"I feel fine," she said. "Can I go home now?"

"Not yet. Let's give it until three o'clock, as your mother and I agreed earlier."

"Okay," Sara said grudgingly.

"Alice is following your instructions," Sadie told him, "and this is Sara's father. I don't know if you've met Cliff Macomb."

"I don't think so." Dr. Conroy shook his hand. "Quite an ordeal your daughter went through."

"She was just telling me about it. Unbelievable."

Dr. Conroy took out a flashlight and stepped up to the bed. Sadie and Cliff moved their chairs back. The doctor shone the light in Sara's eyes and took her pulse.

"So far, so good," he said. "How's the headache?"

"Gone, unless I touch the bump," Sara said.

Dr. Conroy smiled. "I still want you to take it easy for a couple of days. Let's say you don't go back to school until Thursday."

"But I feel fine."

"*Hmm.*"

"Sara's been concerned about her blood work," Sadie said. "Do you have the results of that yet?"

"Everything looks good. Nice and normal." Dr. Conroy looked at Cliff. "We wondered if Sara had been drugged while she was confined. The lab didn't find any trace of narcotics. If she was given something to make her sleep, it was probably an herbal infusion that metabolized quickly. Our tests don't show any nerve damage either. The fact that she was able to get herself out of there on that ankle tells me she's a strong, healthy girl."

"Glad to hear it." Cliff's voice broke, and he cleared his throat. "Doctor, thank you so much for all you've done for my family. Sara told me you got out of bed at two o'clock in the morning to go and tend to her."

Sadie chuckled. "That was the classic house call, eh, Doc?"

"It sure was." Dr. Conroy patted Cliff's shoulder. "No worries, Mr. Macomb. I'd do it anytime. I'm just glad things turned out well in this case. Now, if you'll excuse me, I'll go put the discharge papers in order, so that she can walk out of here at three if nothing else comes up."

Sadie chatted with Sara and Cliff for another hour, and finally Alice came in.

"Well, hi, honey," Sadie said. Alice didn't look truly rested, but Sadie supposed she probably didn't either.

Cliff stood and kissed Alice's cheek. "Hi. Get some sleep?"

"A little."

"I'm really sorry about the phone business."

"It's okay," Alice said, subdued. "You had no idea I'd need to reach you."

"No, but I still should have told you where I was going. And I suppose I should have called you or Nancy when I got to the hotel, just to tell you I didn't have my phone and would be out of touch for a couple of days. I'll make sure that doesn't happen again."

Alice nodded and walked over to the bed, putting on a smile. "So. Has Doc Conroy been in?"

"Yes, and he said I can go at three," Sara said. "Can I get dressed now?"

"Oh, sweetie, it's not even noon. The nurses will probably need to check all your vitals a couple more times. Let's not rush it." She turned back to Cliff, frowning. "By the way, what was that 'don't tell your mom' business in the e-mail you sent Sara a couple of weeks ago?"

"Huh?" Cliff's face was a blank for a moment, until Sara spoke up.

"You know, Dad. But don't tell!"

"Oh, that!" Cliff looked from Sara to Alice and back. "I think we have to tell her now."

"I think so too," Alice said. "I had Theo open Sara's e-mail in front of the sheriff, so we could make sure there was no...well, foul play or..."

Cliff's eyebrows drew together. "You thought I had Sara?"

"No," Alice said quickly. She glanced at Sadie for help.

"At first we wondered if you might have picked Sara up," Sadie said. "We didn't really think you had, but we needed to rule it out. We had tons of people out there searching, and if she was with you..."

Cliff sighed. "I get the picture. I really messed up, didn't I? Alice, I'm truly sorry."

"So what are you not supposed to tell me?" Alice crossed her arms and gazed at him, unblinking.

"It's a surprise, Mom," Sara said. "Something Dad and I wanted to do, but we weren't sure we could pull it off."

"Well, it's not my birthday or Mother's Day."

"No," Cliff said. "Sara, honey, we might as well tell her."

"Oh, all right," Sara said, but her lips pouted a little.

"Sara wanted to do something special at Thanksgiving," Cliff said. "I was trying to set up a family weekend at one of the ski resorts."

"For you and me and the kids?" Alice asked.

Cliff shrugged. "Yeah, or just you and the kids if you didn't want me there."

"And Grandma," Sara said. "I just wanted a special time for our whole family. And Dad said he thought he could set it up."

"That sounds expensive. Especially on a holiday weekend." Alice eyed Cliff suspiciously.

"Well, it turns out most of the lodges are booked already for that weekend," he said. "But we could go for a day. If you want."

"Not until Doc says her ankle is completely healed," Alice said, and Sara frowned. "Honey, it was a really nice idea." Alice gave Sara a little hug. "Thanks for thinking of it. And, Cliff, thanks for trying to make it happen. But for now we'd probably better concentrate on less athletic pursuits."

An aide appeared at the doorway, holding a tray. "Well, Miss Sara! You're a popular young lady. I brought your lunch."

"Did you eat?" Alice asked Cliff.

"No, did you?"

"Not really."

"Why don't you two run down to the cafeteria and get something?" Sadie said. "I can stay with Sara, and Cliff can give you the specifics of the doctor's report."

"Well..." Alice looked over at Cliff.

"Sure," he said. "I could go for something to eat."

"Go on," Sadie said. "I brought my laptop. If we get bored, we can play a game."

"All right," Alice said. "I guess we should talk. We'll be back in half an hour, okay?"

"Go on, Mom," Sara said.

"Where's Theo?" Cliff asked as they headed for the door.

"I sent him to school. Do you think I should have let him stay home?" Alice's voice faded as they walked down the hallway.

While Sara ate her lunch, Sadie opened her laptop. She was able to use her cell phone as a wireless connection for her laptop.

"What are you working on, Grandma?" Sara asked.

"Just checking my e-mail for now."

"Did you ever find out anything about that doctor's kit you got at the auction?"

Sadie smiled. "Not really. It's only been two days, you know, and I've been sort of busy."

"Wow." Sara made a face. "It seems like forever since I walked into the store and you showed it to me."

"It does, doesn't it?" Sadie clicked on one of the sites she had bookmarked. "I did do a little research on the army officer who owned the sword I bought the same day. I hoped maybe I'd find a doctor in his family, but no luck so far. I was checking on some of the antique medical instruments here." She turned the screen so that Sara could see it too. Sara moved her tray a few inches, and they settled in comfortably.

"I found some stories about a woman back in the early days of Silver Peak," Sadie said. "The miners called her the Angel of Silver Peak. She helped them when they had an influenza epidemic, and there are some stories—rumors, really—that she may have helped some of those injured in mine accidents."

"That's cool," Sara said.

"I haven't found any hard facts—like her name," Sadie said. "And there seemed to be one point where they were afraid of her." She clicked on a picture of a surgical clamp. "This is almost identical to one of the instruments in the bag I bought."

"What did they use it for?"

Sadie grimaced. "To clamp off blood vessels while they were operating."

"*Ew.*"

"Not the best lunch conversation." Sadie looked at the tray. "Nothing wrong with your appetite though." Sara had eaten more than half of her chicken and vegetables already.

"I was really hungry. I thought hospital food was supposed to be awful, but this is pretty good. Aren't you hungry, Grandma?"

"I'll go get something after your folks come back."

"Mom didn't seem to be mad at Dad anymore. I'm glad." Sara sipped her milk through a straw.

"What do you mean?" Sadie asked.

"Theo said last night that Mom was really upset yesterday because she couldn't get hold of Dad, and she thought he might have kidnapped me."

Sadie smiled sadly. "I sort of wish Theo hadn't told you that. It was a wild thought that came to your mom while she was distraught. She had tried for a long time to reach your father, and she was afraid he didn't want to be reached. Turned out it was all a mix-up because he forgot his phone."

"I've done that before."

"Me too," Sadie admitted. "I'm glad they're having lunch together. I hope it gives them a chance to straighten out any little problems."

"Yeah." Sara's lip curled. "They don't fight much. I really hate it when Mom's not happy though."

"Between us, I think she was entitled to a little crazy thinking this weekend. It's safe to say you gave her the worst scare of her life."

"I wish I'd been...smarter, or something when that woman came along. I sure wouldn't have gone with her."

Sadie shrugged. "People who've just bashed their heads aren't known for being rational. And she offered to help you."

"Yeah." Sara rolled her eyes. "Some help."

"It's a lesson for us all to remember in the future," Sadie said.

"Uh-huh. I just wish we could have had the skiing weekend."

"Maybe another time," Sadie said.

Sara glanced at the computer screen. "What's that?"

"What?"

"That snake thing." Sara pointed.

"Oh, that," Sadie said with a chuckle. "It's a medical symbol called a caduceus."

"A medical symbol?" Sara frowned, her forehead furrowing as she leaned closer to the laptop. "I think..."

Sadie could tell this was somehow important to Sara, and she waited in silence.

"I think I saw that before," Sara said at last. She closed her eyes for a moment. "In that woman's hut."

17

SADIE'S HEART RACED. "YOU SAW A CADUCEUS IN THE WOMAN'S hut?" she asked carefully.

Sara squeezed her eyes shut tight. "Maybe I dreamed it. But no." She opened her eyes and gazed at Sadie. "One of the times she gave me the tea, she knelt down beside me and bent over me, to help me sit up and drink it. And she had this necklace hanging outside her jacket when she bent over. It had one of those on it."

Sadie's mind darted about, trying to haul the possible research avenues into line. "A necklace with this symbol. You're sure?"

"It had a white background, and that thing was red and silver. And she had those pet tags on the chain with it."

Sadie sat up straighter. "Pet tags?"

"I mean dog tags. You know. Soldiers wear them."

"Yes, I know exactly what you mean. Sara, soldiers usually also have a cloth strip on their shirt pocket that has their last name on it. I don't suppose that woman had a name on her clothes?"

Sara started to shake her head and winced. She rubbed her temple and closed her eyes again. "I'm pretty sure I'd have noticed something like that if she did."

"Are you tired, honey?" Sadie asked.

"Maybe a little."

"Can you eat a little more?"

"I don't think so."

Sadie got up and moved the wheeled stand holding the tray and laptop away from the bed. "Why don't we lower your head and let you rest awhile?"

"Do you think that necklace is important?"

"It may be. I'll tell the sheriff about it. If he wants more information, he can come and see you again, okay?"

Sara nodded. Her eyelids drooped.

Sadie touched the button on the bed rail that slowly eased down the head of the bed. She pulled the light blanket up to Sara's chin. "Just close your eyes, honey." She smoothed Sara's hair, thinking.

A caduceus and dog tags. She itched to do more research.

When Alice and Cliff returned twenty minutes later, Sara was asleep and Sadie was immersed in a site displaying military uniforms and insignia. She looked up and smiled at them, holding a finger to her lips.

Alice glanced over at Sara, and her face softened.

Sadie rose and carried her laptop toward the door. She beckoned to them and led them into the hallway.

"What's up?" Alice whispered.

"Sara saw a caduceus on a Web site I was looking at, and she thinks her kidnapper was wearing one."

Alice's mouth opened round.

"That could be a significant clue," Cliff said.

Sadie nodded. "That's what I thought. So I've been researching the insignia on uniforms. The Army Medical Corps uses the caduceus, and their Nurse Corps has it too. But what Sara described was more of a pendant, not part of the uniform."

"We need to tell the sheriff," Alice said.

Sadie nodded. "I can call him if you'd like. Dr. Conroy will be back sometime, and I know you don't want to miss him."

"Thanks," Alice said. "Please tell the sheriff he can see Sara later at our house if he wants to."

She and Cliff tiptoed into Sara's room, and Sadie walked down the hallway to a family lounge. No one was using the room at the moment, and she put in the call to Sheriff Slattery.

"That's interesting," he said, when Sadie had told him what Sara had remembered.

"Well, she did say the woman wore camouflage clothing," Sadie reminded him.

"Do you think it was an actual uniform, then?"

"I'm not sure. She's asleep now, but I thought I could ask her more questions about that later—or you could. But I'm thinking it's likely she has a medical background, and possibly she's been in the military."

"Lots of people wear camouflage in the woods," Sheriff Slattery said, "but the dog tags—now, that's pretty specific."

"I agree. Alice plans to take her home at three when Dr. Conroy discharges her, and you're welcome to visit Sara at home later. Meanwhile, I thought I'd find some uniform pictures of medics and army nurses to see if Sara recognized anything else about them. A lot of them have the red cross on white background as part of the insignia, but she didn't mention that."

"Anything you can come up with would be helpful," Mac said. "I'll see what I can turn up too. You never know what will spark a memory."

As she walked back toward Sara's room, Sadie's phone rang, and she answered it. To her surprise, the caller was June Hyland, a teller at the Silver Peak Bank.

"Hello, Sadie. I heard your granddaughter was found safe."

"Yes. She has a sprained ankle, but the doctor thinks she'll be all right."

"Wonderful. I'm so glad. I expect it will be all over the TV news tonight."

Sadie hadn't turned on the news for two days, but she supposed June was right.

"That's not the reason I called though," June continued. "One of our customers apparently found your bank deposit bag during the weekend and..."

"Thank You, God!" Sadie couldn't contain her exhilaration at this news. "And you too, of course, June! Where on earth was it?"

June chuckled. "Mrs. Remington said she found it on the edge of the street across from the bank, cuddled up to the curb. No telling how long it had been there when she found it yesterday morning. But it makes sense now—that's only a few steps from the Antique Mine's front door."

"Oh, Jane Remington found it? Bless her heart!" Sadie knew Jane and her husband, Jerry, the owners of the Silver Peak Bed-and-Breakfast. "I'll have to call and thank her."

"We didn't realize you'd lost it," June said. "Jane came in this afternoon to see if we'd gotten it all right. She said she saw it as she walked down the sidewalk yesterday morning before she went to church, and she didn't even look inside, though she could tell it wasn't empty. Since it had our logo on it, she figured the bank was the safest place for it. She just dashed across the street and tucked it into our night deposit slot. But she remembered it had *S.S.* written on the front in black marker. I knew it was your bag. I hope you don't mind that I told her."

"Not at all," Sadie said. "That was a pretty hefty deposit. I'm so glad Jane was the one who found it."

When she walked into the patient room a moment later, Sara was awake and talking animatedly to her parents.

Alice glanced at her mother. "You look happy."

"I am." Sadie sat down on the foot of the bed. "The bank just called to tell me a Good Samaritan found my missing deposit on the street yesterday and put it in their slot."

"Oh, I'm so pleased," Alice said.

Sara looked blankly from one to another. "Did I miss something?"

Sadie laughed. "Yes, honey, you missed a whole lot, but it's okay."

———

Sadie ate a late lunch at the Depot restaurant and dropped by the Antique Mine. Julie was behind the counter.

"Come give me a hug," she cried when she saw Sadie.

Sadie laughed and returned her embrace.

"How is Sara?" Julie asked.

"She's doing well. Alice and Cliff are taking her home this afternoon."

Julie beamed at her. "That was the most wonderful phone message I ever got. When Laura called me, I wanted to shout and dance and, well, Roz was here at the time and we *did* shout and dance. So did the customers, when they heard what had happened."

Sadie chuckled. "Thanks so much for filling in for me. I wasn't even going to open the store today, but with Sara found, I figured, why should we disappoint the customers? And I knew there was a bus coming up from Breckenridge."

"You made the right call." Julie leaned toward her and lowered her voice. "I sold that appliquéd coverlet, the beveled mirror, and a slew of small items today."

"Good for you!" Sadie glanced about. The nearest shoppers were down in the kitchen section, so she said softly, "And guess what? The bank deposit turned up today."

Julie's jaw dropped. "Hooray! Where?"

"At the bank." Sadie laughed and told her the story.

"Well, that's terrific," Julie said. "Now, I don't want to insult you, but I'm going to be brutally honest and tell you—you look awful. Why don't you go home and take a nap?"

Sadie sighed. "I've hardly slept the last two nights."

"I figured as much. Now, go on. I can take care of things here. And I'll make sure the deposit gets across the street this time."

"Alice invited me over for supper this evening," Sadie said, considering her options for the intervening hours.

"You'd better rest until then," Julie said.

"You're probably right. The sheriff's going to interview Sara again after she's home. He's hoping for more details about the kidnapper."

"So it was officially a kidnapping? Wow!"

"Sheriff Slattery says so. A woman led Sara off into the woods and kept her at a little cabin somewhere out there. When she said she wanted to go home, the woman wouldn't let her leave."

"Sounds like a kidnapping to me." Julie nodded firmly. "Your Sara's one gutsy little gal."

"I'll say. She had the courage to make a run for it when the woman wasn't around, and then she limped miles on a badly sprained ankle. I'm so proud of her, I may bust a few buttons."

———

An hour's sleep was all Sadie got before her doorbell rang. She opened it to the local newspaper editor.

"Well, hi, Troy."

"Hi, Mrs. Speers. Sorry to bother you. I heard Sara Macomb's been found, but no one's at their house."

"The doctor wanted her at the hospital for observation," Sadie said, carefully avoiding the fact that Sara was probably arriving home as they spoke.

"I see. Well, it's great news, and everyone in Silver Peak will want the details. Could you give me a little information?"

Sadie knew that if she declined, Troy would keep on asking people. He might as well get it straight from her and keep it accurate.

"Sure, I can give you a few minutes. Come on in, Troy. Would you like a cup of coffee?"

"I'd love it. Thanks."

They settled in at Sadie's kitchen table, and Troy took out his notepad. Hank came around to sniff Troy's pant legs and then settled on his cushion again.

"So who found Sara?" Troy asked.

"She walked out of the woods last night, down the mountain a ways. When she got where she had a cell phone signal, she called me."

"Boy, that must have been exciting."

"It sure was. My dog and I went to meet her and got her up here to the house. Dr. Conroy and Sheriff Slattery came here to make sure she was all right and ask her a few questions. And her family came too, of course."

"You said she went to the hospital. So she's not completely all right?"

"Apparently she was thrown from her horse while riding, as we had suspected, and hit her head. She might have been unconscious for a while on Saturday afternoon. Her ankle is badly sprained as well." Sadie hesitated. How much should she tell Troy?

"So where was she all day yesterday, while people were out looking for her?" he asked.

"You know what, Troy? I'm going to let you get the details from the sheriff on this, but I'll tell you this much: A person found Sara after she'd been injured and offered to help her. That person actually took her farther from home instead of closer."

Troy eyed her carefully. "So someone deliberately kept her from being found?"

"I didn't say that. The person may have had good intentions. We don't know yet. The sheriff hopes to locate them and have a little chat. He can tell you more, I'm sure."

"This is quite a story. Can you tell me where he took Sara?"

Troy was assuming the person who found Sara was a man, but Sadie didn't correct him.

"Actually, we don't know yet. Sara was disoriented and confused. After she came back, she tried to tell the sheriff where she had been. He has men out looking for the spot now."

"So...a house? Someplace here in Silver Peak? You said she walked out of the woods not far from here."

"We believe she walked several miles."

"What about that fellow, Pomeroy, who found the hair ornament yesterday? Was he mixed up in it?"

"No. I'm happy to tell you, Lane Pomeroy had nothing to do with Sara's troubles. All he did was hike up a trail at the right time and find a clue."

"So...somebody else."

Sadie sat back in her chair. "Troy, I don't mean to be evasive, but I'm not sure how much the sheriff wants publicized yet on this case. Until he finds the person Sara had contact with, I'd rather not say much. But do talk to Sheriff Slattery."

"Okay, will do. And thank you. You've given me enough to start my follow-up story. I'm really glad we can report this to the readers. Of course, everyone in town has probably heard by now that Sara was found. But they'll want to know more."

"I understand," Sadie said. "Thanks for coming by, Troy."

She walked him to the door. To her surprise, another car was coming up the driveway. The driver parked next to Troy's vehicle and climbed out. Chris Willard.

"Oh, great," Sadie said softly. "Do you know this guy?"

"I met him at Milo's yesterday," Troy said. "He's with that *Colorado Neighbors* magazine."

Sadie waited until the reporter was close to the front porch steps.

"May I help you, Mr. Willard?"

"I hope so." He nodded at Troy. "I see I'm not the first to ask for an interview today."

Sadie eyed him curiously. "You want to do a magazine story about my granddaughter? Isn't that unusual?"

"I'm not sure yet," Willard said. "Mostly, I wanted to help the family if I could. But I heard at the coffee shop that Sara is safe, so I guess that's taken care of. I'm glad she's been found."

"You've spent two days up here when you weren't sure you'd do a story?" Sadie asked.

Willard shrugged. "You can't always tell at first. Now I'm thinking I might do a piece on wilderness searches in Colorado, and focus on the families waiting for news."

"Well, it's true Sara is safe," Sadie said. "I don't think the family is up to doing interviews yet. If you decide to go ahead with the article, you can try to contact my daughter in a week or two and ask if she's interested. Meanwhile, I'm referring people to Sheriff Slattery for details of Sara's case." She turned to smile at Troy. "Thanks for coming by, Troy."

The first thing she did after the two writers drove out was to go to her computer and look up *Colorado Neighbors*. Sure enough,

Chris Willard was listed as a staff writer. Sadie did a little more searching and found that he had a personal profile page. A headline caught her eye on the list of search results, and she followed a link that listed his name in a news article nearly twenty years earlier. *Denver girl missing, no leads.* She skimmed the article, her heart quickening. Chris Willard's eight-year-old daughter had disappeared two decades ago, and as far as Sadie could tell from the follow-ups, she had never been found.

Tears welled in her eyes, and she sat back in her chair. So that was what Chris had meant when he said he'd hoped he could help the family. He didn't want to see another girl lost to her family forever. If they had let him, he would have offered his empathy. He knew the agony Alice had suffered yesterday—but his torture had lasted twenty years. She wished she had known all this when she spoke to him.

Lord, she prayed silently, *please comfort that man.*

She glanced at the clock. She had told Alice she would bring a pan of corn bread for supper. There was time to take Hank out for a nice, long walk before she mixed it up and got ready to go to Alice's. She looked over at Hank, who dozed on his pillow bed.

"Hey, you lazy thing! Do you want to go out?"

Hank rose with an affirmative yip, and his tail began to wag. Sadie laughed and put on a jacket.

Later, just as she pulled the pan of crispy, golden corn bread from the oven, her phone rang. She hoped it was Alice, not another reporter.

"Hey, Sadie, it's Mac."

"Oh, hi, Mac. What can I do for you?" Sadie asked.

"Milo Henderson just called in," he replied. "They've found the hut where Sara was held captive. Would you like to go for a ride?"

18

SHERIFF SLATTERY DROVE PARTWAY DOWN THE MOUNTAIN AND onto a small paved road. They descended a valley and started up the shoulder of another peak. After a couple of miles, he left it for a dirt road that was more of a Jeep trail.

"I didn't want to take Sara out, since she's just getting settled at home," he said to Sadie. "Besides, it may be too traumatic for her to come back here. But she's confided in you a lot. I thought you could be helpful in observing details at this place. That information she gave you about the medical symbol and the dog tags may lead us to her kidnapper."

"So the woman wasn't there when Milo and the others found the hut?"

"No, and they think she hadn't been there all day. Cold ashes in her fire pit, that sort of thing. I'm thinking she went into hiding as soon as she realized Sara was gone. She may have left the area entirely, but if she's out there, I want to find her."

"She must have realized that dozens of people were out looking for Sara yesterday."

"Yeah, I think so too." Mac glanced over at her. "And if she really was in town foraging last night, she might have picked up some information and decided it was time to move on."

"I keep thinking about last night," Sadie said. "Why would she come to my house?"

"I don't know. She may have gone to several ranches and houses on the outskirts of town. Or maybe Sara had mentioned you to her. She said she asked to go home more than once. Maybe she gave this woman her name, and yours, and Alice's, hoping she'd contact the family. I plan to talk to Sara more later and see if we can go a little deeper."

"Good. And I want to show her the camouflage patterns I found online," Sadie said.

He nodded. "Thanks to the info you gave me today, I've put in an inquiry with the marines, the army, and the National Guard, asking about female medical personnel."

"Sara didn't know how old the woman was," Sadie mused. "She could be retired."

"Or someone who spent a tour or two overseas and didn't re-up. There's my deputy's truck." Mac stopped the SUV behind the white pickup and turned the motor off. "We walk from here, and I won't be able to contact the deputies or the Henderson brothers. They said it's about a mile from this point. I hope you're up for it."

Sadie grinned. "Wore my hiking boots. How far is this from my house, anyway?"

"It's almost seven miles by road, but it's a lot shorter as the crow flies. Milo said it's less than four miles, according to the topo map. But Sara probably didn't take a straight line."

"Poor kid," Sadie said. "She did remarkably well in the dark."

"Better than a lot of adults would have done."

The trail the sheriff selected was barely discernible from where they had parked, but following instructions Milo had given Mac earlier and a few flags of yellow plastic tape the men had left on shrubs and tree branches, they had no trouble following the faint track. They had walked for about ten minutes when Wyatt Henderson appeared a few yards ahead, coming toward them through the trees.

"Hi," he called.

"Hello," Mac answered, and Sadie waved.

"We figured you'd be getting here soon, so I came out to guide you in the rest of the way."

"Thanks," Mac said. "We did find your markers. They were helpful."

"We haven't disturbed anything," Wyatt said, "but the deputies have photographed everything, inside and out."

Sadie and the sheriff followed Wyatt swiftly. The path became more apparent, and suddenly they broke into a small clearing at the foot of a steep, rocky mountainside. Milo and the two uniformed deputies got up from the ground, where it appeared they had been enjoying a break.

"Howdy," Sheriff Slattery said.

"You guys did a good job finding this place." Sadie gazed at the small shelter that stood against the base of the rock face. It almost looked like a part of a thicket of bushes that crowded a small stand of aspens. Some of the darker green boughs on the roof were beginning to turn orange.

"Find anything significant inside?" the sheriff asked.

"Maybe," said one of the deputies. "No weapons, but there was a partial box of ammunition. And it does appear that the suspect has lived here for an extended period of time."

"Let's take a look." The sheriff glanced over at Sadie. "You're welcome to come inside. I just ask that you don't touch anything."

Sadie nodded and followed him. Mac had to duck his head to enter through the low door of the hut.

The interior was very dim, with the only light coming through the door behind them, and the deputy turned on a powerful spotlight and shone it about the small room.

"We figure that's where Sara slept." He illuminated a heap of evergreen needles to one side. A wool blanket lay crumpled on top of the pile. "Over here's food." He showed them two covered five-gallon buckets. "One's about half full of rice, and the other had red beans." On a rustic shelf nearby sat a manual can opener and a leather-covered carrying case.

"What's in that?" Sheriff Slattery asked.

The deputy smiled. "Night vision goggles."

Slattery gave a low whistle.

From behind them, Milo said, "Here's the half box of .22 shells we found, Sheriff, but the gun's not here."

"Did Sara mention a gun?" Slattery asked Sadie, turning to examine the box.

She shook her head. "No. At the hospital today she did mention several different food items the woman gave her, though. Apples, a granola bar, herbal tea. And remember, last night she talked about eating an orange and some kind of hot cereal. She thought it might have been corn-based."

"Grits?" Milo asked.

"Maybe. Sara had never had it before, but she knew it wasn't oatmeal or Cream of Wheat."

"I remember," the sheriff said. He took the deputy's light and aimed the beam upward. Hanging from the underside of the roof were several batches of dried plants. One bunch looked like chives, and another Sadie recognized as sorrel. Half a dozen more hung down from the poles that made the roof frame. "That may be the tea makings, up there," Mac said.

"We didn't find those other kinds of food," the deputy told him.

"Maybe she took it with her," Milo suggested. "If she moved out fast after Sara left, she wouldn't be able to carry all this stuff."

"True," said the sheriff. "Could be she grabbed the most essential things—and the most portable. Sara mentioned a green plastic water jug. Did you find that?"

"No," both deputies said.

Sheriff Slattery grunted. "She couldn't carry everything and she had to choose. Any more observations, Sadie?"

"Maybe you could take samples of those herbs. I think we'd all like to know what she gave Sara."

Mac turned to the deputy. "Take a small piece of each type and bag it. I don't suppose it would do any good to leave one of you boys out here tonight."

"She might come back for the rest of her things," Milo said.

The sheriff shook his head. "She'd know if we were here. For all I know, she's watching us right now."

"We've got her night eyes," the deputy said.

Mac huffed out a breath. "She's smart. I don't think she'll come back here for a while, especially if we're sitting here waiting for her."

"But if we're not here..."

"Exactly what I said." Mac walked out into the late afternoon sunlight, and the others followed. He looked back at the door to the hut and stood for a moment, frowning. "All right, let's leave one man. Not for *her*, but there are a lot of reporters in town right now. I'd hate to see evidence destroyed before we catch this woman. I'll set up a relief shift, but anybody new will have to come in before dark, or he'll never find it."

"I'll stay until you get someone else," one of the deputies said.

The others gathered their belongings and followed Sadie and Mac out onto the path.

When Sadie and the sheriff got to Alice's house, the early news was airing on television.

"The Denver broadcast is leading with Sara's story," Alice said as she took them to the living room. Cliff, Theo, and Sara were watching the program.

"The sheriff's office reports that the girl is making a good recovery from her ordeal," the reporter was saying, "and she will return to school later this week. Meanwhile, authorities continue to look for the woman who allegedly held Sara Macomb against her will for a day and a half."

"I saw that reporter woman yesterday," Theo said.

"Are they filming that at Milo's?" Sadie asked, scrutinizing the backdrop, with several horses grazing in a corral behind the reporter.

"Yeah, she's on location in Silver Peak," Cliff said gleefully.

The camera cut to the anchorman. "Thank you, Sharon. Does this suspect they're hunting for have anything to do with the rumors of a wild man making appearances around Silver Peak in the last month?"

The reporter smiled. "Good question, Dave. I spoke to several local residents, and they've all heard the stories of someone lurking around isolated houses at twilight and dogs barking at fleeing figures. The county sheriff revealed that several complaints have been made of food items and small tools going missing from various residences. If they find the woman who held Sara Macomb captive, maybe they'll find their so-called wild man."

"Oh man," Theo said. "Why do people tell them these things?"

"Well, it's all true," Alice said. "Emma Roundy says the night she saw the wild man, a trowel and a bag of walnuts went missing from her shed."

Sadie watched Sara, who held the remote and clicked it off with a frown on her face.

"You all right, Sara?" Sadie said.

Sara nodded. "Why did you give them that picture, Mom? I hate that one!"

"I had to give the sheriff recent pictures of you," Alice said. "Besides, that's a beautiful photograph of you."

"It shows my braces."

"But that's good," Cliff said. "If one of the searchers had found a girl lying unconscious under a juniper bush, and she didn't have braces, they'd know it wasn't you and could keep looking somewhere else."

They all laughed, and Cliff stood up and walked over to Mac. "Evening, Sheriff."

Mac nodded. "I just dropped in to tell you folks we've secured the hideout, but as I told you earlier, the woman wasn't there. My men have seen no sign of her since they located the scene. I wanted to ask Sara a few quick questions, but I don't want to delay your dinner." He sniffed and smiled. "Pot roast?"

"Yes," Alice said with a laugh. "Would you like to join us?"

"My wife would have a fit if I didn't come home for dinner again."

"All right." Alice turned to Sara, who sat in a recliner with her feet elevated. "Are you up to a few more questions, honey?"

"I guess so," Sara said.

Mac walked over and sat down on the end of the sofa. "Sara, in the time you were with this woman, did you ever see a gun?"

Sara frowned and squeezed her eyes nearly shut. "Yeah. One time when I woke up, she was just coming in through the door. She had something in her hand. I thought it was a pistol, and she put it away where I couldn't see it. I could have imagined it."

"No, I don't think you imagined it," the sheriff said. "We found some ammunition in the hut."

"Maybe she uses it for hunting." Sara looked to her father for confirmation.

"Most people don't hunt with handguns, kiddo," Cliff said.

"I didn't see a gun when she first found me and took me there," Sara said slowly. "But I guess it could have been inside her jacket. She didn't threaten me or anything."

Mac leaned toward her. "Think carefully, Sara. You told me earlier that you asked to go home. You told her you wanted to leave. Is that right?"

Sara nodded. "More than once."

"What did she do when you said those things?"

"Just told me that my ankle had to heal, and I wasn't ready."

"She never threatened you?"

"No..." Sara's lower lip quivered. "It seemed like every time I talked about going home, she gave me more of that tea. I couldn't tell how long I'd been there, because I kept sleeping. It seemed like forever, but when Grandma found me, she said it was only the second night. I thought I'd been gone a week, or at least three or four days."

"And she didn't take your cell phone away from you, right?"

"Right. Maybe she knew I couldn't use it there. I shut it off after the first few times I tried to use it, because I was afraid the battery would run down. But if I woke up and she was outside, I'd try it again. It never worked until I got almost to Grandma's."

Sheriff Slattery wrote in his pocket notebook. "One more thing, and then I'll leave you alone. I want you to think about the woman's clothing. Was there a name patch or any other words on her jacket?"

"US Army," Sara said, touching the right side of her chest. "Here."

"Great. How about the other side? On the pocket, maybe?"

"I don't think so." Sara thought for a moment. "There was a patch on the sleeve, but I can't remember exactly what it looked like."

"Okay. Now, you said her jacket and pants were both camouflage."

"Yes."

"Did they match?"

Sara's eyes widened, and she nodded. "I think so. But they weren't like Theo's T-shirt."

"What do you mean?" the sheriff asked.

"Well, her things looked old and worn, but the colors were different."

Mac waited a moment and then asked, "How were they different?"

"I...can't really remember."

"Sadie told me she'd found a Web site that shows a lot of different camouflage fabrics," Mac said. "Could you look at it, please, and tell me if you see the pattern that this woman had on her clothes?"

"I can try." Sara looked toward Sadie.

"I brought my laptop." Sadie took it over to Sara's chair and sat down on the arm. She opened the computer. "It will just take a minute."

"People use different camouflage patterns to help them blend in with different surroundings," the sheriff said to Sara. "Duck hunters might use clothing that has elongated green and brown lines, to look like tall grasses and reeds. In the Arctic, they use patterns of blue, white, and gray, to blend in with the snow. Now, there are a lot of variations out there, but if you can just give us an idea of what kind of pattern she used, it may be helpful."

Everyone was quiet while Sadie brought up the Web site she had bookmarked. It displayed photographs of more than two dozen different camouflage designs. She turned the screen toward Sara. "Here you go."

Everyone waited while Sara looked over the panel of samples.

"Wow, that's a lot of them," she said.

Sadie patted her shoulder. "Take your time."

After a long minute, Sara said. "I think this one is most like it. Her jacket was dirty, though, and kind of...faded, I guess."

Mac rose and walked around behind Sara's chair so he could look over her shoulder. "Are you sure?"

"Not a hundred percent, but that one's the most like it. It had those brown smears." Sara pointed to a sample made of light green and tan shapes, with irregular patches of reddish-brown.

Sadie bent closer to read the label. "That's the Desert Camouflage Pattern, also known as the 'coffee stain' pattern. The army started using it in the early nineties."

"Right," Mac said. "It replaced the Chocolate-Chip Pattern for the desert uniform. But they have a different one now."

Sadie scrolled down. "Yes, here's a picture of the new Army Combat Uniform. It's a lot different. It says they started using that around 2005."

Mac straightened. "Okay, so if the woman was wearing a real uniform, it's probably ten years old or older. But there are a lot of nonmilitary camo clothes out there."

"Anyone can buy a real uniform at the army surplus store too," Cliff pointed out.

"Well, it gives us a place to start anyway." Mac put his notebook away. "Thank you, Sara. How's the ankle?"

"Not too bad. I haven't walked on it since last night, and when it starts hurting, Mom gives me some medicine."

He nodded. "I hope it feels better real soon. I'm glad it's not broken."

"Me too," Sara said.

"Well, I'll be getting home. Enjoy your dinner, folks."

Sadie joined the family in the dining room, her heart full of thanks. She hoped her sleep would be uninterrupted tonight, and tomorrow she would get back into her routine. It seemed forever since she had spent a normal day at the Antique Mine. The questions about Sara's captor would still work on her, as would the less urgent riddle of the Angel of Silver Peak and the old doctor's bag, but she looked forward to an uneventful day.

19

CUSTOMERS FLOCKED TO THE ANTIQUE MINE ON TUESDAY. Everyone wanted to speak to Sadie and find out how Sara was doing. Word had gotten around that Sara had been kidnapped and held against her will. Sadie tried to avoid adding much detail to the rumors.

"I heard she was held at gunpoint," Marge said. She had brought in an old spice chest with a missing drawer pull, and she hoped Sadie could match the others.

"No, I don't believe there's any truth to that," Sadie said, looking closely at the hardware on the small chest. "Do you want to leave this with me while I look for a replacement? I don't think I've got anything in my stock that will match, but I can search online catalogues and get back to you."

"Sure," Marge said. "I'm thinking of having you refinish it too."

"It seems to have the original finish now," Sadie pointed out. "Stripping it could lower its value."

"Oh, I know." Marge frowned at the small wooden chest of many drawers. "I just don't like those scratches and stains on the front."

"I'll clean it up a little," Sadie offered. "But you know, sometimes these old items are worth more if they look a little distressed."

"You always say that."

"Because it's true."

They eyed each other for a moment, and Marge laughed. "All right, Sadie."

Several other customers had lined up behind Marge. "I heard about the girl," the next woman said. "Is she all right now?"

"She's fine," Sadie said. "A sprained ankle is all. Oh, I see you found the millefiori paperweights. Would you like me to wrap this for you?"

"Yes, please."

Sadie smiled as she reached for a sheet of tissue paper in which to wrap the lovely glass item, with its circles of tiny colorful flowers.

The next customer in line leaned forward. "What about that wild man who abducted the girl? Have they caught him?"

"There was no wild man," Sadie said.

"But I've been reading about him on the *Chatterbox*," the customer replied.

"Those were rumors. Now, let's see." Sadie gave the woman her receipt for the paperweight and rang up the man's purchases. "That will be eighteen dollars and fifty-four cents. I hope you'll enjoy the tin and the book."

The questions didn't stop. After two hours, Julie came behind the counter.

"Could you go out back and make us some coffee, Sadie? I'll handle things here for a few minutes."

"Sure. Do you want some from Arbuckle's?"

"Frankly, I wanted to give you a few minutes for a break," Julie said.

"Do I look that frazzled?" Sadie asked.

"No comment."

Sadie gave in and went to the back room. She started the coffeemaker and sat down with her laptop. Sally Henderson had mentioned Harry Polmiller as a source of local folklore, and Sadie knew that was a good place to look. She went to a family history site and put in Harry's name and "Colorado." Because of his unusual surname, it didn't take her long to locate the correct family.

She clicked on a family tree that seemed to have been submitted by a distant cousin of Harry's. Following it back to the Civil War era, she gave each family member a quick look. Andrew Polmiller married a woman with several brothers who served in the Civil War, and Sadie scrolled down the list, though she feared it was only a rabbit trail.

The youngest Klein brother, who was born in 1853, caught her interest immediately. He had served in the Civil War only in its last year because of his youth, and had escaped injury during his stint in the army. But later, while working for a mining company, he had lost a leg. The mine had been located near Silver Peak, and Sadie's excitement grew. Could this be one of the cases she had read about, where the Angel of Silver Peak stepped forward to help? She took out her phone and called Harry.

"Hi. This is Sadie. I wondered if I could drop by later today and talk to you about your family tree."

"My what tree? I've got good apples this year."

"No, your family tree, Harry. I found out something interesting about one of your ancestors, or rather, the brother of one of your ancestors. Can I come by this afternoon?"

"Sure. I've got nowhere to go."

"Great. I'll be over later."

"Oh, Sadie! Wait."

"Yes?" she asked.

"Is Sara okay?"

"She's fine, Harry."

"Good. She's a tough one. Comes from good stock."

"Thanks. I'll see you later, after the store closes."

Sadie hung up feeling better. The coffee was done brewing, so she went over to pour it out for herself and Julie.

Four customers were queued up before the counter. Julie threw her a desperate glance.

Sadie took the mug over and set it beside the cash register. "Sorry. I didn't realize you were swamped out here."

"If you could go and help that lady in the linens section, I'd appreciate it so much. I promised her I'd be right there, but I can't get away from the till."

Sadie hurried to help the waiting patron. The rush continued, and she and Julie had to swap off at the counter in order to grab a late lunch. Finally, after four o'clock, things slowed down a bit.

"Wow. I've rarely seen it this busy after Labor Day," Julie said, "at least not when no tour buses came through."

"It was a good day," Sadie said, totaling up the receipts.

She left at four thirty, after Julie assured her she could handle things. Sadie crossed the street, extra carefully dropped her bank deposit in the slot, and then drove to Harry Polmiller's house.

The old man came to the door and unlatched the screen for her. "Hello, Sadie. Come on in!"

"Thanks. I hoped I could get here earlier, but a lot of people came to the store today. Most of them wanted to know about Sara, and what really happened to her."

"You poor thing, having to answer questions all day. I won't ask any. Would that help?"

Sadie laughed. "You can ask anything you want, Harry. I can tell you right now, I talked to Alice a few minutes ago. Sara's doing fine. Oh, and the sheriff hasn't found the woman Sara met in the woods, but his men are still looking."

"Well, I'm glad she's all right." Harry ushered Sadie slowly into his living room. "I'm moving kind of slow today. Spent two hours out in the garden, getting it ready for winter, and now I'm kind of stiff."

"You put me to shame," Sadie said.

"I doubt that. Have a seat."

When Sadie was settled on his comfortable leather-covered sofa and Harry had sunk into his recliner, he said, "So. You have something to discuss concerning my family?"

Sadie opened her bag and took out a couple of sheets of paper she had printed out. "I found your great-grandmother's family online. The Kleins. Are you familiar with that line?"

Harry nodded. "Her family came by way of Texas," he said. "A lot of Germans immigrated to Texas in the late eighteen hundreds."

"That's right, and Anna Klein married a Polmiller."

"Great-grandpa Andrew," Harry said.

Sadie smiled at him. "I hope my memory's half as good as yours when I hit my nineties."

Harry laughed. "It can be a blessing or a curse. So you're interested in one of the Kleins?"

"Yeah. Anna had several brothers, one of them being Tom."

"He was the youngest, I believe. I've got a picture of him somewhere, in one of the old albums. Only had one leg, you know."

Sadie's pulse picked up a little. "I do know. That's what struck me as interesting. Tom Klein survived the Civil War in one piece, but while he was working at the Tip Top Silver Mine, he was injured so badly he had to have his leg amputated."

"I believe that's correct," Harry said. "And it was done by a woman."

"What was?"

"The surgery."

Sadie huffed out a breath and sat back against the sofa. "Tell me you know about the Angel of Silver Peak."

Harry's eyes twinkled. "Doesn't everyone?"

Sadie glared at him, pretending to be angry. "No, everyone doesn't. I've been trying to learn more about this mysterious woman. I should have known I was looking in the wrong places. Should have come to you first, shouldn't I?"

He laughed. "I don't know a lot, but I do know Uncle Thomas told family members late in his life that she had saved his life when she performed the amputation. He was bitter about losing the leg at first, you know."

Sadie settled in more comfortably. "Consider me ignorant, Harry. Just pretend I know absolutely nothing, and tell me the whole story, if you don't mind."

"All right. There was a cave-in at the mine. They had taken out a lot of ore, and it was a very successful concern, but apparently the owners weren't the most conscientious. Over a period of five years, they had at least three accidents where workers were injured or killed. Tom Klein was one of them. He and two other fellows were trapped in a tunnel for several hours. Tom's leg was crushed, and they didn't think he'd make it."

"How did they get out?" Sadie asked.

"The other miners dug through the rubble and finally hauled them topside. There wasn't any doctor available. As I understand it, the other two who were caught with him survived with minor injuries, but Tom's leg was beyond saving. His wife sent for this woman who had helped out at other times."

"Helped out how?" Sadie asked.

"She had some nursing skills and had volunteered to help during the flu epidemic of 1879."

Sadie smiled. "Yes. I found a newspaper that mentioned it. Go on, please."

Harry shrugged. "She apparently told Uncle Tom Klein's wife that she might be able to save Tom's life by taking the leg off, but if that wasn't done, he would die for sure."

"How did this woman have the knowledge and skill to do something like that? I've searched for female doctors in this area, and I haven't found any records of one at the right time."

"Oh, she wasn't a doctor," Harry said. "Nope, though she might have been. She certainly had the brains and the nerve for it. But her husband was the one who had the training. I understand he was a very fine physician."

"Her husband. I wondered about that possibility."

Harry nodded. "He'd died a few years after the war ended, but she'd helped him in his practice, you see. They say she was one of the best skilled nurses in the territory. And after he died, people came to her, because they knew she had a lot of medical knowledge."

"How do you know all this?" Sadie asked.

"Family lore. And a journal."

Sadie stared at him. "You have a journal and you never told the historical society?"

"Reckon I forgot. It's not Uncle Tom's journal. It's his daughter's, you see, and she married a military man and moved to California. She died in 1950, and the journal made its way to me eventually. There's not a lot in it about Colorado, but she did write down what her father had told her about the mine accident and the trauma of losing his leg. I gathered he didn't talk about it much, but after some time he could see that the amputation was a good thing."

"I should think so," Sadie said. "He lived a good many years afterward."

"Yes, but I guess for a long time he refused to believe it was necessary, and he blamed the woman who did it. Said his wife shouldn't have let her take his leg off, and that she had no credentials or anything."

"What changed his mind?" Sadie asked.

"His daughter wrote that she took him to a new doctor after he was widowed. He had moved to California and was living with her and her husband then. Apparently the new doctor told him that whoever did the surgery knew what he was doing, and Tom told him it was a woman. That doctor told him he should thank God she was there when it happened, or he'd have died back then."

"That's nice to know. Do you happen to know the woman's name?"

Harry scratched his chin. "Let's see, now…I think it's in the journal. Tom's daughter said her father wrote a letter to the woman, not knowing whether she was still alive and living near here. But he wanted to thank her, so he wrote it and sent it off. And his daughter copied it in her journal before they mailed it."

"Oh, how wonderful," Sadie said. "Could I possibly see it?"

Harry nodded. "I think the journal's upstairs, in the spare room."

Sadie jumped up. "I don't want you to have to go to the trouble of going up there. Can you just tell me where to look, and I'll go and get it?"

"*Hmm,* well now, it's probably in a box. I've got three or four cartons of stuff in the closet up there. I should look, really."

"If you trust me to do it, I'll be careful to put everything back the way it was," Sadie said.

"All right, if you'll join me for supper."

"Now, Harry, I don't want you to go to any trouble."

"Nonsense," the old man said. "I've got a rice and chicken dish that Jeanne Sweeting put in my freezer a couple of weeks ago. All I have to do is microwave it. But she always puts too much in a package. I know without looking that there's too much for me to eat in one sitting."

Sadie smiled. "All right, I accept."

He nodded emphatically. "Attagirl! Now, you go up the stairs, and it's the bedroom on the left. Open the closet. I've marked the boxes, and I believe it's in the one that says 'Old Family Stuff' on it."

Sadie chuckled. "I like your approach to filing things, Harry."

"Well, it usually works well enough. If you don't find it in there, look in the other boxes. But it's a small, brown leather book. Quite fragile."

"I'll exercise great care."

"I know you will."

Sadie went out into the hallway and up the narrow staircase. She hoped Harry didn't try to come up here too often. On the landing, she entered the room on the left. A double bed was covered in an old George Washington bedspread, and the dresser and chairs in the room looked as though they had sat there a hundred years. On the wall hung an old portrait of a couple. The bearded man sat in a chair, his back stiff as a poker, staring at the camera. The lady stood behind him, her hand resting on the shoulder of his suit. Sadie lingered for a moment, studying her dress and hat. Eighteen-nineties, she guessed. She wondered if these were Harry's grandparents.

She opened the closet door, and found it neatly arranged. Several articles of clothing hung from the rod in plastic suit bags. On the floor were three cardboard cartons, and some smaller boxes rested on the shelf above.

Sure enough, one of the larger boxes was labeled "Old Family Stuff." Sadie smiled to herself and pulled it out into the room. She loved going through old things. This was almost as much fun as cleaning an attic.

She lifted a packet of papers out of the box, then a couple of old photo albums. She was tempted to browse through those, but she didn't have permission, and she didn't want Harry to wonder what was keeping her. She set them aside and reached into the box again. This time she was rewarded. Her hand closed on the worn leather cover of a small volume. She opened it to the first page and read, "Harriet Klein Atwood." This must have belonged to Tom Klein's daughter.

She placed the other items back in the carton and returned it to the closet. After brushing the dust off her knees, she turned off the light and closed the door on the spare room. As she descended the stairs, the smells of coffee and something savory struck her, and she knew Harry was hard at work in the kitchen.

"Find it?" he asked eagerly as she entered.

Sadie held up the journal. "Right where you said it would be." She placed it in his hands.

"Oh yes, that's it all right." Harry's eyes glittered as he slowly turned the pages. "That letter was near the back, if I remember right. Not the very back, but…" He leafed through the volume, squinting down at the old script. "There! Here's where she tells about her father's accident."

The bell on the microwave pinged, and he handed the book back to Sadie. "That's our dinner. Have a seat."

"Can't I help you?"

"No, I'm all ready. Well, maybe you could get us some water glasses. I've got coffee going too. Half-caff. I can't drink the real stuff in the evening anymore."

Sadie helped him put the finishing touches on the table and sat down opposite him.

"This is a real treat, Harry."

"We'll have to make sure we tell Jeanne on Sunday." He bowed his head and asked a blessing on the food.

They chatted amiably while they ate, and then Sadie insisted on washing up the dishes. When she had finished, Harry said, "Now, sit down for a minute and find that letter. I want to hear it again."

Sadie sat beside him on the sofa and opened the journal to the page he had indicated earlier. She read through the entry detailing Tom Klein's mishap at the silver mine. Harriet had not been born yet, but her mother had told the story many times. She told of her mother's fear that she would lose her husband that day, and her desperation in calling for the doctor's widow. Her father's good recovery was a blessing to the family, she wrote, but it took him many years to admit the fact and take steps to thank the woman who saved his life.

In closing, Harriet had written, "So I helped Dad pen the letter, and this morning I phoned the post office in Breckenridge. They couldn't give me the address, but they assured me that if I sent the letter there, Mrs. Trafton would receive it."

Sadie turned the page. "Here is a copy of what he sent her."

June 7, 1911

Dear Lady,

I take pen in hand to thank you, and to humbly beg your forgiveness for the wicked thoughts I once harbored toward you, and for the words I spoke against you. I owe you my life, and I have come to see that what you did was best. You truly have a gift for ministering to those in need. May God bless you,

Tom Klein

"There now," Harry said. "That's a fine letter."

Sadie nodded. "I'm glad he was able to send it to her while she was still alive. And this Mrs. Trafton—the medical bag I bought at an auction last week could very well have belonged to her husband. The initials RMT are on it."

"Hmm, I don't know what her husband's name was," Harry said.

"It was an estate auction, and I've tried to research the owner's family, but I didn't find any doctors in it, much less with those initials. But maybe now that I have the last name..."

"No doubt that Mrs. Trafton is your 'angel.' She sounds like a woman with a gift, as he said, and one who was willing to face great unpleasantness to help others."

"You know..." Sadie skimmed back over the daughter's account silently.

"What?" Harry asked.

She looked up. "It puts me in mind of the woman who helped our Sara."

"I thought she harmed Sara, or at least kept her from getting help."

"Ah, but did she know that? From what Sara told me, I wonder if she didn't think she was helping. And perhaps the things she did were of some medical benefit. Sara said the woman told her repeatedly that she mustn't try to walk until her ankle healed. And she put a poultice on the ankle. When Doc Conroy first looked at it, we found some plant residue bound around Sara's ankle with strips of cloth. I couldn't tell what it was, but I'm thinking that woman had studied herbs."

"Maybe she fancied herself like this Angel woman, Mrs. Trafton."

Empty Saddle

"Could be. And the tea she gave Sara to dull the pain and make her sleep—yes, I'm sure she knew what she was doing with the herbs."

"Let's be thankful Sara's injury wasn't as serious as Uncle Tom Klein's."

"Amen," Sadie said fervently.

"Do you know what kinds of plants she was using?" Harry asked.

"Some of them. I recognized sorrel, chives, and sage hanging in her cabin. There were a couple of others that I didn't recognize."

"Could be Emma Roundy could help you. She knows all about herbs."

"That's a good idea," Sadie said.

She cradled the journal in her hands. Would insights she had gained from it help her find the woman who had cared for Sara in her odd way?

————

Traffic flow at the store seemed more normal the next day. Sadie had time to catch up on her paperwork while Julie rearranged some of the displays and did a thorough vacuuming. After lunch, Sadie took Marge's spice chest to her workbench and went over it carefully. In her opinion, all it needed was the missing drawer pull and a light cleaning, and she hoped Marge would decide not to tamper with the original finish.

"Sadie, there's a man here asking for you." Julie spoke from the doorway to the back room. "Shall I send him back here? I've got a couple of browsers in the store."

~ 201 ~

"I'll come out." Sadie went to the doorway. A young man about thirty years old stood examining the Civil War sword, where Sadie had mounted it on the wall. He had thick, dark hair and was dressed in Dockers and a chambray shirt, with a lightweight jacket over it. Sadie couldn't quite peg him—he didn't look like a reporter, yet he wasn't her typical antiques buff either.

She stepped forward. "Hi, I'm Sadie."

The young man turned toward her, his brown eyes a bit anxious. "Hello. Michael Whitney." He glanced about as though checking to see who stood close enough to hear. "I was looking for Sheriff Slattery, and they tell me he's out in the field today. The fellow at the post office suggested I talk to you."

"To me?" Sadie frowned. "I don't have anything to do with law enforcement."

"Sorry. I should explain. I heard on the news last night, and again this morning, that the sheriff's department here is looking for a woman who lives alone in the woods. The description they gave…" He broke off, and Sadie sensed that he was distressed.

"I see. My granddaughter was the one who…who met her. Did you think you recognized the description?"

"It's possible she's my sister."

20

"YOUR SISTER." SADIE LET OUT A LONG, SLOW BREATH. "WOULD you like a cup of coffee, Mr. Whitney? There's a wonderful coffee shop next door."

"That sounds good."

Sadie turned toward the counter. "Julie, I'll be at Arbuckle's."

Julie nodded, and Sadie led the young man outside and into the coffee shop. Only a few customers were in the shop, and they got their coffee and took a small corner table.

"Mr. Whitney..."

"Please, call me Michael."

Sadie nodded. "Michael, then. Can you tell me what it was that made you think your sister is the one they're looking for?"

He took a sip of his coffee and set the mug down. "As soon as the news anchor said they were looking for a 'wild woman,' I thought of Maddie. Madison, that is. She's gone off into the woods several times and lived off the land."

"Is she a survivalist?" Sadie asked, thinking of Lane Pomeroy.

"Not exactly. Sometimes she feels more comfortable out away from people, so she goes off the grid. She's not big on hunting though. I think she takes some supplies with her."

Sadie studied his face. Michael seemed sincere, but troubled.

"You're worried about her."

He sighed. "I'm always worried about Maddie. But I've learned that it doesn't do me any good to look for her. If she doesn't want to be found, I won't find her."

"The sheriff has some local men who are expert woodsmen helping him."

"That's good. I hope they find her. But I hope that if they do, they'll treat her gently."

"Tell me more about Maddie," Sadie said. "My granddaughter, Sara, didn't know her name, but she said that the woman fed her and bandaged her injured ankle and seemed to want to help her heal."

Michael nodded. "That sounds like Maddie. I never thought of her as dangerous. Quite the opposite. She wanted more than anything to help people."

"And she was wearing a caduceus pendant," Sadie added. "I thought she might have a medical background."

"She does. She's a registered nurse, and when she's feeling all right, she works per diem at a hospital in Denver. But she has trouble staying with it for more than a few months. Her boss is understanding, but..." He looked away.

"But kidnapping is over the line?" Sadie guessed.

"Yeah. It sounded as though she held your granddaughter against her will." His brown eyes were wide and pleading.

Sadie said carefully, "Sara did ask to go home, and she believes the drinks that the woman gave her were meant to put her to sleep and keep her from running away."

Michael's expression clouded. "That's not good. I'm not saying Maddie wouldn't do it. She doesn't always think straight. But she's never done anything like this before, I swear."

"I thought perhaps that was the case. Is she a veteran?"

"Yeah. She was with the Army Medical Corps. She loved it at first. Felt she had a real purpose. But... she saw a lot of hard things in Iraq."

"I thought as much. PTSD?"

Michael nodded.

"I'm sorry." Sadie took a sip of her coffee and sent up a quick prayer. She wasn't sure she could do anything to comfort this young man. He obviously loved his sister, but felt he was ineffective in finding a solution to her problems.

"I don't know if they'll give her back her job this time," Michael said.

"Her employer has been lenient in the past?"

"Yes, but I had to go in and plead her cause last summer. She always comes back." His voice cracked. "At least she has so far."

"How long has she been gone this time?" Sadie asked.

"Almost two months."

Sadie thought back over the rumors and reports of "wild man" sightings and petty thefts. The earliest ones had surfaced perhaps six weeks ago. Her cell phone rang, and she took it out. Julie's name appeared on the screen. "Excuse me for a moment." She rose and walked to the window. "What's up, Julie?"

"Sheriff Slattery just came in. Shall I send him to Arbuckle's?"

"That would be fine. Thank you." Sadie went back to the table. "The sheriff's come in from the search, and he's on his way here to meet you."

"Probably for the best," Michael said.

Mac Slattery entered the shop and greeted Luz Vidal at the counter. A moment later, he approached their table carrying a mug of coffee and a Danish pastry. "Hello, Sadie."

Sadie and Michael stood.

Sadie said, "Sheriff Slattery, this is Michael Whitney. He thinks he can help you."

They all sat down, and Michael filled in the sheriff on his sister's condition and why he thought she might be the quarry the sheriff's men were seeking.

"First of all," Sheriff Slattery said, "I want to thank you for coming forward. Second, I assure you my people realize the woman we're looking for may need careful handling. But we also think she's armed and hiding from the law."

Michael's face paled. "She has a gun?"

"We found some ammunition in the hut where she held Sara Macomb for a day and a half. Sara said she may have had a handgun."

"Sheriff, please tell your people not to hurt Maddie."

"We'll do everything we can. So you didn't know she had a handgun?"

He shook his head. "Is it a service pistol?"

"No, it's a .22 caliber. Now that you've given us a name, I can check and see if she has a concealed carry permit for it. Of course, that isn't necessary unless one carries it concealed, but it's another piece of the picture. Do you have a photograph of your sister, Mr. Whitney?"

Michael took out his phone and brought up a picture on the screen. He passed it to the sheriff, and Sadie leaned in to see it.

"That's her in her uniform," Michael said.

The young woman in the picture looked idealistic, content, and put together in her dress uniform. It was hard for Sadie to imagine her in the state Sara's captor had been in.

"That's when she first enlisted. There's another, more recent one." Michael took the phone back and clicked to another picture. This one showed the woman a decade older, walking on a beach, the wind catching her dark hair. She wore shorts and a long-sleeved T-shirt in this one, and she was laughing.

"She looks like a different person," Sadie said. The disheveled long hair, she thought, synced with what she had seen and what others had reported.

The sheriff glanced at Michael. "I'd like to show these to Sara Macomb. It would be extremely helpful if she could give us a positive ID on the woman who held her captive."

Michael drew in a breath. "All right. It would be a relief to me too, in a sense. I can't believe it's anyone but Maddie. And if it is her, I might be able to help you. If it's not her by some miracle, well... at least we'll know."

"Is Maddie knowledgeable about herbs?" Sadie asked.

Michael nodded. "She was into natural remedies, as opposed to manufactured drugs." He looked at the sheriff. "The person who took Sadie's granddaughter will face legal charges, won't she?"

"I'm afraid so," Sheriff Slattery said. "The state will have to press charges."

Michael looked down at his coffee. "Maddie wouldn't willingly hurt anyone. She always wanted to help people. It's just... Her mind isn't right when she's like this."

"I'm sorry," the sheriff said. "Has she ever done anything like this before? Interacted with people in the wild, I mean."

"No, nothing. I was just saying as much to Sadie. Maddie just goes off by herself until she gets her head together. And she's had therapy for the PTSD. She hadn't had an episode for months, and then in July she was gone again."

"I'm sure a judge will take her state of mind into consideration. Let's get these pictures to Sara."

"I'll call Alice." Sadie looked to the sheriff for confirmation.

"If you don't mind," he said.

Sadie stepped away from the table and rang her daughter. When she had explained the situation, Alice asked, "Do you think it's her?"

"It could very well be. But Sara is the only person who could say for sure, if she recognizes the photos."

"Sure, send them over," Alice said. "Sara and I are both taking one more day off from school, but she hopes to go back tomorrow with crutches."

Mac was standing beside Sadie when she ended the call.

"Alice says it's fine to go to the house," she said.

The sheriff nodded. "All right, but I'm going out to my vehicle for a minute first. It won't hurt to confirm this Whitney fellow's identity before we go any further."

"I didn't think of that," Sadie said.

Sheriff Slattery shrugged. "He seems on the up-and-up, but you can't be too careful. And if his story is true and this does turn out to be his sister, we may see it resolved soon."

He went out the door, and Sadie went back to the table where Michael sat.

"Will you go with us to see your granddaughter?" he asked.

"I don't think you need me," Sadie said. "But I hope every-thing goes well and you find your sister soon."

After Mac returned to collect Michael, Sadie went back to the Antique Mine.

"How did it go?" Julie asked as she entered.

"Okay. The sheriff did some checking and found that Michael's an upstanding guy who works in the city clerk's office in Denver, and his story about his sister is true."

"So now what?"

"They've gone to show Sara some pictures of the sister, to see if she recognizes her."

"Wow, this has been intense for Sara," Julie said.

Sadie nodded. "She's strong, though. I think she's going to be fine." She gave Julie some details on the conversation and then looked around the shop. "No customers at the moment?"

"No, it's been kind of slow this afternoon."

"I guess I'll try to find the hardware I need for Marge's spice cabinet."

Julie stayed in the front of the store while Sadie went to her computer. It didn't take her long to find exactly what she needed on a Web site run by a salvage and building supply company.

With her order complete, she turned once more to the puzzle of the Angel of Silver Peak. The notes she had made during her session with Harry Polmiller helped, and she was able at last to locate the mysterious Mrs. Trafton on a family tree. After some research and more note-taking, she went back to the counter, where Julie was polishing a pair of old silver candlesticks.

"Found it!"

"What, the drawer pull?"

"No. Well, yes, that too, but I meant the owner of the medical bag."

"Fantastic," Julie said. "Who was it?"

"Dr. Robert Monroe Trafton. He moved to Denver after the Civil War, but died a few years later. His wife had been helping him in his practice. She was a skilled nurse."

"Let me guess. She became known as the Angel of Silver Peak."

"You got it." Sadie laughed. "There's no solid proof, where the Angel is called by her name, but I'm pretty sure she's the one who ministered to the miners, using her deceased husband's equipment. She led me on a merry chase, but thanks to Harry, I've caught up with her at last."

"Actually, it only took you three days," Julie pointed out. "That's not so long. But why was the medical bag in that estate sale?"

"It seems Mrs. Trafton was Major George Watson's niece. His sister's daughter. She didn't have any surviving children, which is kind of sad. I guess her personal belongings ended up with a cousin, and over the years the family lost track of where the bag came from."

"It's too bad she didn't have children to keep her memory alive," Julie said. "At least we know she had a fulfilling life, helping others."

"Yes. Unlike Michael Whitney's poor sister, who wanted to help others and wound up scaring them."

"You don't think Sara's injury is worse because of anything that woman did to her, do you?"

Sadie shook her head. "Not unless you count walking for several miles on that ankle. But I think the sheriff is serious about pressing charges."

"From what you've told me, she may need professional help more than she needs a jail cell."

"I agree. It's a sad case of a heroic young woman who wanted to serve her country and other people, but ended up scarred herself and unable to function sometimes."

"I guess the wild man stories will stop now," Julie said.

"If they find her." Sadie frowned. "The sheriff and his men have watched that hut for a day and combed the woods around it. I'm afraid Maddie has moved on."

21

Sadie sat across from Roz at Arbuckle's on Wednesday morning.

"I'm so glad you suggested this," Roz said. "Roscoe went to the hardware store early, and I was going to skip breakfast."

"I wanted to catch you up on things." Sadie buttered half of her blueberry muffin. "I was sure Mac's men would find Madison Whitney yesterday. Her brother went out to the hut in the woods with them and called to her, but she never showed herself."

"Do you think she's still out there?" Roz asked.

"Not after yesterday. I doubt she knows Michael was here. I think she cleared out after Sara left her and found another place she thinks is safe. But it will be harder to find than the first one."

"And that was very well hidden," Roz said.

"Yeah." Sadie took a bite of her muffin, and the juicy blueberries flooded her mouth with flavor. "*Mmm!* Luz has outdone herself."

"So what are you going to do now?" Roz asked.

Sadie sipped her coffee and set the cup down. "I've been thinking about it a lot. Michael Whitney had to go back to his job in Denver, but he let the sheriff copy the pictures he had of his sister. When they showed them to Sara, she was positive Madison was the woman who took her to the hut. I want to go back there."

"You saw it the other day," Roz said.

"Yes, but now I know more about Madison. I want to look more closely at what she left behind. There may be a clue there as to where she would go if she had to leave her hideout."

Roz pushed her shoulder-length gray hair back behind her ears. "You shouldn't go alone."

Sadie smiled. That was so like Roz. "Are you volunteering to go with me?"

"I thought you'd never ask."

Sadie laughed. "Just what I hoped you'd say. Finish your breakfast and we'll head out."

"Do I need boots?"

Sadie ducked down to look at Roz's feet under the table. "Probably a good idea. Those Birkenstocks wouldn't be so great in the woods."

"No problem. My boots are out in the car. But I'd better pop in to the store and tell Roscoe." Roz frowned. "On second thought, I'll just call him. We're less likely to get delayed that way."

"Okay, and I want to take Hank, so we'll swing by my place."

Twenty minutes later they were in Sadie's Tahoe on the way around the mountain. Hank huddled in the back, barely able to contain his excitement. Sadie drove as close as she could to the rustic hideaway where Madison Whitney had taken Sara and parked at the edge of the gravel road. Roz got out and looked up at the wooded mountainside.

"You did tell someone where we'd be?"

"Yes, I told Julie." Sadie frowned as she clipped Hank's leash to his collar and let him out of the Tahoe. "I did expect to find a sheriff's department car here. I guess they've given up on watching this spot."

"Manpower is expensive," Roz said. "And if the woman isn't coming back here..."

"She might," Sadie said. "She left some fairly valuable things. The night vision glasses, for instance."

She led Roz through the bushes. The path was easier to follow, now that people had used it heavily for a couple of days. Branches were broken and feet had worn a path in the earth. She probably could have found it without the fluttering pieces of yellow plastic tape that graced the branches every few yards. Sadie felt a little bit sad that another wild place now showed the wear of human use.

"I'll bet Maddie went a different way every time she came here, to keep from making a path," she said.

"I hadn't thought about it." Roz looked all around her. "I guess we do leave our mark wherever we go."

Hank barked and pulled at the leash.

Sadie laughed. "He gets all excited every time he sees a squirrel. Not today, Hank. You're staying with me."

A few minutes later, they came out of the pines beneath the rock face.

"There it is." Sadie waited for Roz to catch up with her.

"Wow. I don't think I could have found it by myself," Roz said, staring at the hut in the blackberry thicket. "It blends right in with the rocks and bushes."

"Come on." Sadie led Hank around the cold fire pit, to the door of the crude shelter. "Anyone home?" No one answered her cry. She took her flashlight from her belt and shone it inside.

Everything looked the same. Sadie stepped inside and let Hank sniff around while she and Roz looked at the sparse items that were left.

"She was into herbs," Roz observed.

"Sara said she made poultices and gave her tea to drink." Sadie played the beam of her light over the clusters of dried leaves and roots hanging above them.

"Do you recognize any of those?" Roz asked.

"Sagebrush. Sorrel. Juniper."

"Isn't that poison?"

"Maybe, depending on how you used it," Sadie said. "Indians ate the cones. The sheriff's men took samples of them all the other day, but when I called this morning, Sheriff Slattery said he hadn't heard back from the lab yet. I thought I'd take some of my own and show them to Emma Roundy."

"She knows a lot about herbs," Roz said.

"Yes, and she may be able to tell me more about these." Sadie took two plastic bags from her pocket and handed one to Roz. "Can you get a few stalks of that one over there? I'll get these."

Roz looked uneasily toward the door. "You don't think that unbalanced woman will come back now, do you?"

"I doubt it. Not while people are in here. And we have Hank." Sadie stretched to pull down a bunch of dried leaves. "I've seen this before, but I don't know what it's called." She put two leafed stems in her bag and hung the rest back where they'd been. Carefully she and Roz took bits of each type of plant.

"I don't see those goggles you were talking about," Roz said, shining her flashlight around the little room.

"The night vision glasses? I think the sheriff took them, and the box of ammunition. They didn't want to leave them here for someone else to find. I'm sure he'll return the glasses at least to Madison later, or to her brother."

Sadie took several pictures of the hanging dried plants with her cell phone and then looked around once more, with the aid of her flashlight, to be sure she hadn't missed anything. Hank had inspected every part of the hut and now tugged toward the door.

"I don't see anything else that could help, do you?"

Roz shook her head. "If you can get a clue out of those dried leaves, you're a lot smarter than I am."

"Not me. Emma. And it may come to nothing, but I hope she'll be able to tell me how they're used medicinally."

Sadie stepped out into the sunlight and blinked. She and Roz stood for a moment in the small clearing.

"It sure is quiet here," Roz said. "And a little creepy. She could be watching us."

Sadie looked carefully at the silent trees around the clearing. "It's possible."

"Well, let's get moving." Roz set off down the trail they had come by.

Sadie dropped off Roz at her house and Hank at home. She spent the afternoon at the Antique Mine with Julie. Between customers, she called Emma Roundy. The elderly woman said she would be delighted to see Sadie that evening and examine the dried herbs she had found.

When Sadie arrived at the small, white clapboard house at six o'clock, Emma opened the door with a smile.

"Come right in! I've been looking forward to seeing you all afternoon."

"Thank you, Emma. I brought you something." Sadie held out a paper bag from the bakery at the Market. "A slice of Maggie Price's carrot cake."

"Oh, that's wicked, just wicked," Emma said with a grin. "Didn't you bring a piece for yourself?"

"No, that's for you to enjoy later," Sadie said.

"Thank you! Now, come right in and sit down. I want to see those mysterious plants."

Emma led Sadie into her living room, and they both sat down on the couch. Sadie explained what had happened to Sara and how she had gathered the herbs that morning.

"I know what some of these are." Sadie removed a plastic bag from her tote bag. "This is sagebrush, right?"

"Yes, and that one with it is purple sage, or some folks call it tobacco sage, or mint sage."

Sadie nodded. "Now, what would that be used for, medically speaking?"

Emma pursed her lips. "Well, you can make an infusion for colds and such. Or it makes a good poultice."

Sadie smiled. "Sara said the woman put a poultice on her ankle."

"Yes, I can see her doing that. Some Indians used it for fevers and headaches. Congestion too. General illness. And the big sagebrush is thought to prevent infection."

"Now, that's interesting."

Emma took the plastic bag from her and peered closely at the plants. "*Mm-hmm*. They would put it on wounds. Sometimes they used it for internal injuries too, and for headaches and colds."

"I wonder if sagebrush was in the tea Maddie gave to Sara."

"I hope not," Emma said. "It could make her feel sick."

Sadie took out her notebook and wrote it down. "Do you know what's in it?"

"You mean chemicals? No, can't say as I do." Emma frowned. "You can look it up though. Artemisia, that's the fancy name for big sagebrush. I can't remember what the purple sage is called. Salvia something, I think."

Sadie made notes. "Thanks. I've got some books about plants at home. I can look these up later, or find them on the Internet. Having the Latin names will help." She took the second plastic bag from her tote. "Now, can you tell me what this is? I know I've seen it before."

Emma studied the crumbling dried plants. "Looks like sweet cicely." She opened the bag and smelled it. "Yup." She passed the bag to Sadie.

Sadie took an experimental sniff. "It smells like licorice."

"Anise. Sweet cicely always smells like that. It's part of the same family as carrots and parsnips. Some call it sweetroot."

Again, Sadie made a note. She had an ongoing interest in plants, especially the flora native to the Colorado mountains, but she'd been so busy running her business lately that she hadn't delved into the subject for quite some time.

"The Indians would use this for swelling and cuts and bruises," Emma said.

"In a poultice then."

"Yes. And you could make a tea for fever or digestive problems."

"Where does it grow?" Sadie asked.

"In wooded areas."

Sadie hadn't noticed any growing wild around Madison's hut, but she hadn't looked for it, and she wasn't sure she would have recognized it now that the growing season was nearly over.

"Oh, and this one." Emma tapped the bag. "This grows in more arid places. It wouldn't grow up here. I think you'd have to go down the mountain to find it."

"How far away?" Sadie wondered if Madison had brought some of the herbs with her when she came to Silver Peak.

"Well, I think there's a place down near the old Bisby ranch. Do you know the place?"

"Yes." Sadie frowned. "That's got to be seven or eight miles from where the hut is. But she might have walked that far in her foraging, I suppose."

"Well, it's dry down there."

"What's that one called?"

"Biscuit root. I don't know the scientific name."

"I'll look it up."

"You can eat it," Emma said. "People usually dig the roots in the spring. You can eat it raw, or boil it or roast it. It's quite versatile."

Sadie wondered if that was what Sara's mysterious cereal was made from. She finished her notes. "Thank you, Emma. You've been a big help."

"You're welcome." Emma pointed to the biscuit root again. "I don't know for sure that you'd find it down at the ranch now, but it used to grow there when the Bisbys had the property. I don't know of any other place around here where it grows. But then, I don't know everything."

Sadie chuckled. "You know plenty."

Back at home, Sadie took Hank out for a run and then fixed herself a light supper. She sat down with a couple of books from her library.

"Biscuit root," she muttered, as she scanned the index of an herbal encyclopedia. "*Lomatium dissectum.*" She flipped the pages and studied the entry for the plant. "The Paiute and other Native American tribes used it for a diuretic. *Hmm.* Maybe Madison gave it to Sara to take down the swelling in her ankle."

She read more and learned that the plant was also used to treat flu-like symptoms. She went to her computer and searched for it. "The starchy, edible roots have been a traditional North American food, eaten cooked or dried and ground into flour," she read out loud. "Lewis and Clark were surprised to find that Indians in what is now Idaho offered them large, flat biscuit-like food made from the *lomatium* root." Sadie smiled. "So that's why it's called biscuit root, I guess."

She thought some more about Madison Whitney and the herb collection in the hut. When Madison discovered that Sara had escaped, she knew she wouldn't be safe at the hut anymore. She had probably moved to a new location. It was a long shot, but if she had scouted the area where the biscuit root plants grew during her foraging expeditions, maybe she had found a place near there, where she could take refuge for a while.

Sadie went to the phone and called Julie.

"Hi. I might come in late tomorrow, if that's okay with you."

"Sure," Julie said. "I'll open in the morning. Come in whenever you're ready."

Sadie gave Alice a call to inquire about Sara. To her surprise, Sara answered the phone.

"Hey, Grandma!"

"Well, hi, honey. How's the ankle?"

"Good. I'm still taking ibuprofen for it, but the doctor says I can go back to school tomorrow."

"Fantastic."

"Guess what?" Sara said.

"You're going to be interviewed on the *Today* show?"

Sara giggled. "No! Dad sent me a book about the birds of Colorado. He said he thought I needed some reading material. It has gorgeous pictures."

"That's nice, sweetheart."

"And he's coming here again this weekend."

Even better, Sadie thought. Nothing like a crisis to bring families back together. She chatted with Sara for a few more minutes and then prepared for bed. She knew she wouldn't be happy until she had been to every spot she thought Madison Whitney might have been recently, and she would start with the old Bisby ranch.

———

A "For Sale" sign stood in knee-high weeds at the end of the lane leading to the Bisby ranch. Sadie drove in slowly, looking around. Emma had told her where to look for the plants she wanted.

The house had been vacant for several months. Sadie parked in the front yard and got out of her vehicle. A light wind blew through the valley, and the deserted ranch had an eerie feel. She had left Hank at home, so that he wouldn't give away her presence. Now she wished she had brought him along.

On a hunch, Sadie walked to the house and tried the front door, but it was locked. She strolled around to the back and found the kitchen door also secure. She was glad to find no evidence that the empty house had been broken into. Still, with no one living here, Madison might feel safe to camp on the grounds.

She walked past the weathered post-and-beam barn and opened the pasture gate. Emma had recommended that she cross the pasture and go through the fence on the other side, then look along the tree line, where alders and blackberries blurred the division between woods and open ground.

Sadie could imagine horses or beef cattle grazing here. She wondered why the property hadn't sold yet. The Bisbys had moved away last spring, after Harland had a mild heart attack. Sadie had heard that they were retiring to Arizona.

She reached the fence on the farther side of the pasture. There didn't seem to be a gate nearby, so she pushed down the bottom strand of barbed wire and held up the top one while she ducked through, mindful of her jeans and khaki shirt. She walked along the outside of the fence row, looking for the fernlike leaves of the biscuit root.

She came to an area where bushes grew as high as her head, and a few had encroached on the pasture, growing inside the fence line. She looked around cautiously. Anyone could hide out here easily and have no fear of discovery. Was there a water source nearby? There must be something for the livestock that used to graze in the pasture. She had not noticed a watering trough near the house.

Listening carefully, she thought she caught the sound of running water. She walked slowly toward it through the bushes. Soon she came out on the bank of a stream that flowed into the eastern end of the pasture. She glanced about and then studied the ground. Had anyone passed here recently?

Walking slowly, Sadie tried to keep her steps quiet as she moved along the bank, even though she'd had no indication that anyone else was within a mile of her position. The woods thickened, and she couldn't help thinking this would be a great place for a hideout.

She looked up into the branches of the pines above her. A treehouse, maybe? Most of these trees weren't tall enough or thick enough to support a structure, but she wouldn't rule it out. There was no cliff face here, and no bluffs that would hold caves. She let out a big sigh. There must be a thousand places within ten miles of Silver Peak that would be at least this good for someone trying to keep out of sight.

She decided to head back to the ranch house, but to walk through the woods this time. By circling away from the stream and then back toward the fence, she would at least get a look at more of the forest before she headed home.

Pushing aside a low-hanging branch, she stepped into the woods and then looked back. For an instant, she thought she saw a glimmer of light—a reflection, maybe, from a thicket across the stream. She stood still and held her breath. A person wearing camouflage would blend in with the foliage over there, even better than she did in her khaki and denim. What would throw off a glint like that, a yard or so above the ground? Had the sun reflected off binoculars? Eyeglasses? A rifle scope?

MYSTERIES *of* SILVER PEAK

After half a minute or more, she noticed a gentle swaying among the thicket's top branches. None of the other bushes or trees nearby was moving. Maybe it was time to move faster.

She tiptoed through the woods as quietly as she could, but about fifty yards from the stream, she caught the toe of her boot on a vine and stumbled. She lay on the carpet of pine needles for a moment, catching her breath and wondering if she had discovered Maddie's new sanctuary. Somehow she couldn't believe that an animal had made those bushes move. But if Maddie had seen her, no doubt she would flee again, probably farther away. Sadie's hunch might have backfired.

Bringing Mac here seemed the wisest course. She would go now. Sadie shoved to her feet. Just as she started forward, someone seized her from behind. Arms encircled her neck and pulled her head back. She gasped for breath and clawed at the muscled forearms.

"What do you want?" a voice rasped in her ear.

22

SADIE SUCKED IN AIR WITH DIFFICULTY. SHE TRIED TO SPEAK BUT couldn't. At last the arms, clad in camouflage, relaxed.

"Don't try to run," the voice said. Her captor shoved Sadie hard, and she fell to the ground again.

She turned slowly and looked up at Madison Whitney. The woman stood with her feet spread a foot apart. Her tangled hair and faded camo suit were unmistakable. Sadie tried to see in the planes of her face some trace of the idealistic young woman whose picture Michael had shown her. The hunting knife Madison held made it harder.

"Maddie?" It came out a hoarse whisper.

Madison's eyebrows lowered, nearly touching, and she eyed Sadie cautiously.

Sadie put a hand to her throat and gently massaged the skin over her windpipe.

"What do you want?" Madison said again.

"I wanted to find you."

"Why?"

Sadie breathed slowly, deliberately, trying to maintain a calm expression.

"You helped my granddaughter, Sara. I wanted to thank you."

Maddie's scowl deepened. "Is that why you took the police to my place?"

"I didn't take them there," Sadie said. "They found it without me."

"Did she tell them?"

Sadie figured she meant Sara. She shook her head. "Sara couldn't remember how she got there, or what path she took home in the dark."

Maddie stared at her for a long moment. "She shouldn't have left. Her ankle wasn't healed."

"She wanted to get home to her mother. She's getting better now."

"I would have taken her, after she was better."

"I'm glad to hear it," Sadie said.

Maddie looked away for an instant, then back at Sadie, determination hardening her face. "I wouldn't have hurt her. I was tending her foot."

"Sara told me what a good job you did. The poultices, and the tea." Sadie attempted a smile, but her lips trembled. She pressed them together and looked around at the trees. "You must be having a hard time, since you left some of your supplies behind in the cabin."

Madison said nothing.

"I could bring you some food," Sadie said. "You wouldn't have to forage so much." Was the excuse good enough that it would persuade Maddie to let her leave?

"What kind of food do you have?"

"*Uh*, well, I have bread and milk and fresh fruit. In my freezer, I have some beefsteak, and a couple of packages of hamburger. And chicken." She managed a smile this time. "You could cook up some chicken, if you like that. And I have frozen vegetables, and some muffins. And ice cream!"

Maddie's eyes flickered. "What about canned goods?"

"Oh, sure. Soup, vegetables, chili, ham salad, peaches, condensed milk." Sadie mentally ticked off the cans in her larder. "Do you like peanut butter? I have some. And homemade jam."

"Do you have coffee?"

"I sure do. Would you like me to bring you some? I could be back here in two hours, and I'll bring you whatever you want."

For a moment, she thought Maddie would let her go.

"Where's your car?" Maddie asked.

"In front of the house. I was going to go back through the woods and cross the pasture closer to the house."

Maddie slid her knife into a sheath on her belt and pulled a pistol from behind her back. "Let's go. I'll be right behind you, so no tricks."

Sadie plodded through the woods, her mind racing. *Lord, show me what to do.* She paused to get her bearings.

Maddie stepped up near her and waved her pistol. "That way. We're not far from the fence."

Sadie went the way she indicated, and soon they broke out of the trees. The barbed wire was only a few yards away. She looked over her shoulder apprehensively, not liking the idea of Maddie climbing through a fence while holding a gun, but her captor stuck the pistol in the back of her waistband and held the strands of wire apart.

"You first."

Sadie climbed through.

"Now walk away."

Sadie walked and didn't look back. She had already decided it would be useless to try to overpower or outrun Maddie. Better to take her back to her house and give her the food she had promised. Maybe she would find a way to alert someone. *Lord, send somebody to my house!*

She heard footsteps behind her and knew Maddie followed. Turning her head, she said, "That red Tahoe in the front yard is mine."

"You didn't bring anybody with you, did you?" Maddie asked.

"No." Sadie hated to admit it, but she wouldn't lie. She considered offering Maddie her vehicle. She could call the sheriff on her cell phone as soon as she drove away. But no, she had a feeling Maddie wouldn't take it. It would be too easy to trace, for one thing.

Sadie walked diagonally across the empty pasture toward the gate. They both passed through it, and Maddie closed the gate. She had the pistol in her hand again.

"Is it locked?" She nodded toward the Tahoe.

"No."

"Wait here." Maddie walked over to the vehicle, keeping an eye on Sadie, and took a couple of quick glances at the interior. "Okay, get in. And no funny business. We go straight to your house."

"Agreed," Sadie said. She pushed down all the warnings she had heard about getting into a vehicle with a gunman. *I'm trusting You, Lord. Let this turn out well, I'm begging You.*

She fastened her seat belt and started the engine. "Do you know where I live?"

"I've seen you there. And the dog."

Sadie nodded. She was right that Maddie had hung around her house at least once. And maybe she had seen the gathering on the night Sara came home.

She turned to look Maddie square in the face. "I'll drive straight there, and we'll get you something to eat." She then told each road she would take, and the turns she would make on the way.

Maddie nodded. "So drive."

Sadie backed the Tahoe around and nosed into the road. After a couple of minutes, she said, "I've got some cookies at the house. Chocolate chip. Do you like them?"

"Sure."

"You can have some. And if you want, I'll fix you a hot meal."

Maddie said nothing.

"Or if you'd rather just pack up some stuff and bring it back here, we can do that."

"Do you have any pizza?"

Sadie almost laughed, but she managed to keep a straight face. As she pulled up at a stop sign, she said, "Yeah, I've got some pepperoni in the freezer, and maybe a four-cheese."

"Pepperoni," Maddie said.

"You got it. I'll put it in the oven first thing." She glanced over at Maddie. "Sara said you gave her some hot cereal."

"Millet travels easily. I cooked some of that while she was there."

"Millet." Sadie smiled. "I haven't had that in years."

"Did she like it?"

"I think so."

"She didn't say?"

Sadie pulled out onto the road that wound up to Silver Peak. "I think she was pretty scared. She wasn't sure what you were going to do."

"Make her better. I was helping her get better."

"Of course," Sadie said. "Sara didn't know that. She's very young. She wasn't sure you would let her leave."

"She wasn't ready." Maddie turned her face to the window.

A few minutes later, Sadie drew up before her house. To her disappointment, the yard was empty. Hoping someone else would be there had been unrealistic.

"Here we are. Come on inside."

Maddie fumbled with her buckle. "Wait. How…"

A quick vision of her leaving Maddie trapped in the unfamiliar seat belt and dashing inside flashed through Sadie's mind.

"Take it easy," she said. "I'll help you." She waved gently at the pistol, and Maddie turned it so that it pointed toward the windshield. Sadie leaned over and pushed the button on Maddie's buckle. "There you go."

They both got out of the Tahoe, and Sadie walked over to the porch and up the steps. Inside the house, Hank barked.

Maddie's pistol swung into position, the barrel pointed at the door. "Secure the dog."

"He won't hurt you," Sadie said.

"Hook him up or shut him in another room. Do it now."

"Okay." Sadie had her key ready, and she went to the door and inserted it in the lock. "Settle down, Hank!" She opened the door cautiously. Hank snuffled her hand and tried to shove past her. "Hold on!" Sadie grasped his collar. He barked and strained against her.

She looked over her shoulder. Maddie stood at the bottom of the steps, the gun still at the ready.

"He's been cooped up for a couple of hours. He needs to go outside."

"Not yet," Maddie said. "Shut him in another room."

Sadie couldn't see any good coming of disobeying, so she pulled Hank away from the door. "I'm sorry, boy. Come on, you need to come with me." She got him into the hall bathroom and shut the door on him. "All right," she called. When she turned, Maddie was right behind her.

"Does he go out by himself, or do you need to hook him?"

"He can go out for a quick run."

Maddie looked around, then stepped into the living room, behind the sofa. "Okay, let him out. But you stay in, and don't try anything."

"Thanks." Sadie appreciated Maddie's lenience where the dog was concerned. She opened the bathroom door and latched on to Hank's collar. He whined and barked and tugged toward Maddie.

"No you don't. Come on. Outside." Sadie managed to drag him to the front door, though he turned his head and growled at Maddie. She opened the door, and he bounded outside. Sadie exhaled deeply and shut the door.

"Now, where's the food?" Maddie asked.

"Right this way." Sadie led her into the kitchen. "Have a seat." She opened the freezer compartment and took out a pizza. "You want the pepperoni, right?"

Maddie went to the kitchen window and moved the curtain aside just a little, peering out into the yard. "Yeah."

While Sadie turned on the oven and took the pizza out of the box, Maddie walked restlessly from window to window. She even stepped into the living room for a moment to peek out from the windows there. Sadie started to take her cell phone from her pocket, but Maddie came back to the kitchen.

"You got something I can eat while that cooks?"

"Sure." Sadie opened the cookie jar and put half a dozen cookies on a plate. She took that and her fruit basket, which held bananas, apples, and a lone orange, to the table. "Would you like a glass of milk? Or I can make you some coffee or iced tea."

"Milk would be nice." Maddie laid the pistol on the table. "And maybe some coffee after."

"No problem." As she poured a tall glass full of milk, Sadie said, "If you tell me what you want to take back to your camp, I can pack it up for you while we wait."

"What have you got again?"

Sadie opened the cupboards where she kept staples and canned goods. Maddie had already gobbled down three cookies and drunk half the milk. Sadie listed off the items in the cupboards, taking her time. Maddie interjected "I'll take that," and "Yeah, give me that" several times. Sadie set each item she wanted down on the counter.

She turned to face Maddie. "Oh, and I've got homemade pickles and jam down in the cellar." She smiled at the young woman, hoping Maddie now felt they were friends, or at least allies. "Would you like some of those?"

"How much time left on the pizza?"

"*Uh*…eight minutes."

"Start the coffee first."

"Oh, sorry," Sadie said. "I forgot about that." Quickly she put a filter and some ground coffee in the coffeemaker and filled the reservoir. "There we go. Now—jam and pickles?"

"Yeah, go get some," Maddie said. She shoved back her chair and took her pistol to the window. "Be quick about it."

Sadie opened the door to the cellar and scurried down the stairs. She hurried to the farthest corner of the basement, behind the furnace, and took out her cell phone. The signal indicator showed only two bars, but she thought it was enough to get a message out.

Even this far from the door, Maddie might hear her if she called someone. Sadie decided to text instead. She had talked to Edwin the evening before and told him about Michael Whitney's arrival and news. Typing rapidly, she sent a message to Edwin: HELP. MADDIE AT MY HOUSE. She sent it and glanced toward the doorway. Was there time for another? She keyed in the sheriff's phone and typed the same thing, hit Send, and dashed to the shelves that held her preserves.

"Hey!" Maddie stood at the top of the stairs, pistol in hand. "What are you doing?"

"Oh, sorry," Sadie said. "I didn't know if you wanted strawberry or plum jam, or apple jelly, so I was getting some of each." She grabbed a small box from the shelf and loaded three jars into it. "What about pickles? I've got dill and watermelon and bread-and-butter."

"Just get up here." Maddie's voice sounded testy. Sadie snatched two jars of pickles and stuck them in the box.

"This should keep you going for a while," she said, heading for the stairs. "Now, I don't need the jars back." Even to her, that sounded silly in this context, but she hoped to distract Maddie from wondering what had taken her so long.

Up in the kitchen, Sadie plunked the box on the table. "There! Now, we can put some of these cans in here with the jam and pickles. And I can give you some biscuit mix. It just stirs up with water, and you can cook it over a fire if you want. Wrap it around a stick, even, and cook it like a hot dog."

The coffee was still dripping into the carafe, but she took down a mug and got the cream out of the refrigerator. "Do you take sugar?"

"No."

Sadie went to the stove and opened the oven partway. "Looks like the pizza's almost ready." She got out plates, a pot holder, and the pizza cutter. All of the cookies she had put out were gone, and Maddie's glass was empty. "Would you like more milk with that?"

"Be quiet." Maddie cocked her head to one side.

Sadie heard it too. Tires crunching on the gravel in her driveway.

Maddie waved toward the corner near the back door. "Get over there. And don't get any ideas about skipping out on me."

"No problem." Sadie held both palms up. "That door's locked anyway. But I'd better get that pizza out, or it will burn." She opened the oven door again.

Maddie went to the window and peered out cautiously, through the leaded-glass pane. Sadie knew she couldn't see the driveway from the kitchen window. Sure enough, Maddie headed for the front room.

The doorbell rang as Sadie set the pizza on top of the range. She turned and walked softly to the doorway. Maddie was peering out the crack between two panels of the curtains.

"It's a silver car."

"Oh, that's just my friend Edwin," Sadie said. Relief and dismay swept over her. Had she put Edwin in danger by summoning him here?

"Don't answer it," Maddie said.

"But he knows I'm here. He can see my Tahoe sitting out front."

Outside, Hank barked, and she heard Edwin's hearty, "Hello, Hank! Where's Sadie?" He climbed to the porch and pressed the doorbell. The ringing sounded loud inside. "Sadie?" Edwin called. "It's me."

Maddie scooted over and flattened herself against the wall so that she would be behind the door when it opened. She pointed with the pistol toward the door. "Open it."

Sadie's pulse throbbed in her throat. She opened the door about a foot and leaned into the gap. "Well, hi, Edwin. What brings you here?" She rolled her eyes to the side, hoping he would catch on that Maddie was only a step away.

"Well, I..." He hesitated. "Are you okay?"

"Fine. I'm planning to go in to the store later. Julie's covering for me this morning."

He sniffed. "You must be cooking lunch."

"Oh yes. Pizza." Sadie wasn't sure whether to ask him in or not. She wished she knew whether Sheriff Slattery had received her message.

"That sounds really good," Edwin said. "Smells good too."

Inviting himself for a meal was so unlike Edwin that Sadie knew he understood the situation and was trying to help her out.

"*Uh*, well…would you like to join me?" She gritted her teeth.

Edwin said gravely, "Why, yes, that would be nice."

Sadie's knees shook as she stepped back and opened the door wider.

"Come on in."

As soon as Edwin was over the threshold, Maddie stepped from behind the door, pointing her weapon at him.

"Put your hands up."

Edwin complied, eyeing her pensively but without surprise. "Hello."

"Maddie, put that gun away," Sadie said. "I told you, he's a friend."

Maddie's eyes narrowed. "You sure he's not the enemy?"

Sadie almost laughed, but she knew the situation was far from funny. "I'm sure. He's a friend. He's…one of us."

Slowly, Maddie lowered the pistol. "All right, but don't let him eat all the pizza."

"I won't. He can have one slice." Sadie started to shut the door, but she caught a glimpse of Sheriff Slattery's SUV creeping up her driveway. Could she distract Maddie for another minute? She closed the door and hoped Maddie wouldn't notice that she didn't lock it.

"Edwin, this is Madison. Maddie, this is Edwin. Come on out to the kitchen," she said with a shaky smile. "I was about to cut the pizza. After we eat, we can help Maddie get her supplies back to where she's staying now."

"Hold it." Madison raised her pistol, leveling it at Edwin. "Someone else is coming." She glanced out the window and back at him. "Who did you bring?"

"Me? No one. But I'm sure it's just friends," Edwin said.

Maddie scowled and looked out the window again. Sadie opened the door again and looked out. Sheriff Slattery, in his uniform, was getting out of his SUV. Someone else sat in the passenger seat.

"Enemy approaching!" Maddie ran behind the sofa, ducked down, and raised her head over the back of it, aiming her pistol at the door. "Get down!"

"Maddie, no," Sadie said, more sharply than she'd planned. "It's not the enemy."

"That's right," Edwin said, his hands still in the air. "It's a friend of ours and Michael."

So Edwin had talked to the sheriff, Sadie realized, and Mac had Michael Whitney with him.

Maddie's wild eyes seemed to focus for a moment. "Michael."

"It's your brother," Sadie said. She walked slowly toward Maddie. "Put the gun down, Maddie. Michael wants to see you. Let him and his friend come inside."

Mac came up onto the porch with Michael behind him. "Everything all right, Sadie?"

"Mostly." She threw him a wan smile. "Madison thinks you're the enemy. It could be the uniform. I think she'll talk to Michael, but you should know that she has a gun."

Mac's expression darkened. "I don't want Whitney going in there until the situation is neutralized."

"You mean, until she gives up the gun?"

"That's right."

Sadie grimaced. "I'm not sure she'll do that."

Mac looked past her into the living room. "Edwin, you all right?"

"Oh, I'm fine," Edwin said, but he didn't put his hands down.

"Miss Whitney," Mac called, "I'm County Sheriff Slattery. Lay your gun on the floor and come on out here."

"First you let my brother go!"

Mac frowned at Sadie. "What's she getting at?"

"I think she's confused," Sadie said.

Sheriff Slattery unsnapped the flap on his holster. "Miss Whitney, I'm not holding your brother, so I can't let him go. He wants to talk to you. Now put down the weapon and come out here."

Michael pushed up beside the sheriff and peered into the house. "Maddie! It's me, Michael. What are you doing, sis?"

"I'm just protecting myself and...and this lady." Maddie didn't sound sure.

Sadie turned toward her. "Honey, you don't need to protect me. These fellows are all friends of mine. And I know that Michael loves you dearly. He's taken time off from work to come and find you. He wants to take you home."

"No, that's not right."

"What do you mean, Maddie?" Michael called through the open doorway.

Maddie wiped her sleeve across her forehead and steadied the pistol. "My enlistment's not up."

"Sure it is," Michael said. "Remember? We had a party when you got home. Aunt Shelley and Uncle Roy came over from Las Animas."

Maddie frowned. "That was a long time ago."

"It's been a while," Michael agreed.

"But..." Maddie looked at Sadie blankly.

Sadie took a couple of steps toward her. "It's all right, Maddie. You can put the gun down and sit at the table with Michael. You can eat pizza together and talk. Nobody wants to hurt you."

Maddie's lower lip trembled.

"Come on," Sadie said. "The coffee's ready. Let's get some and talk."

Maddie gazed at her for several heartbeats. "Tell Michael to come in." Her voice was a hoarse whisper.

Sadie turned to the door. "She wants to see Michael."

Mac's arm shot out, blocking the doorway. "And I want to see the gun on the floor. I mean it, Sadie. I don't want this to end badly. I'll call in backup if I need to."

Sadie gazed over at Maddie. The young woman still stood with her gun at the ready, aiming in her general direction.

"Madison," she said quietly, "the sheriff doesn't want to let Michael come in while you're holding the gun. He's afraid you'll hurt Michael."

Maddie stared at her for a moment and then said, "I wouldn't."

"I know you wouldn't, but the sheriff doesn't know that. He doesn't know *you*."

"What's he doing here?" Maddie asked.

"He wants to make sure everyone is safe."

"Why wouldn't they be safe?"

"Your gun. He's afraid you might use it."

Maddie drew in a deep, shuddering breath. In slow motion, she laid her pistol on the back of the sofa. "Let Michael in. But not him."

Sadie arched her eyebrows at the sheriff. He hesitated but finally lowered his arm. "Okay, Whitney. I don't like it, but if you think it's okay…"

"She won't hurt me." Michael strode into the room. "Maddie, it's just me. I've been so worried about you."

Maddie's eyes filled with tears, and she walked slowly out from behind the couch and raised her arms to her brother. Michael folded her in his embrace and hugged her close.

"It's okay," he said.

Edwin lowered his hands and walked quietly over to the couch. He removed the pistol and carried it to the sheriff in the doorway.

"Thanks," Mac murmured. "Does she have any other weapons, Sadie?"

"A knife," Sadie whispered.

"Did she threaten you?"

"Not directly, but she did hold the gun on me and tell me to drive and get her food, things that were useful to her. But in all fairness, I offered the food to her first, hoping to get on her good side."

"Did you feel at any time she might fire the gun at you?"

Sadie pulled in a deep breath, thinking that over. "I was pretty scared at first. Yeah, there were moments. She's definitely not stable."

She turned to the siblings and raised her voice a notch. "Michael, Maddie, why don't you come into the kitchen with Edwin and me and have some of that pizza?"

Maddie glanced darkly toward the sheriff. "Not him."

"Okay. But could you please give your knife to Michael first? The sheriff is nervous about letting us eat until you've put away your knife."

Maddie said nothing, but pulled the knife from its sheath and handed it to her brother, hilt first. Michael took it.

"Thanks." He walked over to the door and passed it to Mac.

"I'll be right here," Mac said.

Michael nodded. He walked to Madison and put his arm around her. "Come on. Let's get some of that pizza. It smells awfully good."

It took Michael half an hour to convince his sister to go with him and Mac, but finally she gave in to her brother's gentle pleas. With some misgivings, Sadie stood on the porch with Edwin and watched them drive out in the sheriff's vehicle.

"Are you still all right?" Edwin asked.

Sadie sighed. "I wish I knew what was best for that woman."

"It's a difficult case," Edwin said. "Let's pray that the people dealing with her will exercise wisdom."

"Yes. She said she only wanted to help Sara. I believe she meant that. At least, she believed it was true, even if she didn't realize her methods of helping might not be in Sara's best interests."

"And Sara admitted that Maddie didn't directly hurt her," Edwin added.

"Do you think she understood what Mac said—that holding Sara against her will is illegal?"

"I'm not sure. I'm glad her brother was here." Edwin reached for her hand and gave it a squeeze. "It's out of your hands now, but you did the right thing. I'm very proud of you."

Sadie shook her head. "I keep thinking maybe I could have done something different—something better. I just don't know."

"That's the way it is sometimes. We have to do what seems best at the time. And Mac Slattery is a good man. He said they'll have her examined right away. You heard Michael say he had contacted Madison's doctor?"

"Yes. She's driving up from Denver to do whatever she can for Maddie." Sadie smiled at Edwin. "Thank you. I wasn't sure either you or Mac would get my text right away, so I sent it to both of you. But I admit I sent it to you first."

Edwin's eyes twinkled. "I called Mac immediately. He said he'd just gotten a text as well. I happened to be closer, so I got here first."

"Well, I was mighty glad to see you. I wasn't too happy about Maddie holding the gun on you."

"Neither was I, but I could see she had made a connection with you, so I wasn't too frightened. But she's not stable. She clearly needs more treatment."

"Come on in," Sadie said. "One slice of pizza wasn't enough lunch. I'll make you a sandwich, and then I think I should go to the store and relieve Julie."

"I tell you what," Edwin said, eyeing her soberly. "I'll agree to that if you promise me one thing."

"What's that?"

"Next time, don't go off looking for an armed person with a psychiatric illness all alone."

23

—————

THE POSTMAN STOPPED IN AT THE ANTIQUE MINE A COUPLE OF weeks later and handed Sadie a sheaf of bills, catalogues, and sales flyers. One envelope was hand-addressed, and she opened that first.

Dear Mrs. Speers,

Madison and I wanted you to know that she is doing well. She spent a week as an inpatient, but is staying with my wife and me now. She has a new therapist and medication, and it may take some time to get everything regulated, but we see progress.

She has a court date in about four weeks, but her lawyer has every hope that the judge will be sympathetic and consider Maddie's mental state, and also the fact that Sara's family has asked for leniency. We very much appreciate you and Mrs. Macomb offering to attend the hearing in support of Maddie. Of course, no one wants to see a similar incident occur in the future, but I think we all agree that our main goal is to see my sister whole and well again.

I also wanted to tell you that the army liaison is working with us to help Maddie find the right doctors and receive compensation for her treatment. While she is not yet ready to resume work, her boss has assured her that when she is found to be fit, she will have

MYSTERIES *of* SILVER PEAK

a position in some capacity. It may not be in direct contact with patients for a while, but that remains up to her employers. Maddie is contrite and willing to accept this. She wants more than anything to think clearly and not endanger others. The note she received from Sara a few days ago touched her deeply. We are both thankful that Sara's ankle is so much better, and that she doesn't hold a grudge against Maddie. She is a brave girl, and also a gracious one.

Again, thank you for all your help.

Sincerely,
Michael Whitney

Sadie smiled as she read, though tears filled her eyes. So many prayers had been answered. Alice, who was helping her tend the store that day, came to the counter with an apple peeler-corer in her hands.

"That lady from Denver wants this." She looked closely at Sadie. "Mom, are you okay?"

Sadie smiled bigger and held out the letter to her. Alice set down the antique kitchen tool, took the sheet of paper, and scanned it.

"What a nice letter! I'm so glad she's doing better."

"So am I. Sara will be too."

Alice nodded. "She mentions Maddie every day and wants to know if we've heard anything. She's very concerned about what Maddie's future will be like."

"With the right medical treatment and loving care, I think it looks brighter than it has for a while."

The customer buying the apple peeler-corer approached the counter with more items in her hands.

"Did you find something else?" Alice asked with a smile, thrusting Michael's letter back into Sadie's hand.

"Oh yes!" She laid a nineteenth-century nutmeg grinder and two matching salt cellars on the counter. "May I leave these here while I keep shopping?"

"Of course." As the woman turned away, Alice winked at her mother. "Looks like it's going to be a good day for the Antique Mine."

Before Sadie could reply, the bell over the front door jangled, and Harry Polmiller walked in. He leaned on his cane and turned slowly to shut the door.

"Hello, Harry!" Sadie hurried from behind the counter to meet him. "How are you doing?" She gazed at his cane with concern.

"Not bad," the ninety-four-year-old said. "This stick is just to make sure I don't have one of those stupid falls old people have. A preemptive measure."

"Of course," Sadie said. "Very wise."

He held out a plastic grocery sack with the Market's logo on it. "Brought you a few little gourds. Some people like 'em to decorate." He shrugged. "They're nice, but I've got 'em coming out my ears. Thought I'd share the wealth."

Sadie peeked into the bag. At least half a dozen gourds were in it, all of different shapes and color patterns, in greens, yellow, and orange. "Oh, they're lovely! Thank you so much, Harry. I might even make a display here on the counter. Look, Alice. How do you think they'd look in that big yellowware bowl?"

Alice took the bag and looked into it. "Oh yes. That will be stunning. Thanks, Harry. I'll get the bowl." She laid the sack on the counter and bustled off toward the kitchenware section.

"So," Harry said, eyeing Sadie with significance, "can I see it?"

Sadie smiled. She knew what he was talking about. She and Harry had talked about the medical bag a couple of times at church since she'd visited his house.

"It's right here." She took it down from a shelf behind the counter and set it before him.

Harry touched the worn leather case and traced the initials with his finger. "All right to open it?"

"Go right ahead."

He unfastened the buckle and looked in at the instruments. "She was quite a lady."

"Yes, I agree. And with your help, I've definitely confirmed that the Angel of Silver Peak was Elizabeth Trafton, the widow of Robert Monroe Trafton. She's the one who amputated your great-uncle Tom Klein's leg."

Harry sighed. "To think she may have used that scalpel in there when she did it."

Sadie shivered but smiled. "I try not to think about that day in too much detail, but yes. She may very well have had this bag with her and used some of these instruments."

Harry looked up at her, his eyes glittering. "I want to buy it."

"Really?"

"What's a fair price?"

"Well…" Sadie had been researching current market prices for each item in the bag, as well as the bag itself, with its provenance. But for Harry, she was willing to give up some of the profit she might make elsewhere. She named a price that would make her time worthwhile but still give her friend a bargain.

"Done." Harry took his checkbook out of the pocket of his wool jacket.

Sadie cleared a spot on the counter, and he bent over it to write his check. Just as Sadie placed it in the cash register drawer, Alice and her customer came toward them, both carrying several kitchen items.

"Oops, I'd better clear out," Harry said. "This looks like a big sale, and I'll just be in the way."

Sadie laughed. "You're never in the way, Harry, but come on. I'll help you take this out to your car."

She gave him the receipt and carried the medical bag out to the curb, where Harry had parked.

"Thanks, Sadie. Come see me again."

"I will," she promised. "We'll have a cup of tea."

She watched him pull out onto the street and waved, then headed back inside. Alice had rung up her customer's purchases.

"That's a hundred and twenty-two dollars and nineteen cents," Alice said.

Sadie went past them and into the back room. She had taken an old Windsor chair in to refinish for a client, and she took down a can of stripper and a rag.

A moment later, Alice came in. "The store's empty. Thought I'd get some coffee from next door."

"Lovely," Sadie said. "And if Luz has any interesting-looking squares today, I'll take one of those."

"I heard a rumor this morning that she has cranberry-walnut bars."

"Perfect." Sadie looked up from her work. "Oh, Alice, I thought I'd call Sara and see if she'd like to take a little field trip with me next Saturday. Do you know if she has any plans?"

"Not that I know of."

Sadie nodded. "It will only take a couple of hours."

————

Sadie and Sara walked out of the Breckenridge town office with a printed sheet of paper. Sara hardly limped now, and Sadie smiled.

"Your ankle has healed."

"Pretty much," Sara agreed. They got into the Tahoe, and Sadie drove to one of the oldest cemeteries in town. They got out, and Sara held the map the town clerk had given them. Sadie took a bouquet of yellow, orange, and gold chrysanthemums from the back of the vehicle.

"It shouldn't be too hard to find," Sadie said. The cemetery was fenced, and the graves neatly kept. Some of the stones looked very old, of slate, and the inscriptions were fading and hard to read unless one stepped close. Newer granite markers stood out with their lighter color. Outside the fence, evergreens whispered. Hardwoods waved their last leaves of yellow and gold, with a few splashes of red here and there.

"It's a pretty spot." Sara looked out over the fence, toward the town and the mountain that shadowed it in the west.

"It's gorgeous," Sadie agreed. "Which way to the Trafton family lot?"

Sara studied the cemetery map and pointed. "Over there, I think."

They walked along slowly, gazing at the old gravestones and the few more pretentious monuments.

"There it is!" Sara pointed to a thin slab of slate that stood up beneath an overhanging pine tree.

Sadie joined her in front of the stone and read the faint inscription. "Dr. Robert Monroe Trafton, beloved by many. Elizabeth, devoted wife and an angel of mercy to the sick and wounded."

"That's nice," Sara said. "It kind of reminds me of Maddie."

"I've thought that myself," Sadie admitted. "They both truly wanted to help others who were suffering."

"And in some ways, Maddie did help me." Sara brushed back a strand of her strawberry-blonde hair.

"I never thought she wanted to hurt you," Sadie said.

"No, but she could have hurt you and Mr. Marshall." Sara frowned. "Why do you think she held the gun on you, Grandma?"

"She was scared. When I showed up near her new hideout, she was afraid I'd harm her. It also told her that we folks of Silver Peak were still looking for her. That probably had kept her from foraging or hunting as much as she normally would have. She wanted the food I offered, but she knew she was taking a risk in going to my house to get it."

Sara nodded. "I'm glad they didn't put her in jail."

"Me too, honey." Sadie put an arm around Sara's shoulders. "I think she's getting the care she needs now."

"I'd like to see her sometime. Do you think I could?"

"I don't know," Sadie said. "Why don't you ask your mom about that? It might be better to wait awhile and not keep reminding her of what happened."

"Okay. I don't want to upset her."

"I'm sure that after Maddie's had time to rest and settle into her new treatment, she'd love to hear from you."

"Okay. But I think about her a lot, and I pray for her."

Sadie gave her shoulders a squeeze. "So do I." She shifted the bouquet of mums and held them out to Sara. "Would you like to arrange these on the grave?"

Sara took them and laid the flowers artistically on the dying grass before the headstone. She stood and gave a deep sigh. "I'm glad we came here, but do you know what I'd like to do this afternoon?"

"What?" Sadie asked.

"Go riding. I don't suppose you'd go with me?"

Sadie thought of the projects she had waiting for her at the Antique Mine. She was supposed to relieve Julie at noon, but Julie wouldn't mind working a few extra hours. Sadie smiled. "I think that would be terrific. Shall we call Milo and tell him we'll be there around one o'clock?"

Sara nodded, grinning. "We can ask Theo if he wants to go, but he'll probably say no."

"Oh, I don't know," Sadie said. "Your brother has an especially soft spot for you lately."

"That didn't last." Sara turned, and they started walking back toward the parking area. "Did I tell you what he did to me yesterday?"

"I can hardly wait to hear it," Sadie said, smiling.

About the Author

CAROLE JEFFERSON IS THE PEN NAME FOR A TEAM OF WRITERS who have come together to create the series Mysteries of Silver Peak. *Empty Saddle* was written by Susan Page Davis. Susan is the author of more than fifty novels and novellas in the historical romance, mystery, and suspense genres. She is the mother of six and grandmother of nine. A Maine native, she now lives in western Kentucky with her husband, Jim. Visit her Web site at susanpagedavis.com.

Read on for a sneak peek of another exciting book in Mysteries of Silver Peak!

Reunion Dance

SADIE STEPPED THROUGH THE DOOR OF THE DEPOT, ONE OF THE favorite restaurants of Silver Peak's locals. It had been so long since she'd last seen Ann. She wondered if she'd recognize her.

But even before the door swung shut behind her, Sadie realized there had never been a reason to worry. The instant she saw the attractive older woman with the smoothly layered blonde haircut sitting in a booth near the door, she recognized the face of her friend, familiar even over the decades. And the smile Ann broke into at the sight of Sadie wasn't just familiar. It was exactly the same as it had always been, warm, welcoming, and slightly mischievous.

She rose to her feet as Sadie entered, and the two women shared a long hug.

"You don't look a day over seventeen," Ann told Sadie as the two of them took their seats.

"I'm not going to call you a liar," Sadie said with a grin. "Not when it's been this long since I've seen you, at least."

Ann grinned back. "I took the liberty of ordering Spaghetti Western for both of us before you arrived. They haven't changed the recipe, have they?"

"I think the people of Silver Peak would tolerate a change in the town charter before they'd tolerate a change in the recipe of the Depot's Spaghetti Western," Sadie said. "And thanks for going ahead and ordering. I'm so sorry I was late."

Ann shook her head. "To tell the truth, I was a little late myself. There's just been so much going on with the planning for this reunion."

"I've been hearing about that a bit from Roz," Sadie said. "I guess the two of you are co-captains for the planning?"

Ann's brow creased slightly, but she kept her tone bright, with evident effort. "We are," she said.

"Roz is wonderful at these kinds of events," Sadie said. "She's always got such a great vision for things."

Ann's brow creased even more deeply. "Yes." she said, but with a tone that made it clear that she didn't completely agree. "Roz has definitely got a strong vision."

"So can I get a sneak preview of what it'll be like?" Sadie asked, nodding her thanks as a waiter put a glass of water down at her place. "Where is it going to be?"

"That's one of the details we haven't worked out yet," Ann told her.

"That sounds like kind of a big detail," Sadie observed.

"You could say that," Ann said. "Actually, we do have a place reserved already. I found a beautiful ranch outside town with a gorgeous event space, and ponies for the children to ride, and four-star catering. It's very sophisticated, but still with a country feel. They've even got a dance floor that they'll lay out for us in one of the old stock pens. They string those big, old-fashioned incandescent lights around the perimeter, and there's dancing under the stars. I thought it was perfect, and they book up quickly, so as soon as I found it, I made the reservation. The deposit was hefty. But I figured it shouldn't be a problem, if we got the numbers we thought we'd see for this reunion."

"It sounds lovely," Sadie said.

"That's what I thought. And I thought Roz agreed with me. But when I got here, I discovered that she'd taken out a permit to have the reunion right here in town, in the square."

"A lot of events do happen in the square," Sadie said, trying to stay evenhanded in what she was quickly realizing was a serious conflict between her two friends.

"Exactly!" Ann said with an air of triumph. "That's what I said. All the events in town happen in that square. Pep rallies. Bake sales. Political events. I want this reunion to be something special. Something different."

"I know Roz wants it to be special too," Sadie said.

"Yes," Ann said, with a strong hint of disgruntlement. "She's made that clear."

"So what are you looking forward to most about the reunion?" Sadie asked, trying to get the conversation onto a more positive track.

Ann looked surprised at the question. "You know, I've been so caught up in the details that I haven't thought much about that," she said. "It's a good question."

She smiled as their waiter returned to place heaping plates of Spaghetti Western in front of each of them, along with side salads.

"It's not exactly health food, is it?" she said.

"It makes me happy," Sadie said, digging in. "And my doctor says that's good for my health."

Ann nodded, taking a bite herself. She savored it, then gave a satisfied nod. "Just as I remembered."

For a few minutes, the two of them enjoyed their Spaghetti Western in companionable silence.

But then Ann broke it. "I'm not sure what I'm looking forward to," she said. "Seeing you again was definitely high on my list."

"Oh," Sadie said, smiling. "Likewise."

"I've really enjoyed seeing where people I've connected with by social media have ended up," Ann said. "And what about you? Anyone you're interested in seeing in particular?"

Sadie looked around the restaurant thoughtfully for a moment. Then she shook her head. "I can't think of anyone," she said. "But I'm excited to go," she hurried to assure Ann. "It'll be great to see everyone all at once."

"There's no one in particular you want to see?" Ann asked.

"Is there someone I *should* be looking forward to seeing?" Sadie asked.

"I can't believe you don't know who I'm talking about," Ann said, her eyes dancing with even more mischief than usual.

In a flash, Sadie realized who Ann was talking about: Sadie's high school sweetheart. Edwin. She was fishing to see if Sadie was hoping to rekindle that old romance at the high school reunion.

Sadie broke out in a ringing peal of laughter.

"Is it that ridiculous of an idea?" Ann asked, somewhat taken aback. "I mean, I know things change over the years. And I'm sure some things change too much for us to ever go back. But Edwin always impressed me as one of the good ones. And those don't come along every day."

Sadie's laughter finally subsided. She shook her head.

"The thing is," Sadie said. "I've actually seen Edwin recently."

"You *have*?" Ann breathed. "*When?* What was it like?"

"It was lovely," Sadie said. "He came and picked me up just as I was closing the shop, and we walked down here to get a scoop of ice cream for dinner. Then we came back up to Los Pollitos and had some enchiladas for 'dessert.'"

Ann's eyes widened. "Sadie," she said. "That sounds for all the world like a date. Do you think he's interested in you?"

"We've been seeing each other for a while," Sadie said simply. "And I'm very happy about that."

Ann's face broke into a grin. "I think that makes me happier than I would be if I reunited with my own high school sweetheart," she said.

"Jimmy Rhinebacker?" Sadie asked. "Didn't he run off and join the rodeo?"

Ann shrugged. "I don't know. He was one of the ones we couldn't get a certain address for when we were trying to send out the invitations. I left a message at an e-mail address someone had for him, but we never heard anything back. I don't think he's coming. And if he's spent all this time in the rodeo, he's probably walking with two canes now, if he's walking at all."

"Still," Sadie said. "I've always thought cowboys were kind of romantic."

"Not as romantic as the town mayor," Ann said, her voice teasing.

Sadie took her last bite of Spaghetti Western and leaned back in her seat. "It's so good to see you," she said.

Ann smiled. "You too," she said.

"And I'm so glad you're helping head up this reunion," Sadie said. "I know it's a lot of work on your part that the rest of us are just going to get to enjoy. To tell the truth, I'm a little surprised to see you in town so soon. I mean, I was sure you wouldn't miss one of our big reunions. But spending a week in town is a lot for a girl who couldn't wait to get out of here. Especially now that you don't have family in town anymore."

For the first time since Sadie had sat down, Ann didn't meet her eyes. "Well, once you buy the ticket from California, it just makes sense to have a bit of a stay, I guess," she said.

This didn't ring true to Sadie. Ann's parents had passed away years ago, but even though her younger brother Jasper lived on the family ranch outside town, Ann was hardly a regular visitor to Silver Peak. And she was hardly hurting for money. From connecting with her over the Internet, Sadie knew Ann had done very well professionally, building her own personal shopping business with some of the biggest names in Los Angeles—as well as some customers who were so powerful that they managed to keep their names out of the press almost completely.

"So I guess you're enjoying catching up with Jasper, then?" Sadie asked with a smile.

Now Ann stared down at the remains of her Spaghetti Western, as if she couldn't bear to meet the gaze of anyone in the place.

"Ann," Sadie said gently. "Is something wrong?"

"I was trying to decide whether or not to tell you this," Ann said her voice low. Then she looked up and met Sadie's eyes, her own full of questions, and something else—maybe even pain? "But it's becoming clear I can't do it all on my own. And you might be just the person to help me."

"Do what?" Sadie asked.

Ann took a deep breath. "I'm not just in town for the reunion," she said.

By now, Sadie had all but figured that out for herself. But she kept silent. It was clear Ann was carrying a heavy weight, and she needed to tell her own story at her own pace.

"My niece is quite sick," Ann began. "They've been trying to manage her condition for years. But now she needs a kidney transplant."

Sadie's mind whirred, but she didn't immediately see what this had to do with Silver Peak. Jasper's daughter was in Denver, miles away. And although Silver Peak had a wonderful hospital for a town its size, it was hardly the place you'd pick to have a major, complicated procedure like a kidney transplant.

"So, of course, everyone in the family got tested to see if we were a match," Ann said.

Sadie nodded. She could understand why Ann might be especially emotional about something like that. It could be a huge disappointment to find out you couldn't help someone you loved, no matter what sacrifice you were willing to make. And on the other hand, some family members might feel pressured to make a sacrifice they weren't ready for if they proved to be a match for another family member in a life or death situation.

Ann gazed up at Sadie, a plaintive look in her eyes, as if she didn't know how to go on.

"And were you?" Sadie asked gently.

Ann shook her head. Suddenly, tears stood in her eyes. "Sadie," she said. "The tests told me I wasn't even a member of my family."

"I don't understand," Sadie said. She had tons of memories of Ann with her family: her father picking her up from school in his beat-up ranch truck, her mother teaching all the girls how to make themselves look bigger in case they ran into a mountain lion on one of the trails outside town during Girl Scouts. Of course Ann was a member of her family. What could she be talking about?

"Genetically," Ann said. "I'm not a match with anyone in my family. Not mom's siblings, or Dad's. Or even Jasper." At this, her voice broke. "They said we don't have any recent common ancestors," she almost whispered.

"You were adopted?" Sadie said, reasoning through it for herself.

Ann nodded. "I must have been," she said. "That's the only explanation. But mom and dad never said a word about it to me. And Jasper was born just five years before I was. He doesn't remember anything."

"Nothing?" Sadie said. "Nothing at all?"

Ann shrugged in despair. "That's all he'll say, that he doesn't remember anything. But he doesn't want to talk about it at all. As far as he's concerned, he says, I'm his sister, and Mom and Dad are our parents, and he doesn't see why I'd want to know anything besides that. But Sadie," she said. "I have to know."

"I can understand that," Sadie said.

Across the table, Ann fingered the chain of a necklace at her throat. As she did, a distinctive charm peeked out from the collar of her shirt, a delicate chain holding a thick ornament. It looked strangely familiar to Sadie, but she didn't have the time to think about it now. She could ask about it some other time, when Ann wasn't struggling with such a serious question.

"I came back to town so early to see if I could get some answers," Ann said. "You've been here in town so long. You know so much more than I do about how things work around here. And you've always been so good at getting to the bottom of things. I can't do it on my own. I'm too emotional. And I don't even know where to start. I know it's a lot to ask, but I don't know where else to turn. Sadie, will you help me?"

Sadie stared back across the table at her friend. Then she took Ann's hand, squeezed it tightly, and nodded. "Of course I'll help you."

A Note from the Editors

WE HOPE YOU ENJOY MYSTERIES OF SILVER PEAK, CREATED BY the Books and Inspirational Media Division of Guideposts, a nonprofit organization that touches millions of lives every day through products and services that inspire, encourage, help you grow in your faith, and celebrate God's love in every aspect of your daily life.

Thank you for making a difference with your purchase of this book, which helps fund our many outreach programs to military personnel, prisons, hospitals, nursing homes, and educational institutions. To learn more, visit GuidepostsFoundation.org.

We also maintain many useful and uplifting online resources. Visit Guideposts.org to read true stories of hope and inspiration, access OurPrayer network, sign up for free newsletters, download free e-books, join our Facebook community, and follow our stimulating blogs.

To learn about other Guideposts publications, including the best-selling devotional *Daily Guideposts*, go to ShopGuideposts .org, call (800) 932-2145, or write to Guideposts, PO Box 5815, Harlan, Iowa 51593.